When reading this edition of Horror Gems you will find Darkness, Evil, and the Supernatural. It will make you think most profoundly about what is real—and what is not.

In " Sin's Doorway" and "In This Dark Mind", evil will try to win its nefarious games, playing havoc inside the darkest recesses of the human soul.

In reading "Call Me Monster" and "Four Men and a Suitcase," you will discover that your mistreatment of other humans or even "creatures" can torture your soul in ways unimaginable.

To enjoy "Midnight" and "The Altar" you will need to peek into the dark, perverse side of your imagination to truly feel the horror—two mind-numbing tales for the fiend in us all.

If all this sounds appealing, then get ready for a mind teasing set of horror gems that will leave you breathless in the dark…and wanting for more!

TABLE OF CONTENTS

HORROR GEMS

Volume 10
Manly Wade Wellman
and others

Compiled and Edited by
Gregory Luce

ARMCHAIR FICTION
PO Box 4369, Medford, Oregon 97504

For more information about Armchair Books and products, visit our website at...

www.armchairfiction.com

Or email us at...

armchairfiction@yahoo.com

SIN'S DOORWAY

By MANLY WADE WELLMAN

...and Sin lieth at the door. And unto thee shall be his desire, and thou shalt rule over him. —GENESIS, IV, 7.

IN THOSE DAYS and in that part of the South I tried to keep out of county seats and other towns of any size. Sheriffs and town marshals had a way of rounding up tattered strangers and putting them on chain gangs. That spring I followed a trail, not much more than a footway, between two hills where the live oaks and the long-leaf pine shouldered themselves into thickets. There would be clearings in the hollows beyond, and a cabin or two of simple people. They'd recognize me, I hoped, for someone sad and hungry. I'd be invited to eat corn bread, fried bacon too, if I was lucky, or a stew of squirrel or rabbit. I had not eaten since the morning before, nor very heartily then. Feeling faint, I knelt to drink from a little pencil-wide stream. When I rose, my legs were not so shaky.

Then as I tramped downhill between the path's scrub-grown borders, I heard voices singing an old hymn. Around the bend I walked, and came almost among the people.

There were twenty or twenty-five of them, overalled men, and women in homespun dresses and calico sunbonnets, and some shock-headed children. They stood bunched in front of a shabby little clapboard church—I knew it was a church by the tacked-on steeple that housed no bell. Next the church was a grassy burying-ground, with ant-eaten wooden headboards, fenced by stakes and rails. Nobody stood inside the fence. They all faced toward a homemade coffin of whipsawed pine; rough and unpainted.

I hate funerals. I go to as few as I can manage. But I paused to watch this one. Nobody looked sorry or glad, only intent. Beside the coffin stood a tall mountainy man in worn black, with a grizzled chin-tuft that lengthened his hawk-like face. Perhaps Abe Lincoln would have looked like that, if Wilkes Booth had spared

5

Sin's Doorway

BY MANLY WADE WELLMAN

him for twenty more years. That was the preacher, I decided, for as the singing died he began to talk. As my eyes turned toward him, I saw two figures squatting on the ground beyond him and the coffin. For a moment I took these to be old carven images, like figureheads from ancient sailing vessels. They looked weathered and colorless, face, hair, and clothing. One was a bewhiskered male, the other a wrinkled old female. Neither moved, not even their eyes blinked. But their backs were tense, as though slighting

Illustration by Fred Humiston

the church. I know Southern folklore, and remembered a bit; witches, the servants of devils, always turn their backs to the house of God.

"It was the will and prayer of Levi Brett, our departed—brother—"

The preacher had stumbled over that word as if he had disliked to speak it. "His will," he went on, "that we call at his burial for someone to eat his sins."

I pricked up my ears at that. Sin-eating—the old English had believed in it. There was something about it in *Precious Bane*, a delightful novel I hoped to read again if ever I came among books, and had money to buy them. For pay or for gratitude, a living person assumes the burden of sin borne by a dead one. Then a soul is free to enter heaven, and the sin-eater has years of life in which to expiate that assumed obligation. Once or twice I had heard rumors, just rumors, that some backcountry Americans kept the custom.

The preacher paused again, watching his companions. Nobody stirred, except a couple who swayed a little back, as if they disliked the suggestion.

"Levi Brett gave me money as he died," said the preacher. He produced a wallet. "Here are one hundred dollars. That will go to the one who eats the sin. Also Levi Brett's house on Dravot Ridge."

A hundred dollars in cash must have seemed a fortune to those simple hill folk. A heavy-featured, wide-eyed young man started forward at mention of it. But when the preacher spoke of the house on Dravot Ridge, the young man stepped back among his companions. He shuddered, I think; or perhaps they all shuddered.

I moved toward them. The preacher looked at me. So did something else, that now I saw for the first time.

IT LAY prone by the coffin, brown and motionless. At first I thought it was a hound, then I thought it was not. It was hound-size, and lean like a hound; but its feet were all wrong, big and furry, and its low, close-drawn way of lying on its belly was more like a weasel. Its eyes did not falter as mine met them. I never saw a dog with ears like those, and the face, what I could see between the wide forepaws, was strange.

"Yes, brother?" the preacher said to me.

"Sir, you ask for a sin-eater," I ventured.

He held the wallet toward me. "A hundred dollars and a house," he repeated. "It is a fine house—so I hear tell."

"The dead man's a stranger?" I suggested.

"Not Levi Brett," mumbled a voice in the group. "Not enough of a stranger, anyhow."

I paused and thought, and tried to decide what sort of thing it was that lay and watched me, there beside the pine coffin. Then I looked back at the preacher. I licked my lips, but my dry tongue would not moisten them.

"I'll do it, if I'm allowed," was what I managed to say. Since I cannot explain how I began to be nervous and frightened so early in the matter, I shall not try. "I'll do it," I said again, more confidently.

"Praise the Lord," a deep-voiced man intoned, and "Amen!" said a shrill woman.

As I walked toward the coffin, the preacher stepped toward me and took my hand in his big, strong bony one. "Let me call a blessing on you now," he said. "Later, you may be glad of a blessing, brother." His eyes searched my face. "You are young; you have a look of light. I pray your soul won't suffer out of reason."

"But you're really concerned for the soul of the dead man," I reminded, and someone said, "Amen!" I held out my hand. "Give me the money."

"First repeat," commanded the preacher, "I—and speak your name."

Obediently I did so.

"Do freely," he prompted me, "and before all living things in this world and the next, assume and take to myself the sins that trouble the soul of the departed Levi Brett."

I said it all, and wound up by swearing, as he urged, on a holy name. Then he handed me the wallet. It was simply cut and sewn, of some wonderfully soft dark leather. I opened it. Inside were ten ten-dollar bills, of the old large size.

"Levi Brett stands clear of evil," said the preacher to his little flock. "He may enter holy ground. The Lord's name be praised."

They burst into song, another old hymn, and six men moved forward to pick up the coffin by wooden cleats that served as handles.

The preacher led, and they carried it past the stake-and-rail fence into the cemetery where, I now saw, was a ready-dug grave. The hymn finished, and all watched.

From the wallet I took a bill. I spoke to the nearest onlooker, a tussock-bearded old man who looked like photographs of Ambrose Powell Hill.

"I'm hungry," I said. "Faint with hunger.

I wonder if you would—"

"Take that double-damned money away," he snapped, and his eyes blazed above the hair on his face. "It's the devil's price for what you done. You're a man of sin, young fellow, purely rotting away with the sins of Levi Brett you eaten just now. I had nothing to do with him, and I'll have nothing to do with you."

I felt weaker than ever, and I began to plead. "Then, if you'll take no money, will you be kind enough to—"

A WOMAN came to the man's elbow. She must have been his wife, a tall, strong hill creature. "Young sir," she said, "I never hoped to turn away a hungry creature. But I can't give you food or comfort, less'n your sin may catch onto me. I daren't say more than I pity you. Go on somewhere, where they'll feed you unbeknownst of what you carry. That way, maybe, they'll not lose grace by you."

"Look," stammered a young girl, pointing. "Levi Brett's critter—"

The brown animal had risen from where it lay, on four legs that crooked strangely. It pointed a long nose at me, like a trained hunting dog that shows the prey to its master.

"You've taken Levi Brett's sin indeed," said the bearded man, and the glare in his eyes filmed over with terror. "That thing lived with him on Dravot Ridge, his only family. When he was took sick at the preacher's house, it came and camped under his window. It layed by his coffin—" He broke off and choked, then spat furiously, "Now it's youm. Go—please go! Then it'll go with you!"

Everyone drew away from me, toward the fence. Beyond the rails, the coffin-carriers had lowered their burden into the grave, and three of them were spading earth upon it. I felt icy cold, and tried to lie to myself that it was the assault of hunger. I turned away.

Some children began to jabber a little cadenced sneer, to one of those universal childhood tunes:

"Your soul to the devil,
"Your soul to the devil,
"Your soul to the devil—devil—devil—"

After all, I resolutely said in my heart, they didn't mean that. Maybe this was originally an Irish community. I knew that Irishmen sometimes said, "Your soul to the devil," for nothing but a joke. I turned and walked, to get away from staring, repelling eyes.

Beyond the clearing where stood the church and the burying-ground I could see trees, denser thickets than those among which I had walked so far. Two trails led into the depths of the timber, and I turned my steps toward one. Something sounded beside me, pit-pat, pit-pat—the brown animal had joined me. It had a long thin tail, and it seemed awkward on all fours, like a monkey. It looked up at me once, more eloquently than dog or cat could manage, and headed for the other trailhead. I went with it.

As the two of us entered the woods, along the dim green-bough-roofed arcade that was the trail, I sagely decided where I had seen something like my companion. Charles R. Knight's paintings, as are to be seen in New York's Museum of Natural History, or in books like Scott's *History of Mammals in the Eastern Hemisphere*, include several things like that, particularly his restorations of the very early mammals of a million years ago and more. Such things, as I consider them, were developed amorphously, could be ancestors to the monkeys, the dogs, the cats, the hoofed beasts, or to all of these.

I DO NOT want to dwell too long on the specimen that now padded the trail with me. Its snout was long, almost raccoon-like, but its brow bulged in a way that suggested considerable brain volume to go with those expressive eyes. Its forelegs had elbows, its rear legs had knees, and the feet that had seemed like big, hairy lumps bore long toes that could, if necessary, clutch like fingers. I wished it would go away, but did not care to shout or gesture at it.

When I heard human feet behind me, I was relieved, but for a single moment only.

THE two who had sat with their backs to the church were following me. As I glanced back, the man waved a skeleton scrawny arm and the two broke into a run, uncouth but fast, to catch up. Both grinned, showing broken teeth.

"Let them scary folk huddle together and die of the shivers," said the man, breathing hard with his exertions. "We'll see that you get food, Yop, and shelter. That is, we'll see you to your own proper house."

"You did a pure brave thing in taking the sins of Levi Brett," added his companion, "I always say, the young got courage and helpfulness."

I could feel nothing but gratitude in this proffer of help and friendship. In my hand I still carried the bill that I had taken from the wallet, and I held it out.

"Thank you, no," said the man, drawing away. "We're doing it for love," and he flashed his broken teeth in another grin. "You're one of us now."

"You mean neighbors?" I asked, for I thought they might live on Dravot Ridge.

"Just one of us," said the woman. "Hasn't Parway taken you up?"

She meant the brown animal, which stood close to my side, faced toward them but with eyes ever upon me. So its name was Parway—I suppose that is how to spell it. A long moment its eyes held mine, then it turned and trotted ahead.

"Follow," said the man. "It will lead you home."

The three of us went along. I was glad for what I thought was human companionship. They chatted to me genially enough, asking my name and my home. I gave a false name, and said I had no home.

"You have now," said the old woman, and she and her companion blended their cackles, as at a delicious joke. I like that sort of rudeness as little as anyone, and I spoke sharply:

"You mean Levi Brett's house? The one on Dravot Ridge?"

"Well, yes." The old man made a drawl of it. "Only not exactly. It's yours now, by Levi Brett's spoken will. And it's not a house. It's a gardinel."

That word was strange to me. The world will be happiest if it remains strange to the world. I repeated it, rather stupidly: "Gardinel? What kind of a house is that?"

"A gardinel only looks like a house," the old man informed me, "and it can only be used like a house by a few people. There's lots of gardinels, young fellow, in towns sometimes, and sometimes in off-way country places like this one."

"You ever walked along a street, and seen something like a house: not built quite true, that seems to look at you with eyes instead of windows?" demanded the woman, blinking up at me; "Houses generally with nobody living in them, that everybody stays away from?"

Of course I had seen such houses. Everyone has. "Usually somebody tells me such a place is haunted," I replied.

"And usually it's no more than that," she rejoined. "But once in a while it's not a house, it's a gardinel."

THEY were having fun with me, or were they? The beast named Parway had run ahead, and now it gamboled uncouthly at a bend of the trail some yards ahead. There was light, which meant a clearing of sorts. I walked toward it, and my companions followed at my heels.

The clearing was not large, and lofty trees grew thick around it. In its very center was exactly the sort of house I had been prepared for, with all that mocking mystery of the old man and the old woman.

I was never to decide what it was made of. Living wood, perhaps, hard and massive; of living rock, very living rock. On its solid walls were marks as of carving tools. Its two windows had sills that were of one piece with the house front, and the low-drawn roof, which was like a hat pulled down to the eyelike windows, was of a different color but seemed to be part of the same piece, too. The doorway had not been cut oblong, but irregular, rather like a cave-mouth, and all was dark inside. Parway padded up to the threshold, looked back once to me, and darted in. At once a dim light went on, as if Parway had kindled it. My uneasiness was braced by angry mystification. Like the proverbial fool rushing in, I followed Parway.

"I've been waiting for you," said a deep, cultured voice, and there sat a human figure on a blocky stool.

The one was a man of indefinite age, with everything forked about him—his little divided beard, his joined and upslanted brows, his spiked moustache, hornlike points of hair at his brow. These things were probably makeup to a certain extent—Satan himself wouldn't have been so lavishly theatrical. The face was gaunt and mocking, with eyes as brilliant as Parway's; but to look intelligent, there would have to be more forehead. He held out a hand, which I had the instinct not to grasp. His gaunt figure was wrapped in a sort of gray gown.

"You'll be wondering," he said to me, "just what is expected of you."

"I do indeed," was my reply. "If you'll be good enough to tell me—"

"Tell me first," he said gently, "how much you know."

I cleared my throat, and wished for a drink of water. "I came to where they were burying someone called Levi Brett. It seemed he couldn't go into a proper grave until someone, by the old custom, assumed his sins. I did so, because I was poor and hungry, and there was a sum of money offered. Levi Brett's sins must have been considerable, because nobody wanted anything to do with me. And I let myself be led here, simply because it seemed easier than to go somewhere else. That's the sum of my knowledge to date, and I'd like to know more."

"Ah," said the man with the forked beard, "you deserve to know more, for the sake of the important things you're to do."

I TOOK time to look at other things than his face. The inside of the house was not properly angled. Walls curved, and junctures at ceiling and floor seemed blunt. There were beams and rafters interestingly tacked on, like ribs enclosing the body cavity of a disemboweled carcass. Beside the stool on which my new acquaintance sat there was only a desk, covered with papers. In a corner Parway had slumped down into that strange prone position of rest, eyes glued to me. I had a sense of growing disgust, as though I smelled something rotten.

"Permit me," said the man with the forked beard, "my name is Dravot, of the family for which Dravot Ridge is called. And you?"

I gave him the name I had invented for the unsavory couple outside in the clearing. He nodded.

"Let me be simple, though I doubt if the situation can ever be simplified enough to be explained in ordinary words. Levi Brett was—shall we say—brilliantly unusual? Or unusually brilliant? He knew many things, of the sort that weaklings of the ordinary world call forbidden or horrific. This dwelling is the repository of much knowledge. I know relatively little, for I was only his—well, his secretary, his aide. And the two outside are, frankly, stupid underlings. But let us not belittle their courage in accepting Levi Brett's acquaintance and leadership."

"You promised to be simple, and you're not," said I. "Was Levi Brett some sort of sorcerer or wizard? Is that why the people at the church hated his sin?"

"That is exactly the explanation that will do for the moment," smiled Dravot, as if in applause. "You will know better and better, as if dimensions are added to your mind. You have gifts, I daresay, that he lacked. You will carry on what he strove for, the bringing of people hereabout to our way of interesting truth."

I HAD actually forgotten my hunger. About me was a close warmth, a sweaty smell that seemed to go with the carcass-cavity form of the apartment. "I take it that Levi Brett did not make many converts to your beliefs," I said.

"It was deliberately that he set up in this community," said Dravot. "Knowledge that supernatural powers exist is part of the Southern hill culture. But with that knowledge goes fear. For many years Levi Brett did his wonders, and he attracted only me and the two out there. We know what power is possible, but the others refuse to know or even to surmise. They hated him. And even I—a native, of a respected family—haven't dared go among them for years."

"Levi Brett turned against all these things you tell about," I said suddenly. "He died at the preacher's, and left money to buy someone to take over his sins."

There was a sudden storm of cackling laughter from outside, where the old couple was listening. Dravot laughed, too, and pointed his finger.

"Ah, ah, ah," he said, "that took in the fools, but I thought you'd see. Must I explain that, too?"

"You must," I told him, "and seriously, I don't like to be laughed at, Mr. Dravot."

"Forgive me, then. We'll be good friends later. But to explain: Levi Brett knew he must die. He hoped for a son to inherit his knowledge and work, but, for many decisive reasons, he never fathered one. He only pretended to repent—he sought out the preacher deliberately when he felt his last hours upon him. That old ceremony of sin-eating made you his heir, my young friend. You take over his possessions, his knowledge, his work. Good fortune to you."

I gazed at him, uncomprehending. He waved his hand at the papers on the desk.

"Some of these things you may read, but not all. Paper wouldn't contain them. The knowledge, I say, is in this house. Sleep here, dream here. Levi Brett's knowledge will grow within you."

I shook my head. "This has gone far enough," I said. "I dislike practical jokes. For you, as I see it, there is only one way to teach you manners."

Stepping forward, I lifted my fist. I was going to hit him.

HE DID not move, but Parway did. The lithe, strangely made body swooped in front of me. The long jaws opened, and triangular teeth; lead-colored and toxic seeming, grinned at me. I stopped, dead, staring.

"Parway disagrees," said Dravot. "Meanwhile, if you think this is all a joke, how do you explain Parway?"

"Some sort of freak or hybrid," I said lamely.

Parway glared, and Dravot chuckled.

"He understands. He is not complimented, and I don't blame him. Parway has an interesting origin—you'll have read of such things, perhaps. Old demonologists called them familiars."

I had heard the word. Strange entities, given as companions and partners in evil to such persons as contracted to serve hell…but nobody had imagined anything like Parway.

"Suppose you think these things over," Dravot went on, rather patiently. "I'll leave you. It's evening. I wish you joy, young sir, of your first night in your new quarters."

He got up and strode away. The two outside followed him from the clearing. Light was dying there, but strengthened inside. I saw its source, a great candle in a wall bracket, a candle black as tar that burned with a strong white light like carbide.

My early faintness returned to me, and I sat on the stool. If I could but have some food…

And there it was, on the desk at my elbow.

Parway looked from me to the well-filled tray. Had he brought it from somewhere? I could not see clearly at first, then stared. One steaming dish held a sort of pilaf. Another cutlets half-hidden in savory sauce. There was a crusty loaf with fruits baked into it, a massy goblet of yellow metal that held dark liquor. In a deep bowl nestled fruits I did not know, but the colors were vivid and they gave off a delicious odor.

I started to reach for the tray, and paused, for my hand trembled so violently. That was when something—somewhere—betrayed its eagerness clumsily.

For the tray edged toward me on the table, as if it crawled on slow, tiny legs.

I sprang up, sick and dizzy with startled fear. The movement of the tray ceased abruptly, but I had seen. I would not have touched the food then, not though final starvation was upon me. I kicked out at the desk and overset it, tray and all.

The tray vanished, and the dishes, before they struck the flat, dull, solid floor. Parway looked at me bitterly, then reproachfully, and slunk to a corner. I sank back on my stool, wondering furiously.

That feast that had come at my mind's silent bidding, had vanished when I rejected it—there was precedent for such things in the history, or pretended history, of magic. Did not the witches gorge themselves luxuriously at their meetings, which the scholars call sabbats? Was not such gorging a kind of infernal sacrament, which bound the eater to his nasty worship? I congratulated myself on my refusal.

For now I was believing the things that had been told me.

THE NIGHT that closed in would be chilly, I knew, but inside the room the air grew warmer, if anything, and closer. Parway, still crouched in the corner, gazed at me expectantly. I hated that steady stare, direct but not honest. Turning my head, I saw the papers spilled from the overturned desk.

The first word my glance caught was "gardinel," and at once I began to read with deepest interest:

"They may be small or large, conventional-seeming or individual, according to the words said and the help asked. Choose I the place where one will grow, mark the ground plan, scatter the meal of the proper plant, and say—"

There was considerably more, but I would do humanity a disservice to write it here, even if I remembered correctly. Suffice it to say that it spoke of houses, or things like houses, being rapidly grown from nothingness like a sort of fungus. I remembered what I had heard earlier on the trail to Levi Brett's lair, the words of the old man: *"A gardinel only looks like a house, and it can only be used like a house, by a few people.* Was I to be one of such people? Had my declaration that I assumed Levi Brett's sins made me a creature of sorcery, whether I wanted it or not?

"I won't have this," I said. "I'm going."

Rising, I started for the door, but again Parway moved before me. His teeth bared, he crouched low on his rear haunches and lifted his forelimbs. His paws spread their toes, like clumsy hands to strike or grasp, and I could not find the resolution to attack him.

"What do you want?" I demanded, as if he would understand. And he did understand, and pointed with a paw, to the scattered papers. One blew toward me, or I thought it blew. Perhaps it crept of itself. I did not touch it, but bent to read the writing:

"Prepare the mind to receive knowledge. Empty yourself of your own thoughts. Then—"

My eyes read those words, and in the same moment my ears heard them—whether from without or within, how shall I say now? It's all very well to accuse me of hysterical imagination; but if it's easy to be cool and analytical in such a crisis, try it yourself some time. What I do remember well is the script on the page, crabbed but clear and black, and the quality of the speaking, deep and harsh and metallic, like the voice you would expect from Frankenstein's monster.

I straightened up and turned away, muttering a curse. Probably I should have spoken a prayer instead. Empty myself of my thoughts—and what would take their place? The thoughts of another, the things Levi Brett had known, thoughts that still crowded, bodiless, in this awful room and waited for a mind into which to slide themselves. Then I'd be Levi Brett.

I DID not want to be Levi Brett. I did not want the knowledge with which his thoughts were freighted. Anyone, even a skeptic, could see how fatal that would be. "You take over his possessions, his knowledge, his work." Dravot had told me that I would live in this house that wasn't a house, eat foods of which I knew not the name that came from I knew not where. My companions would be Dravot, Parway, one or two of the God-forgotten among the natives. I wanted no such legacy. How to reject it, and remain what I had been, a starved and wretched wanderer?

The food, I remembered, had vanished. That was because I had refused it. Perhaps I had a due to the procedure. I turned toward Parway.

"Go away," I commanded. "Go away, and let this house—what they call a gardinel—go, too. And everything else. I reject it."

Parway showed his teeth. This time he smiled, worse than any human being could manage. He laughed, too—no, someone outside laughed. Dravot was lounging just outside the door.

"Show grace," he bade me, tauntingly. "You can't turn back from us now. Accept. How else can we have you for our chief?"

"I'm no chief of yours," I said. "I refuse to be."

"Too late." He pronounced the words with a satisfaction that was downright smug. "You can't give back what you've taken. From now on you'll live here, think here, work here. Open your mind, and cease to be a fool."

From the darkness beyond him came a patter of voices. The disgusting old couple had come back with Dravot, and they prayed. I'd rather not repeat the prayer, or the names it invoked. I put my hands over my ears.

"I'll not listen!" I shouted. "Let me out of here!"

Jumping to the threshold, I struck at Dravot. He bobbed easily out of danger, and I started into the open after him. At the same time something clawed and clutched at me from behind—the paw of Parway. It scrabbled and wriggled like a knot of gnawing worms, indescribably filthy. Then, I thank heaven, my ragged old jacket tore in the grasp he fastened upon it, and a moment later I was out in the clearing.

I wanted to run, but I knew I must not. I could not endure another seizure from behind. Anyway, the horrid old man and woman stood at the head of the one lane through the thick-grown trees. Abruptly I threw off the remains of the torn jacket and kicked them aside. With both hands I caught a stub of dead branch and wrenched it free from its parent stem. I poised it like a club. There was a strange flowing into me of resolution and rightness.

"Come on now," I challenged Dravot. "I'll flail the grin off of your face. Bring those two swine with you, and Parway if he dares. I'll fight you all four."

But they did not come. They stood where they were—Dravot nearest, the two oldsters by the trailhead, Parway squatting uncouthly in the lighted doorway. Their four pairs of eyes gazed at me, glowing greenly, like the eyes of frightened flesh-eating animals.

"You're not being fair," Dravot stammered, and I found the strength to laugh at that.

"Fair!" I echoed. "Fair, after you tried to trick me into this deviltry?" I lifted the stick. I felt strong.

"He did it," mouthed the old man beyond Dravot. "Chance, or some butt-in power from somewheres—he grabbed a hazelnut branch!"

"But we called lightning to blast it dead!" quavered the voice of the old woman.

"It stood because, dead or not, we couldn't touch it," Dravot flung at them. "Shut your mouths, or he'll guess."

I HAD guessed Hazelnut. I had armed myself with hazelnut, a tree of force against ill magic. What says Albertus Magnus? I've looked it up since, and found it in his writings, not once but in many places. *Cut a hazelnut stick, and therewith strike the witch or wicked being*...something like that...

"You're all dirt," I raged at them, "and I'll plant hazelnut over any of you that dares face me."

Dravot had sidled forward, but kept out of reach of my stick. His foot gingerly touched my torn jacket, kicked it toward me. "It's yours," he said. "Take it back."

"Let it lie," I replied, wondering why he insisted on such a thing at such a moment.

"Take it back," he repeated, and lifted the rags on his toe. For an instant light from the doorway picked out something, the dark wallet of Levi Brett that protruded halfway from a pocket.

"I won't," I snapped. "That money is one of the things I want to give back."

"He knows!" squealed the old woman, and the old man slapped his skinny hand over her mouth. Dravot cursed her in words that made my scalp tingle. With a kick of his foot, he threw the jacket at me. It soared like a tatter-winged bat.

I struck at it with my club. It caught on the end and flapped there for a moment, then went sailing back, full into Dravot's face.

He screamed, as shrilly as the old woman could have managed, and pawed at the fabric with his hands. It had wrapped itself around his face like a net. I heard his muffled pleading that someone set him free, but nobody moved. The old man and woman had run away up the trail, and Parway drew back inside the house-thing. I stepped close to Dravot and began to beat him.

"Why didn't you take the money, if taking it meant such great power?" I yelled as my stick thumped on his swaddled head.

"You were afraid—of what? Things too evil for you?"

He tried blindly to defend himself. His out flung hand once grasped my stick; but he let go at once, with a howl as though electric current had run through him.

"Parway! Parway!" he cried, and Parway emitted the one sound I heard from him in all the incident. It was like a sound, human in quality but wordless. Dravot, still pawing at the clinging coat around his face and head, turned and stumbled in the direction from which Parway's voice had come.

"I rejected that money," I called after him, "and it has fastened on you. Now you can't let it go. Suffer from your own sins and those of Levi Brett!"

As Dravot reached the threshold, Parway ran from him, back inside. I saw him as he lurched against the wall, and he jarred the great black candle from its bracket. Dravot stumbled blindly, sprawled through the door, and lay still there. He must have fainted.

THE candle no more than struck the floor when flames burst and bloomed like flowers from a stage magician's trick rose-tree. Something in the construction or material fed those flames like suet. They sprang and spread everywhere. Parway, cut off by them from the one exit, scrambled back into a corner that would not long remain unkindled. Dravot lay, still motionless, even when tongues of fire lapped eagerly across him. The fire was dark, giving off oily wisps of smoke. I retreated, toward the lane up which the old couple had run away.

I departed, feeling my path in the dark with the hazelnut stick. I tried to rationalize, even though the matter was not rational.

Everything had centered around Levi Brett's bribe-money, which had doomed me when I accepted, which freed me when I thrust it away. The evil had been desperate when Dravot, as unprepared as I, came in contact. It had fastened upon him like a snake.

What now happened to him, in the heart of the burning, meant that I was spared the curse. I groped along as swiftly as I could. After moments, I heard a noise, a long quavering whoop or wail— not Parway, certainly not Dravot. The house, the thing called a gardinel—if it lived, could it feel? If it felt, could it scream its pain of fire?

I made myself run. I kept running until I was beyond earshot. Then I slowed to a walk again.

My weakness and hunger returned, and I had to brace my spirit to endure them. I must keep going until morning. By then I might have come to some other · district among the hills, where nobody would guess that for an hour I had been in the grip of cursed magic. People would see me for a starved stranger, and offer me something to eat.

THE END

IN THIS DARK MIND

By ROG PHILLIPS

*Is murder ever justified? He knew the answer—no! But he was the most
desperate of men and somehow
he would find justification for killing his wife.*

THE early light roused him, striking his face, finding his closed
eyes. He stretched wearily, protesting against consciousness. His
forehead was throbbing with slow ferocity, and he groaned. It was
the sound of the nightmare from which he had awakened. For a
sleepy moment, he couldn't remember. Then his hand rubbing his
cheek touched something sticky.

His hand fell, and his sleepiness was gone. With sickening
clarity he knew the stickiness on his cheek was blood. He had
killed Alice! God help him, it wasn't a nightmare. It was true. He
put his head in his hands, seeing even as he did so, the long deep
scratches on his bare arms. He couldn't believe it. He had killed a
woman!

Now he could remember everything. How she had struggled,
clawed, and fought. And how quiet it had been. Violence without
sound. Alice didn't have time to scream.

Ruth, the only other person in the house, had slept through it
all. And when he had finished his work, when Alice's body went
limp and resistance ceased forever, he had come back to this room.
He had fallen onto this bed, happily finding the sleep of the
innocent.

Now the throbbing in his head grew and he groaned again. In
an hour Susannah, the cleaning woman, would be here. He must
get rid of Alice's body before then. He must find a way, some way,
out of this horror. He must not panic. He had killed Alice. That
was all that really mattered. He had destroyed her in time.

From the first night he'd known she was wrong for this place,
that she would bring disaster. Instinct had warned him and made
him wary.

He remembered the first night, a month ago, when he had met her. That night he'd gotten off the 7:10 train, as he always did, clutching his brief case and thinking about supper. As he said good night to his commuting acquaintances and walked to his car, he felt the city-bred tension within him ease away before the peace of the suburban village.

He drove, as always, with careful expertness through the main street traffic. Then leaving the town behind, his car began to climb the long hill up to Roseberry Lane.

For the past four years, heart trouble had imprisoned his wife, Ruth, in their home. So that for four years George had driven to and from the station alone. And alone had entered his home by key, without a welcome or greeting at the door.

Tonight, however, for the first time, he did not need his key. But he didn't know it, and the key was in his hand as he walked slowly up the path from the garage.

He was a tall, rangy man in his early forties. His hair was scattered with gray but still thick. Though he walked with a tired step, his eyes were the seeking, eager eyes of youth, and his glance quick and restless. Still some distance from the front door he stopped.

The door was not shut. A ray of evening sunlight pierced through into the shadowy vestibule.

Something must have happened to Ruth! The doctor must be here. He ran up to the door and inside. He heard music. Impossible, but from the living room came the rich, pulsing melody of a waltz. Thank heaven Ruth was all right. But who was playing the phonograph? And why was the kitchen dark? Susannah should be in there, preparing supper.

He dropped his hat and brief case on the table, took the few steps necessary to reach the living room. On the threshold he stopped in disbelief.

A girl, dark-haired and slim, was dancing dreamily, whirling in lazy circles. She was beautiful, with eyes half-shut, arms held out, caressing, embracing the empty space through which she swayed.

For an uncomprehending minute he watched her. Then he strode to the phonograph and shut it off.

Silence shook her from the dream. Her arms fell, and she turned in annoyance. Something about her features was familiar, but he didn't waste time wondering. He said, "I'm George Parker. This is my house. Mind telling me who you are?"

Illustration by Garner

"Not at all, George," She sank into an armchair. "I'm Alice, your sister-in-law. Sorry to be the bearer of bad tidings but I've come to stay. Ruth wrote and said she needed me."

Maybe to an outsider the words might sound sensible, but to him they were a jumble of nonsense.

"Ruth's sister? But she didn't say anything about your coming." Ruth hadn't said a word, not even that morning. He couldn't remember the last time she had spoken of Alice. "I didn't even realize you two corresponded."

Once years before, Ruth had shown him her sister's picture and mentioned that she lived out West—Oregon or Washington. There was no doubt this was the girl in the picture. She was younger and, of course, prettier than Ruth. Her eyes were wide, with a disturbing depth, and her lips had a sulky fullness. She stood taller than Ruth and held her head differently, almost defiantly.

"I came a few days early," said Alice. "Maybe Ruth meant to tell you tomorrow. Who knows why she was mysterious about it? Anyway she sent me the fare, and here I am, toothbrush and all."

She took a cigarette from the box on the table. He leaned across to light it for her.

"Although I must admit," she continued, "it's not what I expected. The house is much smaller and the furniture so depressing. It has all the sparkle of a funeral parlor." She sighed, exhaling a delicate spiral of smoke. "I should have remembered how uninspired Ruth's taste always was."

He stared at her. He couldn't believe she had just insulted his home and his wife. And yet she had, with a casual assurance and insolence that left him wordless.

"Ruth's waiting," she said. "Hadn't you better run up and see her?"

He didn't trust himself to answer. With one darting look of disapproval he left the room. Going up the stairs he could hear music begin again below.

His wife raised herself from the pillows on the chaise as he came in.

He bent down to kiss her pale cheek. "Hello, darling. How was it today? You look fine and rested," he lied.

She clutched his hand and asked with nervous hesitancy. "Did you meet Alice? Did you like her? I know you will. Did you get a chance to talk?"

"Yes, dear, I met her. It was a bit of a surprise, seeing her without warning, but she introduced herself. I guess it's what you want, Ruth, but do you think it will work out?"

"Of course, darling! It will be perfect," Her enthusiasm was pathetically child-like. "She's wonderful, so full of life, and she'll be such company for me during the day. I told Susannah just to come in the morning and stay till three. Alice will cook supper. Anything she needs she can order by phone. She doesn't need the car."

Ruth chattered on, but in a short while her animation faded, and weariness settled across her drawn features. "Forgive me, darling, but I guess the excitement has tired me. I think I'll rest a bit."

He helped her from the chaise to her bed and adjusted the pillows, as he'd done every night for four years.

She raised a thin hand and patted his arm. "I'm glad you're home, dear."

Every night she patted his arm just that way and said those same words. They were his signal to leave.

Downstairs the kitchen was still dark. Undoubtedly Alice was waiting to see if he wanted his dinner scrambled or sunny-side-up. He took a steadying breath and joined her in the parlor. Although the phonograph played a slow, whimpering blues, Alice was not dancing. She sat on the window bench, combing her hair.

"Dinner's been ready for hours," she said, smoothing back the shimmering mass of hair. "We're eating on the back porch. A cold supper. The Sauterne is on the tray in the pantry if you'll take it out."

He said, "We don't usually take wine with our meals."

"No? Well, I do," She rose and switched off the phonograph. "Quite a record collection you've got there. Too bad Rudy Vallee isn't a big favorite of mine."

She crossed the room, her green silk dress flaring about her knees. With its provocatively fitted lines, the dress was obviously designed for something more exciting than supper at Roseberry Lane. George smiled to himself as he followed her down the hall. Poor Alice, he thought. She didn't know that despite her more than adequate performance and costumes, the theater was empty.

On the porch she'd set up a table with their best china and crystal. A silver bowl was filled with garden flowers. All the scene lacked was candles and a gypsy fiddler.

Alice brought out fried chicken, tossed salad and rolls. "Aren't you going to pour the wine?" she asked, seating herself.

He filled her glass and his own. As he was about to drink, he noticed her questioning half-smile.

"It's fine. Very nice," he said. "But I should explain we don't use this crystal and china every day. Only on special occasions."

She tore a roll apart and buttered it. "I saw some Woolworth crockery on the shelves, but I had no idea you used it."

"We use it," he said coldly.

"Since you're a visitor, you won't mind my acquainting you with our habits. That way it'll be easier for us all."

He went on to explain what hour he liked his breakfast in the morning, when he left the house, and so on. He was patient but her manner was nearly impossible. She interrupted constantly, introducing pointless humor that upset his train of thought. Also, she ate voraciously. He had never seen anyone clean a plate so fast. Or perhaps through the years he had become over-used to Ruth's dainty dawdling over food.

Alice began to peel an orange. "I'll need some money," she said, without preamble. "For clothes. I didn't tell Ruth, but I'm pretty stony. A trunk of mine is coming Railway Express but the clothes in it are about ready for a rummage sale."

He took a minute to think this out. Then he said, "You won't need anything elaborate here. We dress simply, and there are no neighborhood parties or dances, if that's what you're expecting."

She laughed good-naturedly. "Not for parties, George. Just for me. I've only got this one dress. Took my last cent, but I know how important first impressions are."

And she had certainly made hers! He emphasized again how quiet life at Roseberry Lane was, and then reluctantly agreed to give her some money to buy "a few sensible cottons."

"You're an angel," she purred, settling back in her chair. "And Susannah said you were such a cheap skate."

Cheap skate! What was left of his patience was swept away in a gust of rage. Disjointedly he thought, "This vulgar...outrageous creature...is it possible...she has discussed me with the cleaning woman?" His anger was so great he could only sputter incoherently.

"Calm down, George," Alice chuckled in enjoyment. "She didn't really say it...just sort of conveyed the idea."

"In the future," he managed at last, "I'd appreciate it if you let Susannah do her work without gossiping. While you are in my house, as my guest, kindly leave her alone."

"You're cute, George, when you give off sparks. But I get the message." She began to clear the table. "Don't bother the help. Just pussyfoot around in the daytime. I can see life is going to be real cheery."

He lit a cigarette and left the porch without answering. He didn't know where he was going, but he had to get away from her. He found himself opening the front door and glaring out at the summer night. Good idea. He'd take a walk and cool off.

"She won't stay," he told himself hopefully as he started down the steps. She had already criticized the house and everything in it. Without the car she'd be isolated. A few remarks to his commuting neighbors about Ruth's · need for rest would keep visitors away. The community had never, at its best, roared with activity, and now at the summer's height, with families away at the shore, Roseberry Lane had dozed off into a soundless, rhythmic sleep.

But Alice did not languish in boredom on Roseberry Lane. She traveled by bus to White Plains every other day for shopping. The first day she brought back new clothes. The third day armfuls of records. The fifth day an expensive phonograph was delivered to the house.

"That's right. I bought it with my own money," said Alice when George questioned her. "I got a check by mail the other day."

He was unconvinced. "I didn't see any mail for you."

"Sorry, George, but a letter came for me on the two o'clock delivery yesterday," She threw him a smile of pure malice. "What's the trouble? Don't you think I have any friends?"

He was sure she had, but he didn't want to distress himself by visualizing them. So he replied in a manner that would soon become habitual: he shrugged his shoulders and was silent.

On non-shopping days Alice amused herself by rearranging the furniture. George had just become accustomed to the new arrangements when the following week all familiar lamps, chairs, and tables were exiled to the cellar, and strange-looking modern odd pieces were put in their place.

Surveying the living room, George felt like a stranger in his own home. He sought out Alice in the kitchen. "What are you trying to do?" he cried. "That furniture…it's ugly and hideous! Are you deliberately trying to make my home as ugly as possible? And who paid for those monstrosities? Am I supposed to believe you got another mysterious check in the mail?"

"That's right," said Alice. "I paid for it. I replaced that cheery Civil War furniture with something half-way decent that doesn't give me the willies just to look at. Even a blind man could see the improvement, but you can't, of course. Don't bother thanking me for the trouble for the money. Ruthie already did. I told her all about it, and she was thrilled. She thinks it's marvelous, so don't go running upstairs to cry on her shoulder."

So it went on. There was to be no serenity of existence while Alice remained. To get away from the sound of her nightly dance-music sessions in the living room, George retreated every evening after supper to his room or to the outdoors.

He received no sympathy from Ruth who, in her mild way, stubbornly rejected any criticism of her sister. He felt he could not force the issue or give her an ultimatum. Lately Ruth's illness seemed to take all her emotions and to turn her thoughts inward. She had grown more listless and her manner less responsive.

Eventually George decided to telephone Dr. Morell, who paid Ruth a brief house call every week. Morell assured him that Ruth was coming along fine.

"But how about yourself?" said Morell. "Ruth tells me you've been pretty edgy and nervous. Don't think you're driving yourself too hard in this heat, do you? Might be a good idea if you took a few days off from the office."

George mumbled something, a vague promise, and hung up. He'd take some time off all right, but not while Alice was his houseguest.

He went out to the back porch for a cigarette and some silence. He had barely settled down when Alice slammed open the door and clattered a chair over the tiles. She sat down near him, with a rustle of her skirt, but said nothing. A faint perfume reached him.

Finally he cleared his throat and asked, "Dancing over for the night?"

"Maybe," She crossed her legs. "The garden is lovely at night."

He grunted agreement.

"I like the country. The quiet is so loud and steady, it almost throbs, she said. "At night I can feel it throbbing, beating in my blood. Can you feel it flowing through you, like wine?"

He tossed away his cigarette and stood up. She waited till he was at the door before she rose.

"Why are you afraid of me, George?" she said, coming up to him. She put her hand lightly on his arm.

He stared into her shadowy gray eyes and saw the challenge in them. "You don't scare me, Alice," he said.

Her arms went around his neck, and she stood waiting. Here was his chance to fling her aside, to reject her in the only way a woman like Alice could understand.

He put his hands on her shoulders, and then instinctively, as though seized by a strength beyond himself, his grip tightened and he pulled her roughly to him. He covered her red, defiant lips with his own.

As he kissed her, he knew that here, warm and alive in his embrace, was the only woman in the world he could truly want. He wanted her, more than he had ever needed any woman.

He raised his head, and she put her cheek against his, her eyes closed. For a moment they stood motionless together. Then he said, "Don't leave me, Alice."

She stirred in his arms. "No, darling. I never will."

He kissed her again, her forehead, her cheeks, her sweet scented hair.

The days that followed were like the early days of an illness. Consecutive hours brought conflicting emotions, so that the days had a blurred, feverish quality. George's happiness at times was almost unbearable. The fragments of joy, however, were torturingly brief and complete in themselves. They cast no shadow and left him wretched with shame.

But his need for Alice was stronger than his self-loathing. In guilty atonement, he spent more time than usual with Ruth. He brought her new books and candy. Ruth, unlike her sister, was not blossoming. Whenever he came in, her hands were empty and her eyes vacantly tired. She no longer cared about her reading or the radio. She stayed more in bed, going to the chaise only in the afternoons.

Why wasn't she the complaining, querulous type of invalid, so that he could find some shred of justification for his behavior? Her nature had always been gentle, and illness had not changed it. She demanded less of him than Alice, much less.

His own inner anguish was an odd contrast to the untroubled good spirits of Alice. Soul-searching bothered her far less than her wardrobe. Her long-awaited trunk had arrived and brought with it the smartest clothes he had ever seen. He realized belatedly that what he had always called Ruth's "conservative taste" was nothing more than dowdiness. Alice knew instinctively that women should dress for but one purpose: to make themselves more desirable in men's eyes.

She also displayed some costume jewelry that had come in the trunk. He was reminded of Ruth's small collection of jewelry, pieces he had given her through the years of their marriage. Of course, none of the bracelets or brooches he had bought her had been extravagantly showy.

The stones were small but they were the best. And what had happened to them? Ruth had put them away in locked darkness on bits of cotton. She didn't believe in wearing expensive jewelry.

He thought of his last gift to Ruth: a pair of pearl and diamond earrings that had never seen light nor been worn with beauty. Why not give them to Alice, just for a little while?

He had only to go to Ruth's room and take the earrings from her jewel box. He knew where the key was. His watch read eleven-thirty. Ruth would be long asleep.

Alice was at her dressing table painting her nails. He bent to kiss her hair. "Ruth has a pair of diamond earrings that would look beautiful with your blue dress. How'd you like to borrow them?"

Alice shook her head. "Ruth's earrings? Don't bother, darling. I know the ones you mean. She showed me all her jewelry one day, and I didn't want to hurt her feelings. But between you and me, some of those stones you couldn't see with a microscope." She smiled, looking up at him. "I guess Ruthie's easy to please, but I'm fussy. I prefer diamonds you can see with the naked eye."

He stared uncomprehendingly as she laughed. Could she be serious? Were her casual knife-thrusts meant to draw blood? No, she must have misunderstood him somehow.

Her laughter simmered down. "Oh, George," she said, "you're such a big sport. You quite overwhelm me at times. If I had said all right, would you have tiptoed across the hall and stolen those earrings for me?"

So she hadn't misunderstood him. She took his kindness and returned insult. It amused her to shock and pain him. She hated him, and he had never guessed it. All along she had been mocking him, and now she didn't even care if he knew it. He must have been insane to have sacrificed his conscience for her.

He bent his head, covering his eyes from the sight of her. "Get out," he said. The words were low, like a whispered curse.

"Poor George, the truth hurts, doesn't it?" she said. "The big sport was going to steal jewelry from a dying woman!" She laughed again.

"Get out," he said. "I've let you stay here, but now I'm through," He dropped his hands. "Get out of this house."

"Well, now he's become an actor," she said, without moving. "You have so many facets, George!"

"Stop it," he said in a low voice. "Stop it, or I'll kill you. I'm warning you."

"You don't like me anymore, George?" she asked, "because I tell the truth? You prefer hypocrisy and lies, don't you, darling? How upset Ruthie would be if she knew the language of love was dishonesty. She has such illusions," She began to unfasten the back of her dress. "It's after midnight. I'm tired."

He hated her and her smug confidence. She was threatening to tell Ruth. She didn't care if the shock killed Ruth. No, she would ruin Ruth's life and his to amuse herself. She thought she could lie down to sleep and arise tomorrow to continue her evil. She thought he was a fool, a clown. She was right. He hated himself as much as he hated her. He was a poor, stupid, greedy clown, but he wouldn't let her destroy his wife and himself.

He took a step toward her, and she backed away, her smile fading. She stumbled and fell against the bed. Now was his chance. He gripped her throat, and saw that her eyes had become almost glassy with fear. His fingers tightened, closer, cutting off her breath. This was the way, the only way. He had to kill her. It was the price for his self-respect, the price for Ruth. He was a clown, but Alice had forgotten he was also a man.

She struggled, clawing up at him, weakly, futilely, while his fingers held their grip.

So now tomorrow had come. Ruth and he were alive to see it and enjoy it. Alice could threaten no more.

A sound disturbed him. Was it a door shutting? Had Susannah come already? His watch had stopped. He must do something; send Susannah away until he could get rid of Alice's body.

He went into the hall and listened at the head of the stairs. There was no sound. Reassured, he turned towards Alice's room. He took a breath and forced himself to turn the doorknob. He stepped into the room.

The bed was empty. The room was clean, tidy, and empty.

There was not a single, personal article anywhere. He went to the closet. Except for some hangers, it was bare.

She had gone! Somehow in the night she had run away. He hadn't killed her. She was still alive. The threat of her was more dangerous than ever.

He heard the sound again. She must be downstairs; maybe she was telephoning the police or maybe she was pouring her story out to Susannah.

He ran out into the hall, down the stairs. The sound had come from the rear. He tore open the kitchen door, and there was Susannah. She was just removing a faded straw hat. Her black handbag, a large carryall, lay on its side on the kitchen table.

"Susannah!" he cried. "Did you see Alice?"

"I beg pardon, sir?"

"Alice. My sister-in-law. She's gone. All her things are gone."

Where was she? Had she really run away? "Did you meet her? Maybe you saw her as you came from the bus. Tell me! Why don't you say something?"

"About what, sir? Who are you talking about?"

"Alice!" he practically screamed. "My wife's sister. Why do you ask such idiotic questions when you can see I want help?"

She reddened defensively. "Maybe I could help, Mr. Parker, if you'd stop carrying on like a chicken with its head off. And look at your face, all scratched up and marked. If I didn't know you so long, I'd say you'd been in a fight. Now calm down and tell me. Who's Alice? Who's this person you are looking for?"

He forced control of himself. Obviously he had frightened Susannah out of the few wits she had. "Alice is the girl who's been living here for a month. You can't tell me you didn't know her. She's the one who bought all this new furniture…"

Susannah's face twisted as though she were about to cry. Instead she smiled uncertainly. "But you bought it, sir. I know because the first time I called the store when the lamps and those chairs were delivered, I asked Mrs. P. and she said she didn't know nothing about them. So I called the store to say there was a mistake. But they checked and said you'd come in the day before and paid cash for them."

He felt he was in a nightmare of quicksand. Instead of getting free his struggles were dragging him deeper into it. "What's the matter with you? Why are you lying?" He seized her arm. "You must remember Alice and the time you told her I was such a cheap skate. Do cheap skates go out and buy furniture they don't need?"

"Let go my arm, Mr. Parker! I never said no such thing about you, and I don't know no Alice, leastways not in this house. I got no cause to lie to you."

Even Susannah, the solid, the reliable, was crumbling before his eyes. Or was she just pretending to? Maybe she knew something. Of course! She was lying to confuse him. There was some good reason behind her seeming stupidity. Maybe Alice had planned a trap for him and was using Susannah.

"In other words, you don't know anything about the girl who used our guest room for the past month?"

"Nobody's been in the guest room, Mr. Parker. I ought to know. I swept in there day before last."

"I know what you're doing," he cried. "She's paid you to tell these lies, and the two of you are trying to trap me. Don't trust her, Susannah. Don't believe her. She's evil. When she doesn't need you any more, she'll destroy you like she tried to destroy me. I know it!"

A door slammed as he caught his sobbing breath. He was alone. Susannah had run away. She'd seen she had failed. No, he hadn't fallen for that look of innocence on her flat, stupid face.

Ruth would help him. Ruth would remember her own sister. She wouldn't deny the person who'd looked after her the past month. With new hope rising, he ran back toward the stairs.

Next door, at the Fearons, Susannah asked to use the phone to call Dr. Morell.

"This is Susannah," she said, "the daily woman at the Parkers... No, it's not Mrs. Parker. It's her husband... No, not sick, but he's acting strange...I'm not imagining! He was screaming about some woman I never heard of. Said she was living in the house, and you know as well as me, there's only that poor, sick Missus of his... No, not really sudden. He's been acting different for almost a month. You can tell just by looking at him that something's wrong. He's got real thin. I always leave him something cold in the fridge for supper, but lately he hardly ever eats it. And he's been drinking. That's the truth. He started with wine and now it's something stronger. I seen the bottles in the morning with my own eyes. Is that imagining? Oh, yes, just now as I was running out, he shouted at me that this Alice woman was going to kill me! If you ask me, he's lived too long with sickness and stays too much in that gloomy house. All right, I'll wait for you outside. I'm scared to go back in."

She hung up the receiver and had to sit down for a minute. Her legs just gave way beneath her.

George reached Ruth's room and flung back the door. The room was dark, blinds drawn. Ruth was still asleep. How blessed, he thought, to be as remote as she in this upper room, safely distant from the treachery and deceit without.

He approached the bed. "Ruth."

She did not stir. Above the sheet one arm lay, drooping down gracefully, its fingers pointing to the floor. Then he saw the bed lamp.

It was smashed and broken on the carpet, its fragments cast wide.

He stood where he was. He felt frozen, caught on the edge of time. His heart seemed to have stopped, and he felt he could not move. But he *must* go nearer.

Her face was half-hidden by the pillows. Could he bring himself to touch her? "Ruth," he heard himself whisper in a frightened manner.

He put out a trembling hand and raised her arm. It was cold and stiff. Her nails were broken, torn. There was dried blood streaking across them.

Convulsively he dropped her arm, and in a quick, unthinking reflex seized the nearest pillow, jerking it away from her face. Her head fell back, revealed, and he saw her, Ruth! He had strangled Ruth!

With a scream neither of them heard, he fell to the foot of the bed. The pain inside his head seemed to be ripping away at his reason. Had he lost his mind? Was he a mad man? He felt pain blaze up like a light, and by its shattering glare truth flickered for a moment and reached him.

There was no Alice, nowhere, not ever, not for him. There was no Alice, except in the world of his despair and loneliness. There was only Ruth, the dying, the helpless, and he had killed her.

THE END

MIDNIGHT

By JACK SNOW

...and at the stroke of twelve he would climax the years of homage he had paid to the dark powers of evil.

BETWEEN the hour of eleven and midnight John Ware made ready to perform the ceremony that would climax the years of homage he had paid to the dark powers of evil. Tonight he would become a part of that essence of dread that roams the night hours. At the last stroke of midnight his consciousness would leave his body and unite with that which shuns the light and is all depravity and evil. Then he would roam the world with this midnight elemental and for one hour savor all the evil that this alien being is capable of inspiring in human souls.

John Ware had lived so long among the shadows of evil that his mind had become tainted, and through the channel of his thoughts his soul had been corrupted by the poison of the dark powers with which he consorted.

There was scarcely a forbidden book of shocking ceremonies and nameless teachings that Ware had not consulted and pored over in the long hours of the night. When certain guarded books he desired were unobtainable, he had shown no hesitation in stealing them. Nor had Ware stopped with mere reading and studying these books. He had descended to the ultimate depths and put into practice the ceremonies, rites and black sorceries that stained the pages of the volumes. Often those practices had required human blood and human lives, and here again Ware had not hesitated. He had long ago lost account of the number of innocent persons who had mysteriously vanished from the face of the earth—victims of his insatiable craving for knowledge of the evil that dwells in the dark, furtively, when the powers of light are at their nadir.

John Ware had traveled to all the strange land little known parts of the earth. He had tricked and wormed secrets out of priests and dignitaries of ancient cults and religions of whose existence the world of clean daylight has no inkling. Africa, the West Indies, Tibet, China—Ware knew them all and they held no secret whose knowledge he had not violated.

By devious means Ware had secured admission to certain private institutions and homes behind whose facades were confined individuals who were not mad in the outright sense of the everyday definition of the word, but who, if given their freedom, would loose nightmare horror on the world. Some of these prisoners were so curiously shaped and formed that they had been hidden away since childhood. In a number of instances their vocal organs were so alien that the sounds they uttered could not be considered human. Nevertheless, John Ware had been heard to converse with them.

Illustration by
Boris Dolgov

IN JOHN WARE'S chamber stood an ancient clock, tall as a human being, and abhorrently fashioned from age-yellowed ivory. Its head was that of a woman in an advanced state of dissolution. Around the skull, from which shreds of ivory flesh hung, were Roman numerals, marked by two death's head beetles, which, engineered intricate machinery in the clock, crawled slowly around the perimeter of the skull to mark the hours. Nor did this clock tick as does an ordinary clock. Deep within its woman's bosom sounded a dull, regular thud, disturbingly similar to the beating of a human heart.

The malevolent creation of an unknown sorcerer of the dim past, this eerie clock had been the property of a succession of warlocks, alchemists, wizards, Satanists and like devotees of forbidden arts, each of whom had invested the clock with something of his own evil existence, so that a dark and revolting nimbus hung about it and it seemed to exude a loathsome animus from its repellently human form.

It was to this clock that John Ware addressed himself at the first stroke of midnight. The clock did not announce the hour in the fashion of other clocks. During the hour its ticking sounded faint and dull, scarcely distinguishable above ordinary sounds. But at each hour the ticking rose to a muffled thud, sounding like a human heartbeat heard through a stethoscope. With these ominous thuds it marked the hours, seeming to intimate that each beat of the human heart narrows that much more the span of mortal life.

Now the clock sounded the midnight hour. "T*hud, thud, thud—*" Before it stood John Ware, his body traced with cabalistic markings in a black pigment which he had prepared according to an ancient and noxious formula.

As the clock thudded out the midnight hour, John Ware repeated an incantation, which, had it not been for his devouring passion for evil, would have caused even him to shudder at the mere sounds of the contorted vowels. To his mouthing of the unhuman phrases, he performed a pattern of motions with his body and limbs which was an unearthly grotesquerie of a dance.

"Thud, thud, thud—" the beat sounded for the twelfth time and then subsided to a dull, muffled murmur which was barely audible in the silence of the chamber. The body of John Ware sank to the thick rug and lay motionless. The spirit was gone from it. At the last stroke of the hour of midnight it had fled.

With a great thrill of exultation, John Ware found himself outside in the night. He had succeeded! That which he had summoned had accepted him! Now for the next hour he would feast to his fill on unholy evil. Ware was conscious that he was not alone as he moved effortlessly through the night air. He was accompanied by a being that he perceived only as an amorphous darkness, a darkness that was deeper and more absolute than the inky night, a darkness that was a vacuum or blank in the color spectrum.

WARE found himself plunging suddenly earthward. The walls of a building flashed past him and an instant later he was in a sumptuously furnished living room, where stood a man and a woman. Ware felt a strong bond between himself and the woman. Her thoughts were his, he felt as she did. A wave of terror was enveloping him, flowing to him from the woman, for the man standing before her held a revolver in his hand. He was about to pull the trigger. John Ware lived through an agony of fear in those few moments that the helpless woman cringed before the man. Then a shapeless darkness settled over the man. His eyes glazed dully. Like an automaton he pressed the trigger and the bullet crashed into the woman's heart. John Ware died as she died.

Once again Ware was soaring through the night, the black being close at his side. He was shaken by the experience. What could it mean? How had he come to be identified so closely with the tortured consciousness of the murdered woman?

Again Ware felt himself plummeting earthward. This time he was in a musty cellar in the depths of a vast city's tenement section. A man lay chained to a crude, wooden table. Over him stood two creatures of loathsome and sadistic countenance. Then John Ware *was* the man on the table. He knew, he thought, he felt everything that the captive felt. He saw a black shadow settle over the two evil-looking men. Their eyes glazed, their lips parted slightly as saliva drooled from them. The men made use of an assortment of crude instruments, knives, scalpels, pincers and barbed hooks, in a manner that, in ten short minutes, reduced the helpless body before them from a screaming human being to a whimpering, senseless thing covered with wounds and rivulets of blood. John Ware suffered as the victim suffered. At last the tortured one slipped into unconsciousness. An instant later John Ware was moving swiftly through the night sky. At his side was the black being.

It had been terrible. Ware had endured agony that he had not believed the human body was capable of suffering. Why? Why had he been chained to the consciousness of the man on the torture table? Swiftly Ware and his companion soared through the night moving ever westward.

John Ware felt himself descending again. He caught a fleeting glimpse of a lonely farmhouse, with a single lamp glowing in one window. Then he was in an old-fashioned country living room. In a wheel chair an aged man sat dozing. At his side, near the window, stood a table on which burned an oil lamp. A dark shape hovered over the sleeping man. Shuddering in his slumber, the man flung out one arm, restlessly. It struck the oil lamp, sending it crashing to the floor, where it shattered and a pool of flame sprang up instantly. The aged cripple awoke with a cry, and made an effort to wheel his chair from the flames. But if was too late. Already the carpet and floor were burning and now the man's clothing and the robe that covered his legs were afire. Instinctively the victim threw up his arms to shield his face. Then he screamed piercingly, again and again. John Ware felt everything that the old man felt. He suffered the inexpressible agony of being consumed alive by flames. Then he was outside in the night. Far below and behind him the house burned like a torch in the distance. Ware glanced fearfully at the shadow that accompanied him as they sped on—tremendous speed, ever westward.

ONCE again Ware felt himself hurtling down through the night. Where to this time? What unspeakable torment was he to endure now? All was dark about him He glimpsed no city or abode as he flashed to earth. About him was only silence and darkness. Then like a wave engulfing his spirit, came a torrent of fear and dread He was striving to push something upward. Panic thoughts consumed him. He would not die—he wanted to live—he would escape! He writhed and twisted in his narrow confines, his fists beating on the surface above him. It did not yield. John Ware knew that he was linked with the consciousness of a man who had been prematurely buried. Soon the victim's fists were dripping with blood as he ineffectually clawed and pounded at the lid of the coffin. As time is measured it didn't last long. The exertions of the doomed man caused him quickly to exhaust the small amount of air in the coffin and he soon smothered to death. John Ware experienced that, too. But the final obliterating and crushing of the hope that burned in the man's bosom probably was the worst of all.

Ware was again soaring through the night. His soul shuddered as he grasped the final, unmistakable significance of the night's experiences. *He, he* was to be the victim, the sufferer, throughout this long hour of midnight!

He had thought that by accompanying the dark being around the earth, he would share in the savoring of all the evils that flourish in the midnight hour. He *was* participating—but not as he had expected. Instead, *he* was the victim, the cringing, tormented one. Perhaps this dark being he had summoned was jealous of its pleasures, or perhaps it derived an additional intensity of satisfaction by adding John Ware's consciousness to those of its victims.

Ware was descending again. There was no resisting the force that flung him earth ward.

He was completely helpless before the power he had summoned—what now? What new terror would he experience?

On and on, ever westward through the night, John Ware endured horror after horror. He died again and again, each time in a more fearsome manner. He was subjected to revolting tortures and torments as he was linked with victim after victim. He knew the frightful nightmare of human minds tottering on the abyss of madness. All that is black and unholy and is visited upon mankind he experienced as he roamed the earth with the midnight being.

Would it never end? Only the thought that these sixty minutes must pass sustained him. But it did not end. It seemed an eternity had gone by. Such suffering could not be crowded into a single hour. It must be days since he had left his body.

Days, nights, sixty minutes, one hour? John Ware was struck with a realization of terrific impact. It seemed to be communicated to him from the dark being at his side. Horribly clear did that being make the simple truth. John Ware was lost. Weeks, even months, might have passed since he had left his body. Time, for him, had stopped still.

John Ware was eternally chained to the amorphous black shape, and was doomed to exist thus horribly forever, suffering endless and revolting madness, torture and death through eternity. He had stepped into that band of time known as midnight, and was caught, trapped hopelessly doomed to move with the grain of time endlessly around the earth.

For as long as the earth spins beneath the sun, one side of it is always dark and in that darkness midnight dwells forever.

THE END

THE VALLEY OF THE GODS

By EDMOND HAMILTON

Places of death are not feared by an archaeologist—that is, most places!

GARTH ABBOTT was vividly aware of the danger for him in this night-shrouded place of the dead. He did not need the whispered warnings of his nervous companion to tell him what discovery of them here would mean.

It would mean, pretty certainly, the abrupt death of a too-bold young American archaeologist in this obscure little village on the Usumacinta River in upper Guatemala. The primitive folk here would deal swift vengeance to a foreigner whom they caught desecrating their cemetery.

Jose Yanez, the guide whom. Abbott had picked up in Puerto Barrios, very obviously realized that to the full. His flat, swarthy face was pallid in the rays of their lantern.

"Senor Abbott, you don't understand," he persisted. "These people are mostly Indians, still savage. If they catch us—"

"They won't—they're all at the *baile*," Abbott retorted. "Here, give me the lantern. You bring the crowbars."

The rays of the old-fashioned lantern vaguely illumined a jumble of ancient stone crosses. Behind them rose the dark, squat church, and farther behind was the marketplace from which rose a rhythmic dance music of marimbas, flutes, and drums.

Abbott had a rough native cloak slung around his shoulders to ward off the night dew, but his tawny bead was bare. And as he advanced through the solemn aisles of ancient crosses, his strong, rawboned face flared with excitement. He sensed himself on the verge of great discovery.

The somber eeriness of the ancient graveyard did not affect him. He ignored the evil-looking bush-vultures that boldly roosted on the stone markers and eyed the passing lantern like unclean spirits. Places of death were no novelty to an archaeologist, and he was immune to superstition.

Interior illustration by Boris Dolgov

"That's the mound just ahead!" he eagerly told his apprehensive companion. "Quick, bring along the tools!"

The mound rose squat and black just beyond the graveyard proper. It was a grassy hillock a dozen feet high, whose southern face had been partially washed away by recent rains.

Abbott had noticed that earlier in the day. His trained eyes had instantly fastened on the great hewn stones whose edges were exposed by the washout, and which bore chiseled Mayan glyphs.

The hillock concealed a Mayan tumulus of some sort. And Abbott had been set afire by his glimpse of one group of glyphs that spelled a magic name—the name "Xibalba."

Xibalba! That was the mythical lost birthplace of the Mayas, the legendary valley from which their strange race was fabled to have come, two thousand years before!

Did that fabled valley really exist somewhere deep within the unexplored Guatemalan mountain fastnesses? Many scholars had thought so. Stephens himself, the great pioneer of Mayan archaeology, had talked with a man who claimed to have seen Xibalba with his own eyes.

If lost Xibalba could be found, all the riddles of the mysterious Mayan civilization might be solved. The civilization that long ago had reared its mighty monuments and splendid stone cities from the lowlands of Honduras to the jungles of Yucatan, might then yield answers to the enigmas that had puzzled modern men.

THE mere fact that this tomb might be a clue to Xibalba had set Garth Abbott afire to excavate it. But when he had asked permission from the priest of the nearby church, he had met a check.

"I dare not permit that, senor! Pagan superstition still runs deep in many of my primitive flock, and that mound is to them a sacred, forbidden spot. You would risk your life by digging into it."

Abbott had refused to give up. He had told Yanez, "We'll wait until tonight when they're all at the fiesta and open the mound ourselves."

"But when they find out what we have done—" the Guatemalan had objected fearfully.

"They won't find out. I'll simply make flash-photos of all the inscriptions and then close it up again till later."

He had waited with intense eagerness all that day for night and the fiesta to come, feeling himself on the brink of a tremendous archaeological discovery.

Xibalba! The legend-haunted name rang in his mind like a golden bell. If he could find that fabled shrine of the Mayan gods and heroes, what might he not find there?

It had begun to rain softly now, as he and Yanez set their lantern on the ground and studied the raw earth side of the mound. The yellow day almost completely hid the huge stones within.

Abbott estimated that the mound contained a low, round rock vault, most of it buried beneath the present ground level.

"Clear that soil away—that's it," he directed Yanez. "Now we'll pry out one of these stones and see if it opens a way into the vault."

The big block they attacked was inscribed with the word Mayan glyphs. Again, Abbott felt a leap of the pulse as he recognized the symbol for Xibalba—and also the one for "Kukulcan."

Kukulcan was the Mayan god of light and thunder, the great Plumed Serpent. Why was his symbol here? Abbott's eagerness grew.

The block suddenly gave way and slid out onto the wet clay. The lantern showed them a yawning black cavity.

Quivering with excitement, Abbott squirmed through the square opening. In the darkness within, he lowered himself to a stone floor. Yanez passed through the lantern, and Abbott stared.

"Good God, what a find!"

The interior of the vault was a brilliant little treasure-chamber of mystery.

Its chief object was a wonderful stone sarcophagus, over which reared the coils and grotesque head of the Plumed Serpent.

"The serpent of Kukulcan! This is early Mayan, all right. But the Mayans never entombed anyone like this!"

He stared incredulously around the chamber. Its walls were a brilliant pageant of painted sculptures.

Not two thousand years had dimmed the cunning color of those marching figures. They were Mayan of the Old Empire's earliest period, those columns of priests, warriors, and captains.

The pictured pageant represented a great migration. Above the marching columns of stiff figures extended a queer running chart that showed mountains ranges and passes, a great river—

"That river's the Usumacinta itself!" ejaculated Abbott. "The configuration is the same. Why, this is a picture history of the first great Mayan migration!"

He realized the vast importance of his discovery. This long-buried vault was key to the greatest mystery of Mayan archaeology, the riddle of the people's origin.

Eagerly holding the lantern high, Garth Abbott followed the story back around the walls. The painted migration marched bask, up the Usumacinta and then northwestward between two ranges that he knew must be the Ollones and Chistango.

Its beginning was in a place represented as a long, straight valley at the foot of a square black mountain. Here was the representation of a city. And here the glyphs again spelled the magic name.

"Xibalba!" Abbott exclaimed. "The Mayan valley of the gods! Why, with this chart, I could *find* that valley!"

His excitement soared. On that painted chart, in the valley of fabled Xibalba, he perceived two curious dominating symbols.

One was the rearing, fiery plumed snake of the god Kukulcan. The other was the dark, bat-winged figure of Zotzilha, the Mayan Lord of evil. Black bat and plumed Snake were pictured in deadly battle there in the valley!

Yanez had lifted the stone lid of the sarcophagus. "Senor, there is something in this stone coffin!"

Abbott's lantern spilled light into the coffin. There was dust in it, dust that had once been a man. But there was also the gleam of gold ornaments jeweled with jade.

A SWORD lay in the dust. It was a weapon of the most ancient Mayan pattern, a short, heavy copper sword edged with brilliant saw-teeth of green obsidian. The hilt was a miraculous carving of the plumed serpent, whose eyes were two big blazing emeralds.

Abbott eagerly picked the sword from the dust. "Whoever was buried here must have been a king, a great leader—"

He stiffened, his voice trailing off. For as his hand closed around the sword hilt, his senses suddenly swam from shock.

Power, tangible and tingling force, seemed rushing up into his arm and body from the ancient sword!

A roar like the thunder of waves dinned in Abbott's ears. He seemed encompassed by whirling mists, seemed to feel a vast and *alien* personality somehow seize upon his brain.

The mists abruptly darkened and before him flashed a face! A dark, smooth, handsome face with heavy-lidded eyes, which in spite of its unearthly beauty was somehow—hideous.

Repulsion, horror and a bitter hatred shook Abbott. Something in his mind, or in that alien mind that had weirdly gripped him, seemed to recognize that hovering face in the darkness.

"Zotzilha Chimalman!" Abbott heard a voice inside his brain flaring. "So you have watched, evil one?"

Silver-sweet, mocking laughter chimed from the handsome face before him. Its heavy-lidded eyes were taunting, malicious. "Aye, I have watched, for I knew that you would seek someday to return, Kukulcan. But it is too late now!"

"Not while I live!" Abbott heard that mental voice raging. "And I *do* live now and soon I will—"

"Senor!"

Yanez's cry had such horror in it that it brought Garth Abbott back to awareness. He found that he had dropped the sword.

He looked a little dazedly around the low, lantern-lit tomb, and then at the Guatemalan's scared face.

"Senor, your face was strange," shivered Yanez. "It was like one of *those!*"

And he pointed at the fierce-faced warrior-priests pictured on the wall.

"I must have, been dizzy, delirious, for a moment," stammered Abbott. "The air in this place is bad."

He was still quivering from the weirdness of that momentary delusion, but he forced it from his mind.

What the hell, Kukulcan and Zotzilha were mere phantoms, the forgotten gods of a people perished a thousand years ago! The influences of this place had been too much for his nerves, for a moment.

"Come on, Jose—we'll make our photographs and get out of here."

When they squirmed out of the vault a half-hour later, Abbott brought with him that strange sword.

Yanez looked wonderingly, almost fearfully, at him after they had replaced the block.

"And now, senor?"

Abbott's voice rang with excitement. "Now I've got a clue archaeologists have hunted for years—a clue to the lost heartland of the Mayas. We're going to charter a plane and search for Xibalba!"

But why was it, he wondered, that the name of the fabled valley was no longer golden and luring in his ears? Why was it that the very name of Xibalba was now somehow freighted with *dread?*

CHAPTER TWO

THE plane was a stout little two-place job that Abbott had chartered from an air-express line in Barrios. It manfully bucked the tricky currents that swirled low over these blue scarps and ranges of the vast hinterland.

Abbott had been a war pilot in the Pacific, and hunting out an objective in unknown terrain was nothing new to him. But after hours of quartering the tumbled mountains northeast of the Usumacinta, he had to admit himself baffled.

"The valley I'm hunting should be right down there," he said impatiently, pointing. "But it just isn't."

Yanez looked skeptical. "The chart in that tomb was made a very long time ago."

"Mountains and valleys don't shift around," Abbott retorted. "It should be here. We'll circle around again."

He had carefully traced back the route designated by the pictured chart in the tomb—the route from Xibalba that had been followed by the Mayans of long ago. He had gone up beyond the Usumacinta, northeast between the Ollones and Chistango ranges, then on until he had spotted the stark, square black mountain of the pictures.

And the long, straight, narrow valley he sought should be somehow in sight south of that black mountain, but wasn't. There was nothing but a tumbled wilderness of blue peaks and green forest.

Yanez was obviously uneasy. This hinterland was nearly all Lacandone country, and those wild tribes weren't hospitable to fliers who make forced landings in their forests.

The Guatemalan presently uttered a warning. "The sky is getting queer."

Abbott abruptly realized that a strange change had come over the heavens. All around him the sky was growing strangely *dark*.

It was not the darkness of gathering clouds. It was as though the light of the sky was being conquered and submerged by a surging darkness from nowhere.

It was like the weird vibrant darkness that had momentarily enveloped his mind in his strange experience in the tomb!

"Better get out of here!" Abbott exclaimed, banking around sharply. "It's some queer freak of weather—"

Next moment he realized their imminent danger. The unnatural gloom had deepened to such degree that he could barely make out the stupendous peaks that rose about them.

With a startled exclamation, Abbott opened the throttle. There was absolutely no wind, nothing but an unholy stillness in which the shadowy darkness gloomed and thickened.

He took a course to avoid the great square peak, which he could no longer see. Then things happened swiftly.

A blinding flash of lightning seared across the heavens and revealed the black peak looming up just ahead of the plane!

Yanez yelled wildly, and Abbot jerked hard at the controls. The plane started to curve sharply about, but he had a sickening realization that he was too late to avoid crashing into the cliffs.

But a howling gust of storm wind suddenly smote the little ship and flung it bodily back from the looming cliffs.

"Good God!" he cried, as he fought the controls. "If it hadn't been for that storm gust—"

Thunder crashed to drown his voice. Sudden storm was unloosing its fury, spears of terrific lightning tearing the unnatural darkness to shreds, an inferno of winds raging around the little plane.

AGAIN and again, that strange darkness closed in and left Abbott flying blind amid those threatening peaks. And again and again the lightning of the thunderstorm ripped through the gloom!

Lightning that was like fiery serpents writhing across the heavens, struggled titanically with the black-winged darkness that strove to annihilate them! So seemed that infernal battle of the heavens to Abbott, as he hunched over the controls.

A thin wail of terror came from the Guatemalan as the plane sank sickeningly. "The storm carries us downward!"

Abbott saw the altimeter needle rushing back. The plane was helpless in the grip of the howling storm.

Again the fire-snakes uncoiled across the sky.

By their flare, Abbott glimpsed the earth below rushing wildly up at them.

Then he glimpsed something else—a long, straight black line that looked like a mere crack in the earth. It was a narrow canyon, of unguessable depth, invisible from ordinary altitudes.

"That's the valley below!" he yelled. "That long canyon must be Xibalba!"

"We fall!" yelled Yanez, eyes popping from his head.

Invisible giant hands of the thunder storm were dragging the laboring plane down toward that canyon, down into it!

"Bail out!" he yelled to the Guatemalan. "We're going to crash!"

He grabbed up his pack, scrambled to the cabin door. He pushed Yanez out ahead of him and then they were turning over and over in the air as they plunged downward.

Their parachutes puffed out.

As they fell amid lightning-torn wind and blackness and thunder, Abbott had dazed glimpses of lightning-illumined scenes below.

He glimpsed forests, gardens, the walls and terraces of a white stone city. Then with a ripping of silk, the parachute let him down through trees and brush. He felt a shock, and then knew nothing.

When he recovered consciousness, Yanez was bending anxiously over him. The Guatemalan's swarthy face was scratched, and looked wild.

"Senor, I feared you dead!" he stuttered. "This place—"

Abbott sat up. Awe and wonder fell upon him as he looked around.

There was no storm now. Quiet peace reigned here in a green forest of fairylike beauty. Tall ceibas, cedars, and willows waved in the balmy breeze, in a curiously golden daylight.

Abbott looked up. The softened light fell from the crack of sky high above, the mouth of the canyon. Two miles above his head it yawned, and the canyon itself was only a mile in width.

"The merest crack in the surface of earth!" he marveled, "No wonder it's never been spotted by any plane."

Sudden remembrance increased his excitement. "I saw a city as we fell! A city, here in Xibalba—"

Yanez gripped his arm. "There are men around us in the forest, senor. I have heard them gathering."

Abbott scrambled to his feet. As he did so, from the trees around them stepped a score of fantastic figures!

TO THE young archaeologist, it was as though the remote past had suddenly come to life. These were warriors of the ancient Maya!

Copper-red, fierce-eyed men, their garb and weapons matched the sculptures on the walls of Chichen Itza and Uxmal and Copan.

They wore wonderful headdresses of brilliant red and green feathers, built upon light wooden frameworks; short kirtles of jaguar skin and sandals of the same hide; belts of leather gemmed with jade and emerald. Their arms were spears and swords tipped with obsidian, like that ancient sword in his pack.

"Mayans, of the oldest period!" whispered Abbott, his brain rocking. "By Heaven, the fabled valley, the city—is *living!*"

Abbott felt a thrill only an archaeologist could understand. For years, scholars had dreamed of finding a lost, living remnant of the old Mayan civilization.

Many a search had been made, in vain. But the clue of the old tomb, and the thunderstorm that had swept them down into this hidden canyon, had brought him into the heart of such, a survival.

Abbott spoke to the advancing warriors in the Mayan tongue that has remained almost unchanged through the centuries, "We are—friends! We come from above, from outside this valley!"

The warriors stopped, swords raised. Upon the fierce face of their magnificently attired captain came a look of incredulity.

"From outside? You are lying, stranger! No man could descend the walls!"

"It is truth!" Abbott persisted. "Thunderstorm swept us down here—"

The captain's face stiffened. "You say that thunderstorm brought you? That is strange—that is very strange."

Abbott could not understand what the other meant. He watched the play of doubt on that dark red face.

The captain finally spoke, "This matter is not for my judgment. I, Vipal, am but a captain in the guards of Ummax, the king. You will come with us to Xibalba for his judgment."

"This is Xibalba, then?" cried Abbott eagerly. "The valley of the gods, of Zotzilha and Kukulcan?"

His question had an amazing effect. The Mayan warriors seemed to start, and into Vipal's yellow eyes leaped a fierce light.

"What do *you* know of Kukulcan, strangers?" he cried menacingly.

Abbott sensed that he had somehow blundered badly. He should have known better than to start asking questions so soon.

"I meant no harm," he said earnestly. "I thought that Kukulcan, the Plumed Serpent, the lord of thunder, was the greatest of your gods."

"Repeat that blasphemy and you'll not live to reach Xibalba!" hissed Vipal. "Come!"

Abbott, wondering, picked up his pack. More and more, this whole experience seemed dreamlike to him.

Two thousand years might have rolled back for him, he thought. This buried valley hidden in the mountain-guarded wilderness lay untouched by time and Change.

But if these Mayans held true to the ancient civilization, why had his mention of Kukulcan so enraged them? Kukulcan *had* been the most worshipped of the old gods in the Mayan cities of long ago, had been the thunder god, the enemy of dark Zotzilha and his evil powers.

Yanez trudged beside him, the tall, somber-eyed Mayan warriors marching on each side of them. Before they had gone far through the forest, they struck a broad trail that ran northward up the valley.

The forests were green and lovely. A small river flowed down the valley and the trail kept beside it. Looking up, Abbott glimpsed at the north end of the canyon the giant square black peak that blocked its end. Its frowning cliffs loomed stark and brutal.

He thought he could descry a massive flight of stairs leading up the cliff to the portaled entrance of a black-mouthed cavern.

"What is that cavern in the distant mountain?" he ventured to ask Vipal.

The captain looked at him stonily. "It is a place which I think you will soon see, stranger."

The menace in the answer was clear, if the meaning was not. Abbott felt more and more enmeshed in mystery and danger. The trail led them past a giant, ancient stone pyramid-temple that rose in the forest. It looked crumbling, neglected, a terraced pyramid like the great temple at Chichen Itza.

Abbott glimpsed stone heads of gigantic plumed serpents rearing from its terraces, and realized it was the temple of Kukulcan. Why was it so d forsaken, abandoned to the forest?

Then that riddle passed from his mind in a shock of wonder. The trail had emerged from the forest. Before them, beyond gardens and orchards, rose the fantastic white mass of the city Xibalba.

CHAPTER THREE

GOLDEN light of the dying day struck across the city. It was a mass of low, flat-roofed white stucco structures, which were grouped around a central duster of sculptured stone palaces and pyramidal shrines. Biggest of the palaces was a massive, oblong pile surrounded by porticoes of giant columns, rich with grotesque carving.

Toward that barbarically magnificent structure, Abbott and Yanez were led by their fierce-eyed guards. As they entered the paved streets, the American's fascinated eyes beheld a vista of ancient Mayan life such as he had never expected to witness.

Copper-skinned men and women of the lower class were here in great numbers, thronging to stare in wonder at the two strangers. Farmers, potters, weavers, all these were dressed both sexes alike in short kirtles that left their bodies bare above the waist. Here and there brilliant plumed captains and dark-robed priests stood out in the throng.

They crossed wonderful gardens and paved ball-courts to enter the massive palace. Abbott guessed that a runner had gone ahead of them, when they stepped into the long, torch lit main hall.

For Ummax the king sat upon his throne of carven wood awaiting them, and warriors, priests and women crowded the room.

"Now, how came you into Xibalba, strangers?" demanded the king of Abbott, "Long has entrance to our valley been blocked by the great landslide of long ago."

Ummax was a giant of a man, his huge limbs wrapped in magnificent jaguar skins and jeweled leather trappings, the brilliant Plumes of his fantastic headdress falling halfway to the floor. He sat with a massive black stone mace across his knees.

His dark red face was gross but stark in its strength, with brutality and cunning in his eyes as he glared at Abbott.

The captain Vipal spoke before Abbott could answer. "They say that they were brought down into the valley by thunderstorm."

A big warrior beside the throne, a grizzled, one-eyed, scarred-faced captain in white plumes, uttered a loud exclamation.

"By thunderstorm? And this stranger is fair of hair, as legend tells of—"

The king Ummax interrupted fiercely. "What you hint at is impossible, Huroc! The man is lying!"

A girl beyond the grizzled, scarred warrior spoke quietly. "The man cannot be lying when he has not yet spoken for himself."

Abbott looked at her in wonder and quick admiration. This Mayan princess was a figure of wild, barbaric loveliness.

Her slim copper body had for garment but a richly embroidered white linen kirtle, fringed with jade beads. Her soft shoulders and proud little breasts bare, her dark hair crowned by an elaborate headdress, her chiseled features and dark eyes had a compelling allure.

Ummax had turned on her furiously. You, Shuima, are supporting Huroc in hinting blasphemy! I tell you to beware!"

Abbott found his voice. "I do not understand all this. It is true that storm brought me here, yet I was searching for this valley Xibalba. I found a clue to its location in tomb far away."

"A tomb?" mocked Ummax. "A tomb that led you to Xibalba? All lies!"

He raised his hand. "Vipal, you will take these two strangers to—"

"I'm telling the truth!" Abbott broke in desperately. And then he bethought himself of a half-proof he could show.

He stooped swiftly and tore open the pack he had dropped at his feet. From it, he drew that ancient, short, heavy sword. "See, I found this sword in the tomb! There was an inscription, telling—"

Abbott's voice trailed off. A strange and sudden change had come over every human being in the barbaric, torch lit hall.

Ummax, the big one-eyed captain Huroc, the girl Shuima—they and everyone else seemed stricken by a strange paralysis as they stared at the ancient, heavy weapon in Abbott's hand.

"The sword of Kukulcan!" whispered Huroc, his single eye wild, flaming with excitement. "Then the Plumed One after all these ages has returned!"

Ummax bounded to his feet, towering gigantic, clutching his great black mace as he glared at Abbott.

"So it *was* the lord of thunder who brought you here!" he hissed.

And then, abruptly, Abbott saw a strange and awful change take place in Ummax's face.

It suddenly distorted into a wholly different face, into the handsome, heavy-lidded, evil countenance that Abbott had confronted in that strange vision in the tomb.

Darkness seemed to gloom and thicken in the torch-lit hall! Unearthly darkness, something cold, alien, terrifying—

AND then swiftly the handsome, evil face was gone, and it was Ummax's own brutal, raging countenance that looked down at him.

Ummax seemed to struggle for control over himself before he spoke.

"Stranger, that sword is known here," he said finally. "Your tale may be true. At least, we welcome you as a guest until we can speak further of these things.

"Conduct them to fitting quarters," he told Vipal jerkily. And then he added fiercely, glaring around the awe-stricken throng, "And let no blasphemous talk of these things go abroad!"

Abbott, stunned and mystified, put the sword back into his pack and with Yanez followed the captain Vipal from the room.

The face of the tigerish Mayan warrior looked ashen in the torchlight of the sculptured corridors through which he led. He bowed low as he ushered them into a long, white-walled chamber.

"Food and drink will be brought you, lords," he said huskily, and withdrew.

Abbott looked wonderingly around the torch-illumined room. Brilliant feather tapestries woven with familiar Mayan designs hung from the walls. Low stools of carven wood and bright woven mats were the only furniture. Small barred windows looked out into the night.

Quickly, serving-maids appeared with colorful pottery trays and bowls and flagons. The copper-skinned girls, fair bodies bare to the waist, looked with extreme awe at Abbott and Yanez as they set down their burdens.

One, bowing low before him, seized his hand and pressed it to her lips.

"Many in Xibalba have waited long for Kukulcan's return, lord!" she whispered.

Abbott stared after them when they had gone. "I'll be damned! Because of that sword and the thunderstorm, these people have identified me somehow with their god Kukulcan!"

"Gods of thunder and gods of evil—this place is unholy, accursed!" exclaimed Yanez, crossing himself.

The Guatemalan's swarthy face was pale, his hands shaking. Abbott slapped him reassuringly on the shoulder.

"Buck up, Jose. Just because they're superstitious is no reason why it should affect us."

"It is not just superstition, no!" said Yanez feverishly. "You saw that devil-king call hell's demons to him there in the throne-room! You saw his face, saw the darkness that gathered—"

"Hell, will you let a few grimaces and a chance shadow scare you?" Abbott demanded impatiently. "We've found a wonderful place, a place that will make us famous. Forget all this nonsense of gods and devils."

But later, after they had eaten and were stretched on soft malts in the darkened chamber, Abbott found it not easy to forget.

He lay, watching the flickering gleam of torchlight that came through the windows from somewhere outside the palace, and turning over and over in his mind the weird situation into which he had stumbled.

WHY had the chance identification of himself with Kukulcan roused in these people such deep and opposed emotions, of rage on the part of Ummax, of awe in others, of fervent hope in some? What *had* happened there in the throne-room when it had so strangely darkened?

Abbott did not realize that he had fallen into exhausted slumber until he suddenly awoke, alert and quivering. Then he heard a slight, stealthy sound.

A dark shadow was stealing toward him, bending over him. Instantly Abbott bounded upward and fiercely gripped the intruder.

He was thunderstruck to find himself gripping slim, soft naked shoulders, with perfumed hair against his face.

"Lord, it is I, Shuima!" whispered a throbbing voice. "Strike not for I am not your enemy!"

"Shuima? The princess in the throne room?" whispered Abbott, stunned. "What the devil—"

A bigger, dark figure crossed the torchlight gleam from the window, and Yanez awoke to utter a startled squawk.

"Quiet your friend or all is Lost!" warned Shuima swiftly. "It is Huroc, who has come with me on this mission."

Huroc? The grizzled one-eyed captain? Abbott felt more and more mystified but in a hasty whisper he silenced the Guatemalan.

Shuima's soft hand pulled him down to the floor beside the window. By the dim glimmer of light from outside, he could descry her chiseled face and the scarred mask of Huroc.

The girl was speaking quickly. "Lord, Huroc and I have come thus by secret stealth to your chamber, to warn you that at this very moment Ummax gathers the powers of the Bat-winged one against you!"

"The Bat-winged? You mean Zotzilha, your bat-god of darkness? Just what do you mean by that?" Abbott asked incredulously.

Huroc's deep voice throbbed. "Surely you know well. Have you not returned as we have long prayed you would, to crush that evil one? Is it not why you have come, lord Kukulcan?"

Abbott gasped. "You call me Kukulcan? This is all madness. I am no god."

"No, but you are the chosen of the god," Shuima said quickly. "You are the Holder of Kukulcan, as Ummax is Holder of dark Zotzilha."

Abbott mentally damned all superstition. Before he could protest, the girl was rapidly whispering on.

"It is strange that you do not realize these things yourself! For Kukulcan brought you here, his thunders sweeping you down into our valley as you told. And Kukulcan will surely manifest himself in you, for the final struggle that even now impends."

"Struggle? With what? With whom?" Abbott wanted to know.

"With the Bat-winged!" Huroc growled fiercely, his huge figure shaking with hatred. "With the dark lord of evil who for generations has fed and fattened upon our helpless race!"

CHAPTER FOUR

SHUIMA'S soft fingers gripped Abbott's hand passionately as she whispered swiftly.

Twenty centuries have passed since *both* Kukulcan and Zotzilha manifested themselves through living men in our valley. Zotzilha, the Bat-winged, to batten upon the life force of the sacrifices offered him. But Kukulcan, the Plumed Serpent, to teach and help us!

"Kukulcan, though his Holder, blessed our people then. He drove the Bat-winged back into his lair in the black mountain, and he taught us ways of peace and happiness. Then, in a fateful day, the prince of Iltzlan who was then the Holder of Kukulcan led a tribe of our folk into the outer world when this valley became too small for our numbers.

"Iltzlan never returned! And the sword of Kukulcan by which a man could alone become Holder of the god, was lost with him in the outer world. So dark Zotzilha came forth from his lair and dominated our people, and since then has reigned in wickedness over them through sum instrument's as that Ummax who is now his Holder.

"But now you have come back with the sword, and now we know that Kukulcan means to manifest himself through you and to end the tyranny of the Bat-winged and his creatures in Xibalba forever!"

Abbott was appalled. The superstitious dualism of this lost people's faith had involved his own person.

His possession of that sword that he had taken from the tomb, which he now knew was Iltzlan's, had made them think him a chosen instrument of their god Kukulcan.

"I know nothing of gods!" he protested. "By my people, Kukulcan is considered a mere myth."

"Kukulcan is no myth!" Huroc exclaimed. "He is force, invisible but tangible, real, mighty—aye, as Zotzilha is real and mighty. The Plumed Serpent is but the symbol of his lightnings. The real Kukulcan is not of this world."

It sounded almost convincing. But Abbott forced himself to dismiss superstition from his mind. He must keep his head clear.

"Just what do you expect me to do to unseat Ummax-Zotzilha's tyranny? You have some plan?"

Shuima's answer stunned him. "You go with us now to the neglected Temple of the Plumed Serpent. There have already gathered a host of those in Xibalba who still are secretly devoted to Kukulcan—like the two guards at your doorway who let us into your chamber.

"There in his temple, Kukulcan will manifest himself in you as his Holder. And when our people see that, they will follow you to the death against Ummax and his warriors!"

Abbott was appalled. They expected some kind of supernatural possession to manifest itself in him.

It was insane. Yet he had to fall in with the idea, to humor their belief, if he were not to be murdered in this palace-trap.

"All right. I'll go," he said quickly. "But remember that I claim none of the kinship with Kukulcan that you credit!"

He turned to the Guatemalan. "Yanez, it might be safer for you to get clear of this whole tangle once we're out of the palace. I don't want to drag you into further danger."

"I think there is danger everywhere in this valley tonight, senor," whispered Yanez. "And I go where you go."

Huroc opened the door, torchlight from the corridor outside outlining his massive figure. He had a heavy sword in his hand.

"Let us be quick! And forget not the consecrated sword, lord Kukulcan!"

Abbott took the heavy, ancient sword from his pack and followed the huge one-eyed warrior and the slim girl into the hallway.

The two guards on duty outside it bowed to him with deep reverence. "We are of the faith, Lord Kukulcan!"

"Come! This way!" whispered Shuima.

They had taken but ten steps toward the angle of the corridor when there suddenly came around it the captain, Vipal.

The Mayan was not three feet in front of them, and his tigerish face stiffened as he struck with the drawn sword in his hand.

"I *guessed* there might be treachery!" he hissed, as the obsidian-edged blade drove at Abbott's heart.

With a low, warning cry, Yanez shoved Abbott violently aside. As Abbott reeled, he heard a choking gasp.

"Senor—"

HE REGAINED footing, whirled with the ancient sword uplifted. But in that brief moment, it was already over.

Big Huroc's giant arm had whipped around Vipal's throat. There was a dull, cracking sound, and the tigerish warrior went limp with eyes rolling horribly.

"Quieter that way!" panted the one-eyed giant.

"Lord, your friend is hurt!" exclaimed Shuima.

Yanez lay, clutching the ghastly wound made in his side by that swift, saw-toothed sword. His face drained of color.

He whispered a word to Abbott bending frantically over him. The word and his life ended together.

"Damn it. I brought the man to death!" choked Abbott. "He took that sword-blow meant for me—"

"Death is close for all of us unless we get out of the palace at once," warned Huroc. He swung to the two guards who had come racing along the corridor. "Hide these bodies! We go!"

Abbott's brain was whipped with grief, remorse, doubt, as he followed the giant and the girl hastily out of the palace.

Deep black brooded the night over Xibalba, only a thin scimitar of stars across the heavens marking the mouth of the canyon high overhead. He stumbled with his guides across gardens, along unlighted and deserted narrow streets of the low city.

The torch-lit mass of the palace fell behind and presently they were in the forest and pressing along a narrow trail. Birds screamed in the dark trees as they passed, branches whipped their faces.

Huroc looked back and uttered a low exclamation. Abbott descried, far back at the north end of the valley, torches made tiny by distance coming down the stair in that massive mountain-cliff.

"Ummax returns from the Temple of the Bat-winged!" rasped the one-eyed giant. "He will miss you, and then—"

He did not finish, but quickened his pace, Shuima's hand on Abbott's arm urging him ever faster.

Then through the forest filtered red torchlight. There rose before them the looming white terraces of the great pyramidal Temple of the Plumed Serpent.

Men and women numbering many hundreds waited with flaring torches on the terraces, a tense and silent host. Many were warriors fully armed, and the eyes of all fastened on Abbott's face as he went between his two companions up the first massive stairway.

"The sword! It *is* Kukulcan's sword!" he heard them whisper excitedly as they glimpsed the ancient weapon he carried.

"The lord of thunder! The Plumed Serpent!" swelled the cry.

ABBOTT felt dazed when he reached the flat shrine atop the pyramid. Here reared two enormous stone effigies of the plumed snake, great bodies coiled, mighty heads challengingly upthrust. Between them was a stone chair around which their coils writhed protectingly.

He turned and looked down at the hosts on the torch-lit terraces. A deep, taut silence had now fallen upon them, and their faces were like graven masks of utter expectation turned up to him.

"You must sit in the chair of the Holder, and grasp the sword while we make the invocation to Kukulcan," Huroc told him.

"Huroc! Shuima! This is all crazy!" Abbott protested. "What you expect cannot happen."

"We *know* that you are the chosen Holder or you would not have found the sword!" exclaimed Huroc. "Take your place! The invocation begins."

They were chanting, those hosts down on the terraces. Chanting words that were familiar to Abbott from the old inscriptions.

"Bright One, Lord of the Thunder,
Plumed Serpent of living lightning—"

Sitting there above them, gripping the ancient sword, Abbott heard a low roll of thunder up the canyon and groaned inwardly.

"They'll think it the answer to their invocation! And when nothing else happens—"

"Lord of the storm-swept sky—"

The thunder rolled louder as the chant swelled. And Abbott stiffened suddenly on his stone seat.

Force again was rushing up from the sword into his arm and body, as it had seemed to in the tomb. But now more powerfully, his whole body tingling and quivering from its impact!

"Electric influences of that coming storm," Abbott tried to tell himself, his throat dry.

The torch-lit throng below seemed to dissolve in bright mists, the swell of the chant and the roll of thunder to merge into a steady roaring in his ears.

He whirled, spun, was engulfed by shining mist. And again, but more completely how, he felt the impact upon his brain of a mind cool, vast and alien.

"I am he whom these folk call Kukulcan. But I am no god."

He *heard* that cool, quiet voice, in the whirling mists. Yet it spoke inside his own brain!

"You live in a universe that has infinitely many dimensions unknown to you. In those dimensional abysses dwell entities such as you have not imagined, formless, bodiless, yet powerful. And some of them are—evil.

"Long ago, one of those evil ones escaped our watch and penetrated through to the dimension of your Earth. He laired in this valley, became worshipped and dreaded as the Bat-winged, as a god of evil, by these ignorant folk.

"I, whose fault allowed his escape, was sent to force him back into his own dark dimensional gulfs. But he had grown too strong! He has maintained himself here feeding on the life force of sacrifices and utilizing men as his instruments, for centuries.

"And for centuries I have been unable to interfere, because the sword you hold was lost by chance in the outer world. That sword is a cunningly contrived key, which can open the way between dimensions and allow me to manifest myself through the man who holds it. Your finding it enabled me to use you as my instrument against the Bat-winged.

"He must be destroyed, now or never, lest he grow too great for this valley and reach dark arms out over your earth. The black mace of Ummax is the key by which *he* can reach into this world. You must secure and destroy that mace, at all costs!"

Crash of thunder shook the mists that shrouded Garth Abbott's mind, and suddenly those bright mists were fading.

He opened dazed eyes upon the faces and windblown torches beneath him, and saw awe in Huroc's burning eye and Shuima's face. He knew that his own face must have been strange, unhuman.

Down from the gathering storm smote lightning that seemed to dance upon the temple top and outline the great Plumed Serpents of stone beside him, like coiling snakes of living fire.

"Kukulcan!" roared the throng beneath, frantically acclaiming the dazed Abbott. "Kukulcan returns!"

Abbott, brain reeling from that weird mental possession that still seemed partly to grip him, found himself crying out.

"I *am* the Holder of the Plumed Serpent! Kukulcan returns in me! And I say that we march on Xibalba now, to pull down dark Zotzilha's tyranny forever!"

CHAPTER FIVE

DELUSION, hallucination born of waking nightmare that the rush and strangeness of events had brought him? He could not wholly believe that, with that supernal wrath and purpose still possessing his mind.

If an unearthly, evil thing *had* readied into earth from alien abysses, if he himself was really the human instrument by which it must be driven back, he must not linger now to doubt!

"Huroc, gather our warriors!" he cried. "We march back on the city at once."

"We're ready now!" shouted the giant. "Our one chance is to surprise Ummax and—"

Shrill wail from the forest interrupted him, and up onto the torch-lit terraces of the temple staggered a Mayan warrior covered with blood and dust.

"The city's people have risen against Ummax!" he cried. "When the king returned from the Bat-winged's temple and gathered his guards to follow you here, the people rose for Kukulcan!"

"No chance of surprise now! It's started!" yelled Abbott. "Come on!"

Huroc and Shuima were beside him as his host poured through the forest in a torrent of torches and swords.

"The people can't stand long against Ummax's guards!" Huroc was shouting as they ran. "But with you to lead them, all things are possible!"

Thunder of the oncoming tempest rolled behind them as they burst out of the forest into sight of the city.

Xibalba writhed in the throes of battle! Wildly shaken torches revealed the clashing combat in its streets as Ummax's solid masses of guards cut through the seething mob of rebel citizens.

Abbott saw that the raging revolt wavered already on the brink of defeat, that the disciplined warriors were cutting swiftly through the wild mob.

"Slay all with arms in their hands!" roared Ummax's bull voice across the din. "Stamp out these traitors, once and for all!"

Abbott glimpsed the towering figure of the king, his wonderful plumes nodding above the heads of his guards as he brandished and struck with the great black mace that was his weapon.

That black mace was more than a weapon! In Abbott's fevered brain, as he charged beside Huroc, rang remembrance of that mental voice that had seemed to speak to him in the temple.

"The black mace of Ummax is the key by which Zotzilha can reach into this world. You must destroy it, at all costs!"

"Kukulcan! Kukulcan!" rose the wavering cry of the rebels, even as they fell back before the swords and spears of the guards.

"Kukulcan is *here!*" roared Huroc, as he and Abbott with their warriors crashed into the melee. "The Plumed Serpent leads us!"

At sight of Abbott's figure, of the heavy, ancient sword he carried, a thunderous shout roared from the mob. They surged forward in mad new charge.

Abbott felt himself carried as on the crest of a human wave against the solid ranks of Ummax's guards. Saw-edged swords and spears gleamed in the shaken torchlight before his eyes.

He struck blindly with his sword, felt it bite into flesh and bone. He glimpsed awe on the faces of Ummax's men as they fell back, a superstitious dread.

"We're breaking them!" shouted Huroc close beside him, the giant exultant. "On, Kukulcan!"

"Hold firm!" roared Ummax to his men. "The Bat-winged is with us. See!"

Ummax had raised his black mace high in the torchlight. A swift, subtle change was coming over the raging scene.

Cold, malefic darkness seemed rolling down in an awesome wave upon Abbott and Huroc and their advancing horde, smothering their torches, dazing and blinding them.

"The wings of our master fall upon them! Strike and spare not!" howled Ummax, exultant. "But take the false Kukulcan and the traitors Huroc and Shuima alive!"

Abbott felt the pulse of dismay, of dawning terror, through his forces as that chill, rolling darkness deepened over them.

They were giving back, crying aloud in fear! And he too felt a strange dread of that gathering gloom.

He told himself fiercely that he was letting superstition affect him, that it was only a blast of chill air from the storm rolling up the valley that was smothering the torches. And yet—

Ummax's guards were breaking among his shaken forces, swords were striking fiercely at him now, Huroc fighting madly beside him.

"Shuima is taken, our men give way!" the giant cried hoarsely. "Lord Kukulcan, unless you lift the Bat-winged's darkness—"

Shuima captured? Ummax roaring in triumph as he urged his triumphant warriors on? Steady, wrathful anger that was not his own mind's rage seemed to possess Abbott's brain fully now.

"Fear not!" he heard himself shouting. "Zotzilha's dark forces cannot stand against *these!*"

And he flung his hand to point skyward, at blinding lightning uncoiling and searing through the chill darkness.

THE hellish crash of thunder that followed those first lightnings of the breaking storm was punctuated by Huroc's cry.

"The fire-serpents of Kukulcan strike across the sky! The lord of thunder leads us!"

And as the full fury of the tempest crashed upon Xibalba, the warriors behind Abbott surged resistlessly forward.

"Kukulcan leads us!" shrilled the wild, exultant cry.

To Abbot, that battle in the storm-lashed streets became a mad chaos of swords and shouts and ghastly faces, of blinding lightning flaring in battle against sullen darkness.

Battle of gods as well as men? Or not of gods, but of entities from far beyond Earth's dimensions now in death-grapple here?

He could not speculate upon that now. He had but one objective in his mind, and that was to cut his way to Ummax and seize that mighty black mace which the towering king wielded.

But Ummax disappeared from view as the battle lost form and changed into a staggering, swirling melee. His guards were being split up, attacked in groups, overwhelmed by weight of raging numbers.

Abbott found Huroc grasping his arm, leaning to shout to him above the roll of thunder and hiss of rain.

"We've won the city! It's the end of Ummax's tyranny!"

"Not the end until he is dead and his black weapon in my hands!" cried Abbott. "Quick, to the palace! We must find him!"

Wolfishly-shouting, battle-fevered men poured after them over the last remnants, of resistance to the massive palace.

In the torch-lit corridors of the great pile they found no one but scared servants who gave them news of Ummax.

"The king and his last warriors fled past here to the Temple of the Bat-winged! They had the princess Shuima with them!"

Huroc uttered a hoarse exclamation. "We must catch them before they enter Zotzilha's dark cavern! For no man but Ummax himself can enter the Bat-winged's lair!"

Abbott whirled. "Quick, then! We can't wait for the others!"

With the hundred men who had followed them into the palace, he and Huroc plunged out into the tempest and hastened northward up the valley.

CHAPTER SIX

ABBOTT could have imagined no spectacle of such awesome grandeur as the thunderstorm that was moving with them up the great canyon. Confined between those lofty rock walls, its thunders were deafening and each lightning flash appeared to rive the universe.

Wind and rain were wildly rocking the forest along whose trails they pressed. They had no torches and only by light of the recurrent flashes could they finally make out the black looming bulk of the square mountain that headed the valley.

"See, they climb the stairs to the Bat-winged's temple!" yelled Huroc, pointing with his sword. "After them!"

"We follow, Kukulcan!" cried the maddened Mayan warriors behind them.

By the lightning flashes, Abbott saw the stair as a great flight of broad steps cut from the black living rock and leading right up the steep slope of the mountain.

Black stone statues of bat-winged Zotzilha guarded the landing halfway up the stair, and here Ummax's two-score guards had turned desperately with raised swords.

"They seek to hold us while Ummax escapes with Shuima into the Bat-winged's lair!" raged Huroc.

Abbott, by a blinding flash, himself saw Ummax climbing on up the stair and dragging the senseless form of the Mayan girl.

"Crush them down! See, Kukulcan's lightnings assault the evil one's lair!" Huroc encouraged.

The flashes of incessant lightning were indeed striking the face of the black mountain, riving away great masses of rock.

Reason told Abbott that metallic ores in the mountain must be attracting the lightning. But the stunning spectacle seemed to transcend such logic by its supernatural power.

Swords dashed and rang across the stair as they reached the landing and Ummax's guards. Abbott, staggering on the slippery wet stone, ducked one vicious blow and hacked at the distorted face beyond.

The lightning showed six men already cut down when the rest of Ummax's men, unnerved by the appalling flashes, gave up.

"Spare our lives, Kukulcan!" they cried, dropping their weapons. "The king forced us to stand against you!"

"Take them prisoner!" Abbott cried to his shouting warriors. "Now up the stair, Huroc!"

They raced with a score of their men up the last flight of massive steps. The whole mountain seemed rocking and quivering to the continuous lightning blasts as they reached the top landing.

This broad stone platform was a mere shelf cut in the side of the cliff. From it, a high, dark tunnel ran into the solid rock of the mountain. And over that dark portal spread the stone wings of Zotzilha, guarding, warding the lair within.

Abbott gripped his sword and started into the dark passage, and Huroc and the others hesitantly started to follow him.

They stepped into a deep darkness that was utterly cold. A freezing chill smote to Abbott's bones, a feeling of iciness and suffocation as the sullen darkness in the tunnel swiftly thickened.

"The Bat-winged's power is upon us!" choked Huroc. "I cannot move!"

He and the other Mayans seemed actually petrified, either by superstitious terror or by the malign grip of that icy darkness.

But though Abbott himself felt the smothering grasp of the frigid gloom, he was still able to struggle forward along the somber tunnel.

Flash on flash of lightning sent a momentary blinding glare down the passageway ahead of him, and for that moment he found himself able to pitch forward at increased speed.

"Kukulcan goes to slay the Bat-winged in his lair!" he heard Huroc shouting, behind him.

Abbott felt himself two utterly divergent beings as he pressed unsteadily forward through those gloomy cavern tunnels, sword gripped in his hand.

He was Garth Abbott, American and archaeologist, seeking to save the girl Shuima from the brutal savage tyrant who had dragged her here with murderous purpose.

But he was also the unearthly being who was using him as instrument, he was also that bright being from other world dimensions whose century-old struggle with a thing of evil had now reached climax.

"Zotzilha, I come!" he seemed to hear himself shouting fiercely down the tunnels. "Will you meet me, spawn of darkness?"

The part of him that was Garth Abbott rejected that fierce challenge as mere mental aberration born of the influence of storm and battle on his fevered mind.

But the part of him that was Kukulcan drove him forward with raging eagerness against the rolling, turbid darkness.

THE tunnel debouched into a mighty cavern. And here darkness seemed enthroned and supreme, a swirling blackness as of extra-terrestrial abysses that blinded and staggered Abbott.

Hoarse, bellowing laughter like banterings in hell broke echoing around Abbott as he swayed irresolute.

"So you came to meet me, Kukulcan? Then be it so!" it mocked.

A titan thunderclap rocked the mountain as bright lightning flashed from outside along the tunnels into this buried cavern.

The throbbing flare of fiery radiance for a moment illumined the whole interior of the cavernous space to Abbott's eyes.

He saw, across the cavern, the gigantic, looming stone image of a huge bat with outspread wings, whose red jewel-eyes glared down at him and at whose feet Shuima's slim body lay unmoving.

And he saw also Ummax towering beside him, black mace already raised to dash down upon his head!

The lightning flash died—and Abbott whirled away and heard the whistle of the mace as it grazed past him in falling.

Wrapped again in the suffocating cold darkness, Abbott lunged and stabbed with his sword—but stabbed empty air.

"This darkness is *my* realm!" mocked Ummax's voice. "You cannot escape—"

The lightning flared in the tunnels again, and in time to show Abbott that the towering Mayan was charging him.

Abbott struck savagely before the flare should fade, and felt his sword bite into his antagonist's shoulder. But the whirling mace struck his head a glancing blow, this time.

He staggered, felt himself falling, heard Ummax's hoarse shout of triumph. Desperately, as he fell, Abbott caught at the Mayan's legs and brought him down before he could swing the mace again.

They grappled on the rock floor of the cavern, Ummax ferociously choking him into helplessness. And the dancing flares of lightning that were now continuous in the outer tunnels showed Abbott the distorted face of Ummax as the supreme horror.

For it was the handsome, evil *alien* face he had twice before glimpsed that now had usurped Ummax's features.

Face of Zotzilha glaring down at him from the human body it used as instrument? Was his own face in this terrible moment the countenance of Garth Abbott or of Kukulcan?

His shaken senses were fading as Ummax's great hands throttled him. The towering Mayan leaped up, snatching up the black mace to bring it down on Abbott in a final deathblow.

Ummax's wounded shoulder checked him for a moment, forced him to shift his grip upon the mace. And in that moment, with desperate upsurge of last strength, Abbott bounded up and whirled his sword and struck.

He felt the sword crash *through* the uplifted mace, shattering it to fragments! He felt it tear deep into the towering Mayan's breast!

"Beaten, driven, by the Bright One!" howled Ummax as he staggered. "Forever exiled—"

THUNDER rocked the mountain wildly, and the fiery serpents of lightning in the tunnels showed Abbott that as Ummax fell it was the Mayan's own gross face that now was stiffening in death.

And Abbott felt, at the same moment, release from the strange tension of possession that had seemed, to grip him all this night.

Gone dark Zotzilha, forced back into the black abysses from which he had long age crept into earth? And gone too Kukulcan, his mission finished?

Abbott heard the grind and roll of shifting rock, and by the fading flare his dazed eyes saw the giant bat-winged image rocking forward on its base.

He sprang unsteadily and snatched Shuima's slim figure aside as the statue raised of old by Zotzilha's worshipers ponderously leaned and fell and crashed to ruin.

"The Bat-winged!" choked the Mayan girl fearfully when he had carried her into the outer tunnel, and had revived her.

"It has perished, and there is no more to fear," he told her hoarsely.

Shuima clung to him, quivering. "Ummax would have sacrificed me to it, as he has sacrificed many others. Yes, for ages, dark Zotzilha has drunk the life of victims in that dread cavern."

Had it been so? Had, for centuries, some dark and alien being from beyond fed upon the life force of men and women in monstrous vampirism? Or was that only superstition masking brutal murder?

"You have set Xibalba free from that horror, Lord Kukulcan!"

"Kukulcan no more," he told her. "Whatever I was tonight, possessed or mad, I am so no longer."

Possession or momentary madness? He would never know which, for certain. He might come more and more to believe that only the influence of time and place and superstition had given him those queer delusions of having been an instrument in a struggle transcending earth.

But, remembering the strange chain of fate that had brought him from a chance-found tomb to lead the fight against evil tyranny of this lost, forgotten race, he would never be too sure!

He walked unsteadily with Shuima out through the tunnels to the stone landing, and stood there with her in the flare of the dying storm as he faced the frantic acclaim of Huroc and his warriors.

"The Plumed Serpent is victor! Hail the Holder of Kukulcan, the new lord of Xibalba!"

Abbott knew then that whatever had brought him to Xibalba, he would stay here. He could bring these people the best of the outside world, could in time reveal them to that world.

But all that lay in future years. For now, standing with his arm tightening around Shuima, he was content.

THE END

THE ALTAR

By ROBERT SHECKLEY

"Hello. Is this the West Ambrose police station…? My name is Mrs. Robert Slater. My husband failed to come home this evening and it's after nine o'clo— He couldn't have missed every train, and besides, he would have telephoned me to— Don't be insolent! Robert has never taken a drink in his life!

"Acting strangely? Well, as a matter of fact, he seemed a bit upset last night over some strange cults he says have moved into town. But I fail to see— Very well, please call me back."

WITH a sprightly gait, Mr. Slater walked down Maple Street toward the station. There was a little bounce to his step this morning, and a smile on his clean-shaven, substantial face. It was such a glorious spring morning!

Mr. Slater hummed a tune to himself, glad of the seven-block walk to the railroad station. Although the distance had been a bother all winter, weather like this made up for it. It was a pleasure to be alive, a joy to be commuting.

Just then he was stopped by a man in a light blue topcoat.

"Pardon me, sir," the man said. "Could you direct me to the Altar of Baz-Matain?"

Mr. Slater, still full of the beauties of spring, tried to think. "Baz-Matain? I don't think—the *Altar* of Baz-Matain, you say?"

"That's right," the stranger said, with an apologetic little smile. He was unusually tall, and he had a dark, thin face. Mr. Slater decided it was a foreign-looking face.

"Terribly sorry," Mr. Slater said, after a moment's thought. "I don't believe I ever heard of it."

"Thanks anyhow," the dark man said, nodded pleasantly, and walked off toward the center of town. Mr. Slater continued to the station.

After the conductor punched his ticket, Mr. Slater thought of the incident. *Baz-Matain*, he repeated to himself as the train sped through the misty, fields of New Jersey. *Baz-Matain*. Mr. Slater decided that the foreign-looking man must have been mistaken. North Ambrose, N. J., was a small town—small enough for a resident to know every street in it, every house or store. Especially a resident of almost twenty years standing, like Mr. Slater.

Illustration by Ray Cossette

Halfway through the office day, Mr. Slater found himself tapping a pencil against the glass top of his desk, thinking of the man in the light blue topcoat. A foreign-looking fellow was an oddity in North Ambrose, a quiet, refined, settled suburb. The North Ambrose men wore good business suits and carried lean brown suitcases; some were fat and some were thin, but anyone in North Ambrose might have been taken for anyone else's brother.

Mr. Slater didn't think of it any more. He finished his day, took the tube to Hoboken, the train to North Ambrose, and finally started the walk to his house.

On the way he passed the man again.

"I found it," the stranger said. "It wasn't easy, but I found it."

"Where was it? "Mr. Slater asked, stopping.

"Right beside the Temple of Dark Mysteries of Isis," the stranger said. "Stupid of me. I should have asked for that in the first place. I knew it was here, but it never occurred to me—"

"The temple of what?" Mr. Slater asked.

"Dark Mysteries of Isis," the dark man said. "Not competitors, really. Seers and warlocks, fertility cycles and the like. Never come near *our* province."

"I see," Mr. Slater said, looking at the stranger closely in the early spring twilight. "The reason I asked, I've lived in this town a number of years, and I don't believe I ever heard—"

"Say!" the man exclaimed, glancing at his watch. "Didn't realize how late it was! I'll be holding up the ceremony if I don't hurry!" And with a friendly wave of his hand, he hurried off.

Mr. Slater walked slowly home, thinking. *Altar of Baz-Matain. Dark Mysteries of Isis.* They sounded like cults. Could there be such places in his town? It seemed impossible. No one would rent to people like that.

After supper, Mr. Slater consulted the telephone book. But there was no listing for Baz-Matain, or for The Temple of Dark Mysteries of Isis. Information wasn't able to supply them either.

"Odd," he mused. Later, he told his wife about the two meetings with the foreign man.

"Well," she said, pulling her house robe closer around her, "no one's going to start any cults in this town. The Better Business

Bureau wouldn't allow it. To say nothing of the Woman's Club or the P. T. A."

Mr. Slater agreed. The stranger must have had the wrong town. Perhaps the cults were in South Ambrose, a neighboring town with several bars and a movie house, and a distinctly undesirable element in its population.

The next morning was Friday. Mr. Slater looked for the stranger, but all he saw were his homogeneous fellow commuters. It was the same on the way back. Evidently the fellow had visited the Altar and left. Or he had taken up duties there at hours that didn't coincide with Mr. Slater's commuting hours.

Monday morning Mr. Slater left his house a few minutes late and was hurrying to catch his train. Ahead he saw the blue top-coat.

"Hello there," Mr. Slater called.

"Why hello!" the dark man said, his thin face breaking in to a smile. "I was wondering when we would bump into each other again."

"So was I," Mr. Slater said, slowing his pace. The stranger was strolling along evidently enjoying the magnificent weather. Mr. Slater knew that he was going to miss his train.

"And how are things at the Altar?" Mr. Slater asked.

"So-so," the man said, his hands clasped behind his back. "To tell you the truth, we're having a bit of trouble."

"Oh?" Mr. Slater asked.

"Yes," the dark man said, his face stern. "Old Atherhotep, the mayor, is threatening to revoke our license in North Ambrose. Says we aren't fulfilling our charter. But I ask you, how can we? What with the Dionysus-Africanus set across the street, grabbing everyone likely, and the Papa Legba-Dambella combine two doors down, taking even the unlikely ones—well, what can you do?"

"It doesn't sound too good," Mr. Slater agreed.

"That's not all," the stranger said. "Our high priest is threatening to leave if we don't get some action. He's a seventh degree adept, and Brahma alone knows where we'd get another."

"Mmmm," Mr. Slater murmured. "That's what *I'm* here for, though," the stranger said. "If they're going to use sharp business practices, I'll go them one better. I'm the new business manager, you know."

"Oh?" Mr. Slater said, surprised. "Are you reorganizing?"

"In a way," the stranger told him. "You see, it's like this—" Just then a short, plump man hurried up and seized the dark man by the sleeve of the blue topcoat.

"Elor," he panted. "I miscalculated the date. It's *this* Monday! Today, not next week!"

"Damn," the dark man said succinctly. "You'll have to excuse me," he said to Mr. Slater. "This is rather urgent." He hurried away with the short man.

Mr. Slater was half an hour late for work that morning, but he didn't care. It was all pretty obvious, he thought, sitting at his desk. A group of cults was springing up in North Ambrose, vying for congregations. And the mayor, instead of getting rid of them, was doing nothing. Perhaps he was even taking bribes!

Mr. Slater tapped his pencil against his glass-topped desk. How was it possible? Nothing could be hidden in North Ambrose. It was such a little town. Mr. Slater knew a good percentage of the inhabitants by their first names. How could something like this go on unnoticed?

Angrily, he reached for the telephone.

Information was unable to supply him with the numbers of Dionysus Africanus, Papa Legba or Damballa. The mayor of North Ambrose, he was informed, was not Atherhotep, but a man named Miller. Mr. Slater telephoned him.

The conversation was far from satisfying. The mayor insisted that he knew every business in the town, every church, every lodge. And if there were any cults—which there weren't—he would know of them, too.

"You have been deluded, my good man," Mayor Miller said, a little too pompously to suit Mr. Slater. "There are no people by those names in this town, no such organizations. We would never allow them in."

Mr. Slater thought this over carefully on the way home. As he stepped off the train platform he saw Elor, hurrying across Oak Street with short, rapid steps.

Elor stopped when Mr. Slater called to him.

"Really can't stay," he said cheerfully. "The ceremony begins soon, and I must be there. It was that fool Ligian's fault."

Ligian, Mr. Slater decided, would be the plump man who had stopped Elor in the morning.

"He's so careless," Elor went on. "Can you imagine a competent astrologer making a mistake of a week in the conjugation of Saturn with Scorpio? No matter. We hold the ceremony tonight, short-handed or not."

"Could I come?" Mr. Slater asked, without hesitation. "I mean, if you're short-handed—"

"Well," Elor mused. "It's unprecedented."

"I'd really like to," Mr. Slater said, seeing a chance to get to the bottom of the mystery.

"I really don't think it's fair to you," Elor went on, his thin, dark face thoughtful. "Without preparation and all—"

"I'll be all right," Mr. Slater insisted. He would really have something to dump in the mayor's lap if this worked! "I really want to go. You've got me quite excited about it."

"All right," Elor said. "We'd better hurry."

They walked down Oak Street, toward the center of town. Then, just as they reached the first stores, Elor turned. He led Mr. Slater two blocks over and a block down, and then retraced a block. After that he headed back toward the railroad station.

It was getting quite dark.

"Isn't there a simpler way?" Mr. Slater asked.

"Oh, no," Elor said. "This is the most direct. If you knew the roundabout way I came the first time—"

They walked on, backtracking blocks, circling, recrossing streets they had already passed, going back and forth over the town Mr. Slater knew so well.

But as it grew darker, and as they approached familiar streets from unfamiliar directions, Mr. Slater became just a trifle confused. He knew where he was, of course, but the constant circling had thrown him off.

How very strange, he thought. One can get lost in one's own town, even after living there almost twenty years.

Mr. Slater tried to place what street they were on without looking at the signpost, and then they made another unexpected turn. He had just made up his mind that they were backtracking on Walnut Lane, when he found that he couldn't remember the next cross street. As they passed the corner, he looked at the sign.

It read: Left Orifice.

Mr. Slater couldn't remember any street in North Ambrose called Left Orifice. He was certain.

There were no streetlights on it, and Mr. Slater found that he didn't recognize any of the stores. That was strange, because he thought he knew the little business section of North Ambrose very well. It gave him quite a start when they passed one squat black building on which there was a dimly lighted sign.

The sign read: *Temple of the Dark Mysteries of Isis.*

"They're pretty quiet in there tonight, eh?" Elor said, following Mr. Slater's glance toward the building. "We'd better hurry." He walked faster, allowing Mr. Slater no time to ask questions.

The building became stranger and stranger as they walked down the dim street. They were of all shapes and sizes, some new and glistening, others ancient and decayed. Mr. Slater couldn't imagine any section in North Ambrose like this. Was there a town within the town? Could there be a North Ambrose by night that the daytime inhabitants knew nothing of? A North Ambrose approached only by devious turns through familiar streets?

"Phallic rites in there," Elor said, indicating a tall, slender building. Beside it was a twisted, sagging hulk of a place.

"That's Damballa's place," Elor said, pointing at it.

Toward the end of the street was a white building. It was quite long, and built low to the ground. Mr. Slater hadn't time to examine it, because Elor had his arm and was hurrying him in the door.

"I really must become more prompt," Elor muttered half to himself.

Once inside, it was totally dark. Mr. Slater could feel movement around him, and then he made out a tiny white light. Elor guided him toward it, saying in friendly tones, "You've really helped me out of a jam."

"Have you got it?" a thin voice asked from beside the light. Mr. Slater began to make out shapes. As his eyes became more accustomed to the gloom, he could see a tiny, gnarled old man in front of the light.

The old man was holding an unusually long knife.

"Of course," Elor said. "And he was willing, too."

The white light was suspended over a stone altar, Mr. Slater realized. In a single reflex action he turned to run, but Elor's hand was tight on his arm, although not all painful.

"You can't leave us now," Elor said gently. "We're ready to begin."

And then there were other hands on Mr. Slater, many of them, pulling him steadily toward the Altar.

THE END

All the injustices of his past crowded in on him-changed him—until he could only snarl at the world and scream, "Okay! Go ahead—

CALL ME MONSTER

By G. L. VANDENBERG

HE CROUCHED in the corner of the closet, a frightened shriveled up little creature. He hugged his knees close to his trembling body. In his pathetic desperation he wanted to become smaller and smaller until he would be nothing. For, in the torment of those days and hours, in which, he was sure, centuries had passed, becoming nothing was the only escape he could conceive of.

In the forbidding, blackness Time and Space were smothered until he imagined he was no longer in the closet. He was lost. Lost in a terrifying, desolate corner of the Universe, in whose cruel blackness not even the eyes of God could see.

Lost and alone and having nothing, no one to turn to, he wanted to cry. But fear was his master. And the instruments of fear were sadistic and deceptive. They replaced the torment in his sensitive mind with a moment of pride and courage. He was a big boy now and too old to cry. He would be eleven years old in two months, if Time ever began for him again, and now he must be brave and not cry.

She would not like that. She wanted him to cry and if he didn't she might keep him there forever. But he wouldn't cry. He would remain crouched. And the terror would mount. And he would wait, wait for the one excruciating moment she knew he was waiting for. More than anything else he hated the frustrating moments (or was it years or days or months ?) of waiting and not knowing when!

Then, after all the time that had ever been had passed, and it seemed eternity was behind him, she would remove the adhesive tape from the keyhole. A tiny speck of light would gush through, as though God had hurled a star into the midst of his black loneliness, to warm a silent tear on his cold and forgotten face.

Then the door would open. An ocean of blinding light would fall in upon him, forcing him to hug the bare wall and bury his head deep in a corner. He would hear her foot tapping on the hard floor and the terror would multiply a million-fold. When he turned his head and conditioned his eyes to the stinging glare she would be standing there, an ugly vision of triumphant smugness. She would have her arms stiffly folded and her head cocked to one side. He would see the tight grotesque grin and the pale fleshy stepladder of chins that hung loosely above her lace collar. She was a giant of a woman, straight as a steel rod and impenetrable. He could not remember ever seeing her smile.

His father had taught him it was not right to hate. It was only easy. The gift of divine forbearance was something a man should never lose.

He wanted very much, in these awful times of punishment, to hate his Aunt Sarah. But the still fresh memory of a tolerant, warm-hearted old man, whose passing he deeply mourned, was ever present to guide him toward a form of forgiveness.

He would emerge from the closet, stiff and hungry. When she asked if he had learned his lesson he would say yes, though he never was quite sure what the lesson was. In the sanctuary of his own soul he would forgive her. He would tolerate her. But he would never in his lifetime come to understand the insane logic of her discipline.

For Jeffrey Barton the closet remained a coherent, throttling reality. He accepted the punishment and the restrictions she placed upon him. Yet, even as his young mind experienced the first rewards of flexibility, he still failed to comprehend the logic of her actions.

He could not conceivably be as different from other children as she seemed to think he was.

"Sinful! Sinful! A child with your background!" was her reaction when she caught him chewing bubble gum.

Possession of a slingshot brought a more vehement reaction. "A barbaric instrument! You dishonor your father's grave! Infidel! Little infidel!"

And, for sneaking off to play with the kids on Front Street: "Animals! They're nothing but animals! Dirty little street urchins who'd murder you as soon as look at you! How your mother would grieve for you, cheapening yourself this way. You have a little of the animal in you, young man!"

His days stretched into weeks, his months into seasons and years.

And, as Aunt Sarah clipped the wings of Time, she cruelly accelerated the torment of his mind. She was racing the motor while the automobile was standing still. He could not realize he would never be free from 'sin' because 'sin' was anything she chose to make it.

Inevitably the time arrived when he realized it was no longer possible to endure the agony. He would never be able to please her. She was an impregnable fortress that, spiritually and mentally, existed in a world he could not reach, a world totally alien to the one his father had brought him into.

In his pathetic capitulation, unaware that even Aunt Sarah could not bring Time to a standstill, he foresaw for himself a life of exile in the closet; a chamber of horrors in which there would be no peace of mind; and finally a tomb in which there would be *eternal* peace of mind.

It was on a cold, rain-swept October afternoon that a germ of hope reentered his life.

Obeying instructions from his guardian he went to the library, which constituted a separate wing of the house. Aunt Sarah was seated behind the great oak desk that had been his father's. Her hands were primly folded on the blotter in front of her. Her face, as his conscious memory had always known it, bore no expression.

"Sit down, Jeffrey. Take your hands out of your pockets."

She rarely completed a sentence without criticizing him for something. This was her most dominant characteristic and in seven years he had come to loathe it.

He obeyed. He always obeyed.

When he was seated and his hands were folded properly on his lap, she began.

"Jeffrey, you have reached the age of sixteen. If you can learn the lesson of goodness and self-discipline there might someday be valid reason to believe you are an intelligent, growing young man. You are too old now to be placed in the closet for your sins."

It was impossible for him to hold back the smile that parted his lips.

"I wouldn't consider this news as cause for jubilation just yet. There is no reason for me to believe you won't continue to live as errantly as you have in the past."

"Yes, Aunt Sarah."

"Don't interrupt." She gave her hands an angry twist. "Personally I don't believe your confinement to the closet has ever taught you a blessed thing. So you must understand that you will not be immune from punishment when you misbehave in the future. Quite the contrary. The penalty is liable to be even more severe. After all, you may as well face it, you're old enough to know better now."

She went on talking but he was unable to hear her. The severity of future punishment bore no impact. She could draw upon every source of energy in her versatile, pestilent mind and never be able to devise anything as strangulating as the closet had been to him. An unspeakable joy crept through every fiber of his being.

Several million dollars.

The words dashed themselves against the first tender thoughts he had enjoyed in seven years. For a moment all was confusion. Then he was aware that she was still talking, saying something about an enormous amount of money. He listened.

"...and your father was the dearest, kindest person I ever knew in this world. I gave my sacred word to him that you would be reared in the same Christian tradition that has brought dignity and honor to the Bartons since they first landed on these shores. You must realize your father was an immensely wealthy man. Exactly *how* wealthy is not your business at the moment. When you become twenty-one every last penny of that wealth will be yours. And my job will be finished. I pray to God in Heaven that you will take advantage of the upbringing I've given you and uphold your father's good name."

Jeffrey wished she would stop praying to God in Heaven and just tell him *how much* money. He quickly forgave himself for the irreverence of the wish and went on half-listening, half-dreaming as she concluded her lecture.

Two such surprises in one day came close to erasing the bitterness of seven years. But not quite close enough. For as he approached the door on his way out of the library, something impelled him to turn and look at his aunt. She was still sitting at the desk, rigid as always. For just a split second an infinitesimal smile played on her pale lips. Then her face was without expression again. In that moment, in his freshness of mind, Aunt Sarah took on a new aspect.

How curious, he pondered, that on the day she was obliged to inform him of his inheritance she also chose to dispense with the use of the closet.

For the first time in his brief life Jeffrey Barton had a thing to look forward to. Time itself responded to his rejuvenation by resuming a normal pace. That, by Jeffrey's standards, was something akin to lightning-like swiftness.

The five years were by no means pleasant. Only fast.

As a human being Aunt Sarah did not show any improvement. She did grant him limited freedom of movement but her warped devotion to discipline remained unchanged. Chastisement was still available in a variety of forms and for an even wider variety of reasons. She continued to passionately chisel away at his sanity.

At the age of eighteen Jeffrey was thrust headlong into the social arena, a part of his life which had been in the planning stages for as long as Sarah had been his guardian. How many times had that strident horn of a voice pummeled his eardrums, stressing the importance of his future social obligations? And how many times had two days banishment to the closet of correction blighted his comprehension of that importance?

He understood now the why of the closet. He understood but he would never forgive. He understood the discipline, the nurses, the doctors, the tutors, the insipid poise lessons. He understood that all these were necessary to paste together a synthetic body with a remote controlled brain, both to function in a manner befitting his station in life.

But Aunt Sarah had committed a grave strategic error.

The closet.

There was no forgetting that.

His twenty-first birthday Was a social event of grandiose Proportions. He was the center of attention in Hamilton Square, the axis around which the social set rotated. Overnight he had become everybody's *best* friend. He had, as Aunt Sarah informed him five years earlier, inherited "every last penny" of the Barton fortune. There wasn't a richer man in the city of Salem.

Vera Stevens was a vital part of the long-range plans Aunt Sarah had worked out for him. It had never been mentioned but he supposed Vera would someday be his wife just as she would some-day be the richest woman in Salem.

But somehow Vera did not disturb him as much as the others. She was a trifle haughty and prone to shock at the flimsiest display of bad taste, but she showed understanding and consideration. He wanted nothing more than that.

It was at Vera's lawn party that he thought back over the last five years. He recalled the many times, when he should have been studying or practicing the piano, but was actually dreaming of the revenge he would someday wreak upon his Oppressor. How succulent and cleansing revenge would be, he told himself.

The birthday came as a major letdown.

He sought no revenge. Alarm spread through him when he realized he never would.

And there was no release. He felt no more freedom than he had ever known.

He was astonished and disenchanted and then angry. He had been so sure that Aunt Sarah had full knowledge of his intended retribution. She would tremble as he approached her on *his* day. He would delight in telling her he was cutting her off without a cent and putting her in the street. Every part of him would glow with radiant joy as she fainted dead away at the news.

There was no joy. She did not tremble or faint away. He did not cancel her long established allowance.

As a meager substitute he merely escorted her away from the other guests, saying he wished to speak with her. When they were alone he made a determined effort to unnerve her. His eyes narrowed into a resentful stare. His mouth was taut ready to spring open to release his imprisoned feelings. A long, terrible moment passed.

She waited. Not a muscle moved in her grim withered old face. Another moment. He grew rigidly tense. He stuffed his hands into his pockets to conceal clenched fists. He did not speak.

She did.

"You needn't play cat and mouse with me, Jeffrey. Speak your piece and be done with it. And take your hands out of your pockets."

He spoke but his words were without meaning. Their positions were reversed, he told her. He felt there was room enough in a twenty seven-room house for both of them but he would appreciate it if she kept out of his affairs. He would *appreciate* it! How could he use such a word with her? How polite could he be with the person who had so utterly disengaged his individuality?

He had spoken his inadequate piece and now he watched as she walked, proud and erect, back to the guests at the lawn party. She had not even answered him. Her face had not revealed the slightest sign of disturbance or surprise. Nothing. She knew all along he would want his revenge. He was right about that. But she also knew, when the moment came, he would fail. Why did she know! What in God's name was the extent of the injury she had done him!

He stood there gazing after her, his mind frozen with a fear he had once known and thought he would never know again. He wanted to run after her, throw her to the ground so he could tower over her and tell her to get out of his life. He didn't do it. He only felt like a poor fool, thinking of dominance in terms of height. Aunt Sarah thought of it in terms of power. She was right.

The money was his. The position, the mansion, the luxuries, the friends, the tradition, the multitudinous things that would avail him nothing were all his.

Hers was the power.

As he looked across the lawn at the crowded party the guests became blurred and grotesque. Somewhere, lost in that blur, lurked his evil maker, teacup in hand, holding forth over two or three guests, outlining the next stage of his development.

How he hated her! How he loathed her! But how helpless he was to fight her.

Whatever morale he had been able to gather just before the birthday was quickly shattered afterward. There were three servants in the house. Beyond that he was alone with her in the expanse of twenty-seven rooms. She rarely put in a physical appearance anymore, preferring the isolation of her room. But he did not have to see her to know that she remained the source of his living nightmare. He was unable to make a move without her knowing about it. Her advice and comments would then be transmitted to him via the servants.

His enormous material wealth was useless to him in his inner struggle. The money only elevated him to the titular leadership of a ritualistic, tradition-bound society. He wanted neither the leadership nor the society itself. But it was his obligation, his ridiculous eternal obligation to rule the aristocratic roost.

He strove to meet the countless petty demands of his new life, knowing he could never succeed because he could never believe as they did. They were shallow, stagnant creatures. Their flat world began and ended in Hamilton Square and one ventured beyond its limits at the risk of falling into empty space.

But he was born into Hamilton Square and it was as much his world as theirs. In the gloom of this knowledge he sank to the depths of despair. Out of despair grew instability. His nerves were on edge every waking hour. He began to have difficulty sleeping. And when he did sleep he dreamed.

He dreamed about the closet.

Not until after the rumor started did he first see the image.

The rumor didn't disturb him. It was typical of the pettiness of Hamilton Square. In the course of his mental decline his temper had divorced itself from all reason. Every social gathering he attended was sure to witness, at any given time, a display of his temper. Luckily Vera was always with him to prevent physical violence. He was going "eccentric" at a very early age. This was the quaint nature of the rumor and he hated them for having nothing better to do.

The image was a more serious matter. It appeared on a cold February day while he was strolling along the banks of the Weldon River. He was alone and trying to find some manner of relaxation from the bitter turmoil that churned inside him. He had not informed anyone of where he was going.

The brisk New England wind slapped refreshingly at his face. The calm of the river, visible only between the itinerant cakes of ice, was soothing to his tired nerves. Somehow he was immediately aware that here, alone in the pure, open air, he could think clearly again.

A man's loneliness, he reflected, was so dependent upon where he lived it. Beside a river lined with trees, guarded by age-old rocks, he could feel the warmth of security, for a small portion of the world was there for him to see. In the concealment of a closet he could rot away, for there there was a portion of nothing.

He continued his stroll until he came within sight of the old Grover wharf. There was a group of men hauling supplies into an old warehouse. He started to walk toward them. His attention was arrested by a towering elm tree. Its height was awe-inspiring. Glistening icicles bejeweled its regal cape of snow.

One of the icicles near the base of the tree caught his eye and held it. More formidable in appearance than the others it was, nevertheless, dripping lazy pellets of water that formed a tiny crater in the soft snow. It was both intriguing and sad how, at precise intervals, another drop of its life slipped away forever. He could not remove his eyes. It staggered him to know that he had so much in common with a frozen, dagger-shaped piece of water. Each day something of his own life was slipping away and he had always been as helpless as the icicle to prevent it. He watched it dripping...dripping...dripping...

"Hey, fella, watch yer step there!"

The voice was fuzzy, as though it was coming through a mouthless mask.

"Hey, what's the matter with you anyway? You in a trance or something? That water's mighty chilly. You fall in there and don't know how to swim yer a dead duck in ten seconds."

Something touched his arm. His eyes opened. Everything seemed warped. He made out the figure of a man...an old bearded man wearing a fisherman's slicker...standing beside him...a bewildered expression on his weather-torn face.

"You all right, fella?"

His clouded eyes found the wharf beneath his feet. He was standing on the edge...another step and... His head turned in a dream-like motion...he was able to see the outline of the giant elm several hundred yards away. It was *there...and he was on the wharf...*why? ...how did he get to the wharf? ...his head throbbed savagely... How much time had elapsed...? He refused to consult his watch...the sun was still shining... it was the same day...good...or had a whole day passed? ...no...no...impossible...

"Listen, fella, are you all right?" the old man repeated. "I think you better get back from the edge."

Jeffrey looked away from him. Through the dullness of his senses came his thick hesitant answer.

"I'm fine...I'll be...all right."

The man forced an unamused laugh. "See here now, you weren't thinking about going in for a little dip by any chance?"

"I won't...jump," he droned. "I'll be...all right. Please leave...me alone..."

The old man retreated to his chores at the warehouse keeping one puzzled eye on the wharf's edge.

Jeffrey found support against a post. His hand rose in agonizing slow motion to soothe his aching skull. He fought to regain control of himself. His eyes refused to focus. Be shook his head violently. A disobedient mind continued to churn dizzily. Sickness erupted in his stomach. He hugged the post. He leaned over the side of the wharf. It had to be a dream. An incredibly realistic dream. It had to be! It was time to wake up. Wake up! Wake up!

The sickness retreated. Clarity crowded the throbbing out of his skull. The dullness subsided. Focus returned to his eyes. The wharf...the post...real...solid. Not a dream at all! He rested his cheek against the post and gazed into the water.

The image gazed back at him!

The image smiled, revealing a cavernous mouth rimmed with gleaming teeth of gold.

The image stared at him through narrow, malevolent eyes.

The image emitted a hollow, gargling laugh, causing its silken facial hairs to bristle.

The image spoke, its gargantuan voice shooting up from the bowels of the icy river. *"Me! Me! Me!"* it roared.

Then, as mysteriously as it had appeared, it was gone!

His eyes were in perfect focus now. He jerked his head in the direction of the warehouse. The old man was still regarding him with concern.

The air was pure again. Everything was back in kilter. He turned and began the long lonesome walk home.

By the time he reached the iron gate outside his home he was in a state of semi-shock. He stumbled into the house, went to his bedroom, and locked himself in.

He spent the rest of the day attempting to wipe the ugliness out of his mind. The incident and the image remained. He wanted desperately to pick up the phone and call Vera and tell her about it. Dear adorable Vera, always compassionate and understanding. He had come to love her, within the context of whatever meaning love had for him, in spite of the fact that she was Aunt Sarah's choice.

No, it would be wrong, he decided. It was too bizarre, too unbelievable. He could offer no logical explanation for it. To confide in *anyone* would surely give substance to the idiotic rumor of his "early eccentric behavior."

Night fell on his room and there was no sleep. Through the waning hours he tossed and turned, dredging the recesses of his mind for an explanation, struggling valiantly to keep a firm grip on his sanity. The rumor could not be true. He would not allow it to be true! His sanity was intact! He knew it!

Maybe he was the only one who knew it!

No! It was impossible! Impossible because alone by the river just twelve, thirteen hours ago he had been the sanest man on Earth! Alone with nature, absorbing the wonder of God's work, he had felt the warmth of inner peace. It was the finest, moment of his life. Yet it was taken away! Why? Why!

He sprang up in his bed. His mind was a labyrinth of frenzied thoughts that crashed into each other and exploded over and over. He put his hands to his eyes and his head between folded knees. And once again he felt and looked like the little boy in the closet.

"Why?" he asked himself softly. And he began to weep.

Why was that moment of happiness torn from him? What was it that made him see the revolting image in the water? If he had never seen the image it would not now be branded indelibly in his mind and he would still know...

Aunt Sarah!

Yes! Yes, that putrescent face of evil was her doing! It was a part of her. The part no mortal soul had ever seen. He had looked into the water that day and seen the reflection of her diseased mind.

His mind rushed forward excitedly supplying answers. What he had really seen, of course, was nothing more than a hallucination. But he was glad he saw it now that he knew what it was. More than anything he had experienced this served to impress upon him how efficiently and savagely she had cornered his sanity.

He could not go on alone any longer. He had to find someone who could help him get to the root of her influence. If it meant discussing the image he would discuss it. He could afford to conceal nothing. The next few weeks or months might be the difference between salvation and utter collapse.

Tomorrow afternoon he would visit Ned Anderson. He would see him for psychiatric treatments seven days a week if necessary but he would be cured! If, on this cold and forbidding night, there was a particle of his sanity remaining he would use it to recapture all the rest.

Sleep came and Jeffrey; Barton had a beautiful dream.

It was his first. And his last.

The harsh insistent knocking hammered at his skull. He opened his eyes. Someone was knocking at his bedroom door. He heaved himself out of bed and unlocked the door.

Poppy, a wisp of a chambermaid, stood frozen in the doorway. Her normally serene blue eyes bulged as though she had just witnessed a murder.

"What is it, Poppy?"

"Begging your pardon, Master Jeffrey, but it's your Aunt Sarah..." Her mouth remained open and nothing came out.

"What about my Aunt?"

"She's...she's gone, sir."

"Gone? Poppy, what are you talking about? Gone where?"

"Oh, we don't know where, sir! That's just the trouble."

"Trouble..." Still half asleep, Jeffrey became annoyed. "Poppy, you're not making any sense!"

The maid was trembling. "She didn't ring for breakfast. She always rings for breakfast, but she didn't ring this morning," She was getting the words out faster than she could say them.

"What makes you think she's gone?"

"Well because, sir, it's close to three in the afternoon and she didn't ring for lunch either."

"Three in the afternoon!" He had not planned to sleep so late. There was the visit to Ned Anderson. He must get that done.

"Yes, sir, and when she didn't ring by two o'clock we...that is the cook and me...we went to her room. We knocked but there wasn't any answer so we took the liberty of going in, sir. And she was gone."

He stood for a moment in ponderous, amazed silence. He decided to postpone the visit to the doctor. He hurried into his clothes and ran to Sarah's room.

Poppy was right. The room was empty. The bed had not been slept in. There was no sign of a note and, to the extent his amateur deductive powers would take him, no indication of foul play. He questioned all the servants. None of them had seen her leave the house that morning.

He was baffled. She couldn't have just vanished. He was sure she would never go away without notifying him…or at least the servants. Where was she?

Terror gripped him. Was this some new psychological tactic she had devised? It was a possibility. Maybe she realized that being controlled while she was in the house had only accomplished ninety percent of the damage to him. So she decided to move to a remote vantage point. Now she could control him but he would *never* be able to see her. The prospect was more than he could bear.

He conducted a frantic search of the house. She was nowhere to be found. He had no choice but to call the police.

By the following morning the police had searched all of Salem and the surrounding area. They did not find her. The afternoon papers gave the story front-page headlines. Day and night for a week Jeffrey was harassed by reporters and police. They would exhaust one area of questioning and immediately start another and then another.

The theory most prevalent in Hamilton Square was kidnapping. Jeffrey found that amusing. There were many things that many people might like to do to Aunt Sarah but whisking her away was not one of them. If it was he feared for the kidnaper.

By week's end the police abandoned the investigation. The newspapers were relegating the story to the middle pages and Hamilton Square was busy preparing for Tessie Borden's coming out party.

Jeffrey had never believed it was possible that Aunt Sarah would ever leave the Barton mansion, let alone the city of Salem. It took him fully eight days to really believe she *was* gone. When finally convinced he expected a great wave of relief to sweep over him.

He was alone in the immense living room. He sat smugly in the huge colonial wing chair before the fireplace. He looked up at the mirror over the fireplace. The room was warm and dark except for the low fire in front of him. His life was going to mean something now that she was gone at last.

Was she gone? He quickly pushed the question outside of his mind. Was she really gone? Again he dismissed the question. But it fought its way back in another form. How did he know she was really gone? The question burned inside him. He *didn't* know. And all the ways of finding out had been exhausted. He *couldn't* know. She *had* disappeared, yes. That was a fact. But the cause of her disappearance and the end result were only frustrating question marks. Why and how danced out of his reach, tormenting him further. Was she dead? If not, where did she go? Would she come back? That was another mystery.

He sat huddled in the wing chair staring at the waning fire before him. The flame danced capriciously up and down...backward and forward...brave dying flame in and out...up and down...drowsy...constant flame...

Then blackness. Inundating blackness, devoid of Time and Space.

He was standing against the mantel, his hand clutching his forehead. His drooping eyes fell on the mirror. There was no reflection of himself or of any other part of the room. The tall Grandfather clock on the opposite side of the room, normally the first thing anyone saw when looking in the mirror, was not reflected.

In the misty depths of the mirror he saw a shapeless, spongy embryo moving toward him, taking form as it approached...closer...ever closer...

The image!

Its gargantuan voice repeated the words it had spoken from the river. *"Me! Me! Me!"* it roared.

With herculean effort Jeffrey tore himself from the mantel and fell with his face to the floor. He dared not look back. He lay there with his eyes squeezed shut and his heart beating viciously. He was unconcerned about how he had gotten from the chair to the mantel. His only thought was that he had been right about her plan of action. It *was* a new line of psychological attack, more diabolical than any she had ever devised.

He waited for what seemed a week. Then he slowly opened his eyes and peeked at the mirror. The mist was gone. He got to his feet. He saw the reflection of the old grandfather clock. He was all right again. He turned the lights on and sat in the wing chair.

From that moment on he was consumed by one burning thought. She was still alive and she would come back! It was the only thought that made any sense. There wasn't a shred of evidence to show that she was dead...or even that she *might* be dead.

She would come back and he must be ready for her. Deep within him he had the conviction that this was his last opportunity to set himself free of her.

He phoned Ned Anderson. The doctor gave him an appointment. He would begin psychiatric treatment the next day.

"The keyhole," he said. "That was the worst torture of all. If only I could have determined just when she would take the adhesive tape from the keyhole to let in the first blinding ray of light it might not have been so bad. But I never could and I'd go crazy."

Jeffrey bolted upright on the leather sofa.

"What I mean is I'd..."

"It's all right, Jeff," Doctor Anderson's voice was reassuring. "I *know* what you mean."

Jeffrey reclined and continued talking.

"Waiting and not knowing when. I read somewhere that's the way they flog criminals in England. A man is sentenced to a year and twenty lashes to be applied one at a time. But he is never told in advance when any of them are to be applied. So he has to sit there and play the cruelest guessing game of all, praying it could happen now this minute. And then it comes and afterward he isn't any happier than before because he knows it will come again...and he doesn't know when. The cycle goes on and on," He was silent for a moment. "I guess Sarah must have read the same book," his tone was bitter.

"Uh-huh," the doctor mumbled. "Go on."

"There was never much after that. Once the light came through the keyhole I only had one thing to look forward to. A few more days with her and then back in the closet again."

"Mmmm." The doctor went to his desk, sat down and began to pore over the voluminous notes he had taken.

Jeffrey watched him intently. A tender-hearted old man...reminiscent of my father...knows what he's doing too...but the treatments have lasted for six weeks now...twice a week...why doesn't he ever do anything but pore over those damned notes? ...what is he thinking? ...if there's been any Improvement why doesn't he tell me about it? ...There hasn't been any, that's why! ...Sarah has been to see him and convinced him the rumor is true! ...No, no, no! ...Mustn't believe that...mustn't get worked up...he's doing his best to help...he's one of the top men in his field...I just haven't told him everything yet...he doesn't know about the image...I should have told him about it long before this...I really should have...why haven't I! ...look at him...he sits and goes over those notes and burns his good mind away trying to find the answer...and the answer hasn't reached those pages yet...or has it? ...what was it he said yesterday? ...something about existing in the inner world...what did that mean? ...maybe I'd better tell him...yes...yes, I *will* tell him...only not today...not today...

Doctor Anderson yawned and slapped his notebook shut.

"I don't blame you if you're bored," said Jeffrey. "How many times have I gone through that closet for you?"

The old man lifted his glasses to his forehead where they perched like another pair of eyes over two protruding eyebrows flecked with gray. He rubbed his eyes.

"Makes no difference, Jeff," came his patient reply. "It *happened* more than once. I expect to *listen* to it more times than it happened."

Jeffrey started to get up.

Anderson waved him back down.

"Do you mind, Jeff? We're not through yet..."

I must tell him!

"I want you to see if you can go all the way back to that first experience once again..."

Tell him! Tell him!

"...and tell me what it was you did that prompted her to conceive of the closet as a penal device."

Not today! Next time! Next time!

"Are you listening to me, Jeff?"

"Huh? Oh, yes…look, Ned, we've been over this so many times. I don't see the point…"

" Jeff," he interrupted soberly, "we can't afford to stop going over it. I realize you could find more pleasant things to do in an afternoon, but you must face a few facts…"

"I know. I'm not a child anymore. I'm close to thirty and somewhere in the heaping mass of eighteen years there is a haystack and in it there's a needle. All we have to do is find it and I'll be in tip-top shape." He got up and paced the room, scowling, restless, trying to shake his irritation.

"That's right, Jeff. I never for a moment wanted you to think this would be easy. We have to keep moving forward, keep pinpointing. And we have to be patient. The only thing we know to be uncontrovertibly true about the mind is the mystery of it. Our work is like the cycle you spoke of. Each great discovery is countered with a new phase of the mystery. It's never easy, Jeff. Never."

Jeffrey sat on the sofa and looked at the floor.

"I'm sorry, Ned."

The doctor picked up a small chair, placed it in front of him, and sat.

"If you feel a resistance we can call it off for today. But bear in mind we'll start the next session where we left off today. Between now and then you should prepare yourself," He paused and then spoke with intense concern. "Jeff, there is no better indication of how much help you need than what happened last night."

Jeffrey's eyes flared with anger. "I told you that wasn't my fault!"

"All right, we both know it wasn't your fault," he remained calm. "But today Sam Lawrence is nursing a broken jaw."

"He's lucky it isn't a broken neck!"

"Why did you hit him, Jeff?"

"He doesn't know how to behave with women."

"Isn't that his business?"

"Not when he's in my home and the woman happens to be my fiancée!"

"Do you think Vera approved of your hitting him?"

Jeffrey wanted to bellow the answer at him. His reply was almost inaudible.

"No."

"What about the other guests? Do you think they understood why you did it?"

"They *couldn't* understand!" he said fiercely.

"Why couldn't they? If Sam had been that obvious in making a pass at Vera it seems to me they should have sympathized with you."

"They don't know what sympathy is on Mother's Day!"

"Is it possible that Sam didn't actually make a pass?"

"No!"

"Perhaps it was just the way he *looked* at Vera, the way he smiled. And you interpreted it to mean..."

"Now listen to me, Ned..."

"No, Jeff!" The doctor was firm but not harsh. "As an old family friend I think *I* had better do the talking."

Jeffrey's eyes were cold deadly holes, spitting hatred at the man across the room. In that instant a sudden loathing boiled in him. He wanted to leap from the sofa and...

An old family friend.

The gentle truth and sincerity of the words caused him to avoid the doctor's straightforward, penetrating look. He lit a cigarette.

"All right, Ned, I'm listening."

"Did Sam Lawrence make anything resembling a physical pass at Vera?"

"No," he whispered. It hurt him to say it. It hurt bad!

"What made you hit him?"

There was an unendurable silence as Jeffrey searched for a way to explain.

"The party began at eight. It lasted until two or three this morning. Sam hounded her all that time. He kept taking her off into a corner alone..."

"Do you think you were jealous?"

"It wasn't jealousy. Vera belongs to me. I don't have to worry about her. I kept watching him, the way he operated, the shallow insipid laugh, the pseudo-intellectual speechmaker, the professional gentleman, the courageous musketeer. He's a mass of bubbles, Sam is, and every time a lady says no one of the bubbles breaks and Sam is that much closer to floating away from this Earth."

Doctor Anderson smiled. "You've analyzed Sam Lawrence rather well. Now what made you hit him?"

"That's the part that's hard to explain. I know I kept watching him...I wasn't drinking...and suddenly, I don't know just when or how, he changed. He was no longer just a man with an evening of sex in mind...something happened to his face...his mouth curved into the most lecherous smile I've ever seen...his eyes were brimming over with lust...I knew in a flash that he was the personification of evil and I turned away from the mantelpiece and..."

"And your imagination caused you to break his jaw."

Jeffrey rubbed the side of his face.

"I have a dentist appointment later today. He did some damage himself."

"Jeff, I want you to stop seeing all your friends."

The suddenness of the request jarred him, as the doctor had intended it to.

"You want me to do what!"

"Cut yourself off completely from all your friends."

"Why?"

"Why not? You neither like nor respect any of them, do you?"

"No," he replied and then added, "except for Vera."

"Jeffrey, we've covered a lot of ground and we've barely scratched the surface. Your relationship with Aunt Sarah, the way she raised you, your conscious reasons for hating her, and many other elements can be brought to account for your inability to conform to your own society. We know you have a rather mild temper until you are in a gathering of friends. Then it becomes an incredibly violent temper. But Hamilton Square is not your sole resentment. We know you resent being the only Barton left and what responsibility that entails. The family name, the tradition and so forth. And so you've given every indication that you intend to be the last Barton. You've been formally engaged to Vera for eight years and you've consistently avoided marriage for two prime reasons. You love her but resent the fact that she was Aunt Sarah's choice...and you have an overwhelming and, at the moment, quite understandable fear of having children. All this we know and we're in a good position to fight it. But there is one thing we don't know..."

Don't tell him! He must not know!

"Somewhere," the doctor continued, "somehow, during those early years you managed to develop...well, at the moment I shall call it a kind of power. It enables you to see, or at least *think* you see, something in a person that is apparent to nobody else and that unleashes a desire in you to commit physical violence. Naturally, after the strict manipulation by Sarah, you've reached the point where it is impossible to control this power..."

Must not tell him! Make an excuse...have to go to the dental appointment. He is getting too close!

"...to the point where the power practically possesses a mind of its own. That's why I think it would be best if you stopped seeing your friends. Your temperament has always been at its worst in their presence."

"Where do you think I should go?"

The doctor sat behind his desk and consulted his notebook. "In studying the reasons she had for locking you up I find they generally had to do with your having sneaked off to places she had placed off limits."

Jeffrey sighed. "Yes, there was only one place fit for a growing young aristocrat to breathe air in and that was Hamilton Square. Everyplace else was off limits."

"Everyplace?"

He stared at the floor. "Sounds ridiculous, doesn't it? But it's true. I could have fed the pigeons on the Salem Common and it would have been a crime."

"I find the place mentioned most often is Front Street. Any particular reason for that?"

"Many. Front Street is poverty row, crawling with inferior animal types, no place for a little boy with a halo of purity around his head. To associate with poor animal types was to become an animal type."

"Why did you keep going there?"

"She was so dead set against it. With all the frightening stories she told and the long dull lectures that followed, I managed to construct an elaborate mental image of Front Street. I was sure it was a place of dark intrigue, a kind of crossroads of the world, flaming with excitement. One day I slipped out of the house and went there..."

"And your images were destroyed, of course."

"Not completely. True, it wasn't what I had visualized. There was nothing romantic or exciting about it. It was squalid and obscene and corrupt. I remember running like lightning away from it, the only time I was ever glad to get home. But I went back. Somehow it held a strange fascination for me. And I had to keep going back because I wanted to know what that fascination was. But I never did find out what it was...until I was around twenty...and then it was too late."

"What was it?"

Jeffrey walked to the window and looked out over Hamilton Square.

"It was discovery," he said.

Ned Anderson frowned.

"Discovery?"

"Yes. Of certain realities, certain truths. My first shock came when I learned the kids on Front Street wouldn't play with me because I wasn't acceptable to them. *Me*, I thought, having to be accepted by *them!* I had difficulty controlling the urge to run home and laugh in Sarah's face. Eventually I was accepted and I played with them as often as I dared. The next shock came one day when we were playing near the fishing boats. One of the kids, a scrawny little devil with hair sprouting in every direction over his head, told me his great-great-great somebody or other had come over on the *Mayflower*. When I refused to believe him the other kids rallied around him and zealously defended his story. He wasn't a very bright kid and normally the others didn't even like him. But they were proud as hell of his ancestors. I couldn't fully digest it then but my discovery was one of people. Those kids had entered a world without wealth or material possession. They substituted for that by developing the ability to laugh and sing and play", and be proud of what they didn't have. I came into a world paved with red carpets, the material wealth just sitting there waiting for me to take it…and I had to sneak into the other world to find a substitute for my misery. So the discovery was also one of money. Stripped of it I realized Hamilton Square would have been another Front Street and not all of its high-flown tradition could have prevented that. Given enormous wealth the opposite would hold true for Front Street. The kids on Front Street were no less victims of circumstance than I was."

The doctor sucked on a freshly lit pipe.

"When was the last time you went there?"

"About eight years ago, I drove through without stopping."

"Why don't you spend a day there? Talk with people. Maybe you'll see one of the kids you knew. You can talk over old memories. Try it and see."

He was glad Ned had brought up the subject of Front Street. For a while it looked as though the doctor was on the brink of exposing the one secret he wanted curiously to cling to. Thank God he'd gotten away from it.

He put his hand on the old man's shoulder and smiled at him.

"Thanks, Ned. I'll try it. Maybe it'll restore something. I hope so anyway."

The living room seemed to float. Everything was out of proportion. He floundered toward the mantelpiece and gripped it for support. The awful spinning sickness was at his stomach again.

The dentist…he had been to see the dentist…but how did he get home? He couldn't remember coming home…what kind of an injection had the fool given him anyway? …he couldn't remember…no, wait! …there was no injection…there was only the watch…dangling on the end of a chain…bright gold watch…back and forth…steady…a pendulum…fascinating…

Blackness.

The living room…mantelpiece…everything floating. What happened! …a memory cell spilled open…hypnosis! The dentist said he would use hypnosis…no pain…he was right…it worked well…but terrible after affects…

What was wrong with the mirror? …where was the reflection of the old grandfather clock on the opposite wall of the room? …the mirror was a dense mist…reflecting nothing in the room…

He gazed into it and watched the image take shape before his eyes—horrible, unbelievable, but there.

Every responsible part of him was overcome with the desire to run, run out of the house, get to Ned Anderson, tell him she was back, ask him, beg him for help.

The gargled laugh rocketed from its echo chamber roots and shot through him, galvanizing every nerve ending in his body.

"Doctor Anderson can't help you, Jeffrey. He'll find out what you haven't told him. Then he will never be able to help you!"

Jeffrey answered in a soft frightened whisper. "Please go away."

The image smiled. Its thunderous voice softened to a hoarse whisper.

"Forgive me, Jeffrey. One of the servants entering the room might not understand, is that it? Yes, yes, you're right. That mustn't happen!"

"Go away! Please go away!"

The image placed a gnarled, ring-studded index finger to the lipless gash that was its mouth.

"Shhh! The servants, Jeffrey! I can't go away. There are only two people who can help you. You are one and I am the other."

"No, no, that isn't true!" he screamed. "You're trying to destroy me! You *want* me to go insane! You've planned it for years!"

"You do me a great wrong, Jeffrey," came the throaty reply. *"Your rationalization has gone wrong if a mere consonant is the difference between what I am and what you think I am."*

"What do you mean?"

"You're trying to think of me as a fiend. I am really a friend. See what a difference a single insignificant letter makes? Look closer, Jeffrey. Look closer and you will see that I am your friend!"

He was unable to resist. He moved his face closer to the mirror. He was stricken with horror at the close-up of the image. Behind the ravenous eyes there was a long-suffering sadness. Under the silken hair that grew from every pore, lay smooth sensitive skin. The bloodthirsty mouth concealed the gentle soft lips of a child. The hairless forehead was a maze of crisscrossing wrinkles. And in the deep crevice of a scar running just below the hairline he saw a smoldering brand. Its letters were barely perceptible. They spelled his name!

He moved now. He backed away from the mirror, knocking over an end table. But he could not take his eyes from the image.

The image beckoned him to return.

"Now you know, Jeffrey! It will be you and me together now! You see why you can't tell Doctor Anderson, don't you?"

He found himself being irresistibly drawn back to the mirror.

"Yes… I see now…" he droned.

"A good thing, too, Jeffrey, because our two minds are so far superior to any single mind. We outsmarted Sarah's mind, didn't we? We proved we could get along without her!"

"Did we…really prove it…"

"Yes, yes, of course we did!" said the image. It spoke feverishly now as the mist in the mirror began to clear. *"We can do without anyone, Jeffrey. Remember that! Only we have the power now. Go to Front Street, Jeffrey. There is excitement there, a different kind of life. Go there and enjoy the new power! And live! Live… Live…"*

The mirror cleared and the image was gone.

The room was normal again. His head no longer ached. Yet he still needed the mantel, to support him. The revelation had unhinged him. Aunt Sarah had been at the root of all his inner turmoil but the image was not her. It was not any part of her.

The image was himself!

That was the fact. He could not dismiss the fact. *That* was why he couldn't tell Anderson! The old doctor had come close, maybe too close, when he said a power existed almost as a separate being. He knew the image was right. He could never tell Anderson now. He could never tell anyone!

The stink of dead fish was sheer hell on his sensitive nostrils. Front Street was hot and crowded and sticky. The swarming itinerant shoppers elbowed and shoved him. His eardrums swelled with the discordant screeching of fish hawkers. Grimy-faced kids made fun of him and splashed mud on his spotless tailor-made seersucker. The street was filthy, littered with fish heads, old newspaper and wet sawdust.

Front Street. Jugular vein of the waterfront. Source of life to a community in which there was already too much life.

He had been strolling for over an hour, reliving the fascination he had experienced as a child. Their turbulent existence was so completely alien to his own. What amounted, for him, to the ugly realities of life, were only commonplace occurrences to these people. They lived and they were the ugly realities. Unsheltered, he thought. Just as unsheltered as the poor dead mackerels laying row upon row in the bleating sun.

He continued his stroll. He didn't buy anything. He didn't stop to talk to anyone. He didn't know quite how to go about it. Such were the inhibitions that came with maturity. How simple it had been as a child, just a matter of marching up to other children and saying you wanted to play with them. Nothing to it. There was something ridiculous about the prospect of interrupting a man selling fish and saying you just wanted to talk to him. There was the distinct feeling the fish hawker wouldn't be interested.

He walked further, leaving the fish markets and shoppers behind him. The street narrowed into a series of cheap flophouses, tenements, and taverns. This section I was more familiar. It was calmer than he remembered it. There was a group of kids sitting serenely on the edge of the wharf, trying their luck with makeshift fishing poles.

He peered through the window of a tavern. It was empty except for a bartender who was wiping glasses and looked bored to death. Jeffrey thought about going in. It seemed a good way to start a conversation, even though the bartender would necessarily be a captive audience.

He went inside. He stumbled over a beer keg that was sitting with several others just off the center of the room. The bartender looked up long enough to size him up and groan exasperation. The place was cool but had a damp musty odor. There were several booths and tables with chairs turned upside down on them. The ceiling was low, lined with broad oak beams. At one end of the bar there was a narrow flight of stairs. Behind the bottles a mirror ran the length of the bar. The names of drinks and their prices were scribbled on it in soap.

Jeffrey sat on a wooden stool at the bar. The bartender went on wiping glasses, apparently not interested in late morning trade.

Jeffrey waited a moment. He cleared his throat.

The bartender grunted, stuffed his towel into a glass, and came toward him. He was red-faced and pushing sixty. Jeffrey was sure he had one of the beer kegs under his apron.

"What's your hurry?" drawled the bartender. "You are starting early, you got all day," He placed a pasteboard coaster in front of him. "What'll it be?"

"Old Fashioned," said Jeffrey.

"Old Fashioned," the bartender repeated. His lips barely parted for the words to escape.

He took his time with the drink, giving Jeffrey the once over as he mixed. When he spoke again there was a glint in his eye and his words contained a good-natured saltiness.

"You must be a fisherman," he muttered. "Always glad to know when the fleet's in."

Jeffrey couldn't stop his reflexes in time. He looked down at his imported seersucker in complete bewilderment. Then, just as quickly, he looked back at the bartender, embarrassed. The bartender was shaking his drink. There was a mischievous grin on his face.

Jeffrey was at sixes and sevens for a moment. Then he smiled. Being such fair game for the bartender's sense of humor amused him.

The bartender poured the drink and set it on the bar in front of him.

"You lost, mister?"

"Lost?" he said flatly. "I'm afraid I don't..." He caught the bartender inspecting his suit again. "Oh, I see what you mean. No, I was just strolling in the area and...well, I thought I might like to talk to someone."

"Who?"

Jeffrey shrugged. "I don't know...anyone."

"What about?"

"Well, nothing really. I just wanted to get acquainted with someone…" The bartender's stare made him uncomfortable, "…And talk."

"About nothing?"

He answered with a weak hollow laugh. "No, not about *nothing…*"

"Then what about?"

He shifted uneasily on the wooden stool. He couldn't understand why the old guy was so curious.

"Well, about anything… I just want to…"

"You a cop?"

"No of course not," He was dumbfounded. "Why?"

"What business you got here on Front Street?"

"I assure you I'm only visiting. I have no business and I don't want to make trouble for anyone."

The bartender gave him a long steady look.

"You made a mistake, mister, coming to this neck of the woods in those fancy duds."

He was right, Jeffrey thought. Dressed as he was he would have difficulty starting any kind of a conversation on Front street.

"You want me to leave?" he asked.

The bartender laughed. "I said you wore the wrong clothes, mister. I didn't say your money was no good, stay as long as you like. Only be careful on your way home."

"What do you mean?"

"I mean certain people who don't have money form bad habits. They wait in alleys for certain people who do have money. You know what I mean?"

"But it's broad daylight!"

"High noon, four in the morning, it makes no difference. Out on that street the muggers and winos will take one look at you and see a walking vault."

"Thanks," he said. "When I come back I'll know enough to use my head and dress differently."

The bartender's mouth dropped open. "You mean you might come back to this hell hole?"

Jeffrey smiled. "This isn't my first visit."

The bartender whistled in surprise and walked away muttering something about the idle rich.

Jeffrey had two more drinks. When he looked at his watch it was one-thirty. There was plenty of time, he decided, to go home and change clothes. Then he could come back and mingle and never be noticed.

"How much?" he shouted to the bartender, who had gone to the other end of the bar.

"One-eighty," came the reply. He rang up the amount on the cash register on his way to pick up the money.

Jeffrey fumbled through his pockets. His face turned crimson. He smiled weakly. The bartender stood with his hands on his hips and a don't-tell-me-you-lost-your-wallet look on his face.

Jeffrey completed another clumsy search through his pockets.

"I'm afraid something is wrong," he said.

"I'm afraid I know what it is," the bartender muttered, "

I always keep my wallet in my upper right hand coat-pocket. I don't understand."

"I do. Somebody saw you coming, mister."

"Saw me coming?"

"A pickpocket."

"A pickpocket! At this time of day?"

"They keep very irregular hours."

A melancholy frown twisted his features. The bartender was so complacent about it Pickpockets and thugs were accepted facts of life to him. But it wasn't only the bartender. Now that he thought about it the whole street seemed different to him. He wondered if one of the kids he had once played with might have so resigned himself to the ravages of poverty as to resort to a life of thievery...picking pockets in order to exist.

"I assure you..." he began and was interrupted by a bland wave of the bartender's hand.

"I know, I know...you'll send me the money. But it just happens I already rung it up on the register. I don't want to be stuck for it in case you should step out the door into a mild case of amnesia."

"Well, I..."

"It's all right, Fred. He won't forget to pay you," Jeffrey spun around to see who belonged to the third voice.

The girl was young and attractive. A winsome smile played on her friendly mouth. Her hands rested gracefully in the pockets of a light trench coat.

"That's very kind of you Miss, but you don't have to…"

"We've known each other before, Mr. Barton. Won't you let an old friend give you a reference?"

He was confused and speechless. If they *were* old friends he was not aware of it. But he liked her looks whether they were old friends or not. Her skin was porcelain smooth, drawn tight under high exotic cheekbones.

"I'm sorry," he said. "I'm afraid I don't…"

She let him dangle in midair for a moment.

"I'll try to refresh your memory. Shall we sit in a booth?"

"Yes…yes, by all means," he answered dumbly.

The bartender forgot about the tab and went back to the monotonous task of wiping glasses.

They sat facing each other in a cramped wooden booth. She was silent again, deliberately silent. He felt a discomforting warmth in his face. He knew he was blushing.

"You'd better not wait for me to guess," he said with a sheepish grin. "I'm not really very good at guessing."

Her eyes sparkled brilliantly. They were large brown ovals. He liked looking into her eyes.

She laughed.

"What's funny?"

"You're embarrassed," she said.

"No…no, I'm not. Really. I just… I just can't remember, that's all."

"You were twelve and I was ten and we played together not more than a block from where we're sitting." The playful smile returned to her lips. "And I see no reason to tell you my name because you once told me you'd never forget it."

He avoided looking at her. "I *have* forgotten," he whispered. "I'm sorry."

Her smile faded. She reached across the booth and put her finger under his chin. She brought his face level with hers.

"Hey, pull yourself together, Mr. Barton. You haven't committed a crime." She waited until he looked into her eyes. "It's Julie, Julie Noyes. Remember now?"

He nodded.

"You used to tell me how you had run away from your house to be able to play with us. You remember that?"

"I can't forget it."

There was an uncomfortable silence. Her eyes met his. His stare forced her to grin awkwardly. She slipped the kerchief from her head and shook her hair until it fell evenly around her shoulders.

"I've read about you in the newspapers every now and then," she said.

He didn't answer, preferring to be enchanted by the magnetism of her face. Years had gone by and she seemed so vibrant and alive.

She grew uneasy. "You're engaged to that Stevens girl, aren't you?"

"Yes," he said. "Yes, I am." He liked the way her nose wrinkled when she smiled. And how her hair fell in a soft curl over one eyebrow.

"I guess you just don't have much to say to me, is that it, Mr. Barton?"

She started to leave the booth. Something of the radiance was gone. He had offended her. He was furious with himself for not being able to show his enthusiasm for the reunion. He stopped her.

"Please," he touched her arm. "Please sit down. It's just that...it's been so long...I guess I don't know how to talk to anyone anymore."

She sat facing him again, studying his face. She seemed to understand his plight and to sympathize with it.

"I remember you that way. We were always doing things that confused you. And you were always apologizing..."

He grinned. "I remember… You all ran out of patience because I never stopped asking questions. You wondered whether people in my neighborhood sent their kids to school."

She laughed infectiously. "Now you're back on the memory beam."

He felt better now that the conversation had gotten off the ground. He wanted to spend more time with her. She laughed the way he remembered the others laughing.

"Tell me about yourself, Julie. What have you been doing these long seventeen years?"

"You really want to know?"

"Of course. I'm very interested."

"Living," she said and this time he laughed. "What's so funny about living? Sometimes it isn't easy. Only I don't like to think about those times. I just take it as it comes, moment to moment, day to day…"

"Are you married?"

"Am I what?"

"Married."

She rested her head against the back of the booth. The corners of her mouth dipped downward. All at once she looked tired.

"Are you kidding me, Mr. Barton?"

"Why would I want to kid you?" he asked innocently.

She slowly unbuttoned her trench coat, then let it fall open to reveal a string of false pearls and a cheap cotton dress with a plunging neckline. Her firm breasts huddled close together at the neckline.

"Do I look like a girl who could afford to get married?"

"I think you do."

"Let's face it," she said bitterly, "I'd lose a fortune."

"Julie, I don't know what you're talking about."

"Oh, come, come, Mr. Barton. Where've you been all these years? Where were you when they handed out the facts of life?"

Her sudden harshness rattled him. "I'm sorry if I don't understand…have I…have I offended you?"

"Oh, brother, you are kidding me." She buttoned her coat. "Thanks for the afternoon of pleasant memories. If you'll excuse me I'd better leave before I get embarrassed. And if *I* get embarrassed somebody might laugh!"

She got up from the booth and strode toward the door.

He ran after her and took her by the shoulders.

"Please, Julie," he groped for the right words, "I don't know what I've said but I didn't mean to make you angry. Honestly. You've made me very happy...just talking to me. I want to see you again. Please believe that."

"I'm sorry, Mr. Barton," she said in a half-whisper. "I get a little touchy every now and then. Sure you can see me again. Anytime."

"Thank you, Julie."

"Don't mention it. Just climb the stairs to the left of the bar. You'll find me at the far end of the hall on the right."

"You live *here?*"

"You still want to see me?"

"Yes," he replied quickly.

Her large brown eyes closed for a moment as if to wall off tears. She drew his head down and pressed her lips against his.

"When you come by be sure and check with Fred, the bartender," she said. "So long, Mr. Barton."

He stood there, his gaze transfixed where she had disappeared through the door.

He left the tavern. Outside the sun had swung over to the west. Soon it would be evening. A wild sensation swept through him. He had to see her again soon! There was no waiting for tomorrow. It *had* to be sooner. That night!

He walked along the street remembering their conversation and how ineffectual he had been. The desire in him fizzled as he realized she could never appreciate Jeffrey Barton. He needed confidence, a more forthright approach, the ability to laugh as she did and hold up his end of the conversation. He had none of those qualities.

Then he remembered. In his mind the phrase kept repeating itself. Two minds are far superior to a single mind.

He had to get home as fast as possible. At home there was someone who could help him.

The image was still far off in the swirling background of the mirror. But it was already fully formed. As it converged on him he saw all of it for the first time. As if to erase any doubts he may have held it conformed in every way to his physical self.

There was no longer any desire to resist. And if there had been the desire he knew it would have been pointless. The image was irrevocably his and he accepted it. It was the one source of truth he had ever known. He could always depend on it. It was his friend and his benefactor. He needed it and it needed him. Together they represented a whole. Separated, each was helpless.

He stood mesmerized as its hideous frame loomed larger. When it reached the mantel's edge it stepped to one side. Its hair-infested arm gestured toward the hazy background.

"Look, Jeffrey!"

Jeffrey obeyed. His wilting eyes drifted toward the mist.

"Look closely, Jeffrey!"

The mist began to clear.

"There she is!" cried the image. *"See her, Jeffrey?"*

The mist was gone. The Front Street Tavern materialized before his eyes.

"Come in, Jeffrey! Come in!"

A weightlessness came over him. In the next second he merged with the mirror and the tavern became a reality.

"Over there, Jeffrey! On the stairs. She is a lovely creature, isn't she? She was made to deliver pleasure. For you. For you, Jeffrey. You saddened her this afternoon. She wanted you to love her. But you'll rectify that, won't you?"

The image was still with him but no longer visible.

The tavern was crowded with raucous drinkers. Body heat and tobacco smoke combined to smother the atmosphere. He glanced into the annex. The booths and tables were littered with bottles and glasses, overflowing ashtrays and sopping wet coasters. There was a couple at every table. Most of them were making obscene advances at each other. They were all laughing and having a gay time.

"There's no time to waste, Jeffrey. She's not on the stairs now. She's gone to the room. Waiting for you!"

His eyes wandered from the tables and booths, over the bar. Fred, the bartender, and a crowd of seedy looking men were laughing uproariously at someone's joke.

"Up the stairs by the bar!"

His eyes reached the stairs.

"She's waiting for you Jeffrey! To see you again. She is your pleasure. Go up the stairs!"

His eyes surveyed the crowded bar. Nobody was watching the stairs. They weren't even aware of his presence. He darted up the stairs and found himself at one end of a long corridor. The rooms were set close together.

"All the way to the end! On the right! There is your pleasure, Jeffrey! Anytime, she told you. Remember? Hurry, Jeffrey, hurry!"

He stole down the corridor, his pace quickening with every step, the ecstasy piling up inside him. He stopped in front of the last room. He was out of breath. He waited. He would have to catch his second wind before he could make the proper entrance. He could not disappoint her.

He was ready. There was no reason to knock. He knew she was waiting for him, waiting to enchant him. He opened the door. He saw the man and froze.

The man was sitting beside her on the bed. The man was unshaven and obscene in his undershirt. The man was old enough to be her father and was contaminating her mouth with seething kisses.

The shock was compounded when he realized she was not resisting the man. She had betrayed him! His head swelled with blind rage. The room swayed before him. He slammed the door.

They broke apart. She screamed when she saw him. She ran to the corner of the room. The man sprang from the bed and lunged at him.

His claw-like fingers found the man's fleshy bare arm with deadly accuracy. With scalpel precision he opened a gash, releasing a torrent of blood. The man shrieked with pain and scrambled for the door. He clutched the man's neck with iron-strong hands and squeezed until the blood had been compressed into the head. He heard a snap. The body fell in a lump, horrible heap on the floor.

He turned to find her. She cringed in the corner, her thin frail hands knotted together in front of her mouth, her painted face racked with fear. She held no enchantment for him now. The memories had been shattered. She wasn't the same little girl of long ago. She couldn't please him anymore. She was a sorceress, meant to tease and laugh at him.

Her scream lasted only a split second. His hands took her naked white throat. The thick silken hair bristled as his thumb pressed at the jugular vein, choking off another attempted scream. Her eyes bloated out of proportion. The last gasp of life abandoned her limp body. He let her fall to the floor.

He heard voices in the corridor. Voices getting closer. The door! He fled to the door and bolted it. More voices…louder…a knock! He saw the window. The voices were shouting angrily…pushing at the door. He looked out at the alley below…a two-story drop…he crept to the window ledge…he jumped…

Pain ripped through his twisted ankle. His mind was spinning. He heard a crash. Upstairs in the room! They had broken the door down. He crawled into the protective shadow of the building.

"Run, Jeffrey! Run! Run! Run!"

He ran, in tortuous pain, toward the dimly lit street and disappeared into the fog.

The fog evaporated and he saw the grandfather clock on the other side of the dark living room. He turned to the mirror. In the disappearing mist he caught a final glimpse of the grimacing image, its eyes dilating with lurid satisfaction.

"Well done, Jeffrey. Well done!"

His ankle throbbed unmercifully. He limped toward the sofa. He stopped. The sound was faint. Someone breathing. He was not alone in the room!

He turned and saw her standing by the window, her lovely body framed there in the moonlight.

"Jeffrey, where on earth have you been?" Annoyance filtered through her carefully modulated tone. "It's almost midnight, darling."

"What are you doing here, Vera?"

"What am I doing here? I haven't seen you for three days. I'm engaged to you, remember?"

She moved toward him.

"Stay where you are, Vera!"

The deadliness of his command was foreign to her. She stopped.

"Darling, what's wrong?"

"Nothing is wrong. I'm perfectly fine!"

He was caught between the sofa and the mantelpiece with nothing to lean on. He winced as another charge of pain went through his ankle. He had no choice. He hobbled to the mantel.

"You're hurt!" Vera exclaimed, coming swiftly closer to him.

"I told you I'm all right. Go home, Vera!"

"Jeffrey, you're behaving so strangely. You haven't been drinking, have you?"

He turned away from her.

"Go home, Vera. Please go home! I'll call you in the morning."

"No," she answered, sounding a note of concern. "I won't go home. I've been waiting here for three hours. Tomorrow is your birthday and I wanted to surprise you with a present. Now you tell me to go home. What's happened, Jeffrey?"

"Why do you keep asking me what's happened?" he bellowed.

"Darling, you can be a little more civil than that. And a little less mysterious. I only want to know how you hurt your leg."

"I tripped. Coming through the front gate," he snapped.

"Why didn't you say so before?"

"I'm very tired, Vera. Please let me call you in the morning."

"Nonsense. We're going to have a look at that ankle."

Her hand reached out for the lamp switch.

"Don't turn the lamp on!" he shouted. "Leave it alone!"

He heard the click. The area by the mantelpiece was bathed in light. He hobbled to the sofa.

"Now don't be silly, darling. How can I administer first aid if there isn't any li—"

The words died on her lips. A shudder raced through her. She saw the dark red stains on the mantelpiece. Her eyes were drawn to the sofa. His hands were soaked with blood. His eyes turned upward to meet hers. She gasped. His face was sullen, treacherous.

Her mouth quivered. "Jeffrey…" was all she could whisper.

He stood up. "I told you not to turn on the light, Vera," He had to forget about the ankle. That could be attended to later. He had an emergency to deal with.

"Jeffrey," she repeated, forcing the words, "where did that blood come from…"

"I warned you to go home, Vera. I told you I would call you in the morning," He moved toward her. "Why didn't you have sense enough to leave?"

"What are you going to do?"

The answer was in his eyes. She moved. She wasn't fast enough. He jumped in front of her, putting her between him and the mantel. Panic seized her, blotting her coherence. Short uncertain steps brought her closer to the mantel as he closed in upon her.

"Jeffrey, stop it!" she screamed. "Stop looking at me that way! What's wrong with you?"

"Kill her, Jeffrey. Kill her now before she can talk to anyone."

He moved in closer.

"Jeffrey, stay away from me! Stay away!"

Her back touched the mantelpiece. The panic curdled her reflexes. She had retreated as far as possible. The bloodstained hands darted forward and clamped her neck. She mustered up a full burst of energy to scream. His grip was animal-like. It choked off her vocal chords. She clawed at him, digging her nails into his distorted face. She scratched and kicked in a feverish effort to hold on to life. It was useless. The pungent sense of death was all around her. The room got darker. She felt the last dull breath of life slipping away.

She saw the vase on the mantelpiece above her head. There would be only a second or two. Her hand reached up and gripped the rim of the vase. The strength was gone. She was able to tilt it but she knew she could never bring it down on him.

He glanced at the vase. He realized what she was trying to do. That was the end she thought.

His eyes widened. He relaxed his grip. A burst of fresh air rushed into her crippled lungs.

"Leave it alone!" he demanded. "Take your hands off the vase."

Instinct told her to cling for dear life. He released her neck, leaving her choking for more air. The hostility disappeared from his features. He began to whimper like a child. He clutched at her fingers. He could not remove them from the rim.

"Let go!" he cried. "Please let go of the vase!"

She didn't know why he was terrified of it. She couldn't afford to care. She only knew clinging to it was her only way of staying alive.

He put both hands to the task of prying her loose. She tore at his hair with her free hand. He lost his grip and fell backwards, leaving her off balance. The vase started to topple. She couldn't stay on her feet and keep it from falling.

She fell near the fireplace; Jeffrey made a final desperate lunge to save the vase. It was too late. It crashed to the floor, spilling its contents to the rug.

He stood in rapt silence, gaping at it. The electrifying scream that escaped Vera's throat failed to move him. He was mesmerized by the sight on the rug.

Vera stood up. Her hand went to her mouth as if to hold back the sickly feeling that sifted through her.

The vase lay in pieces on the ornate rug. Near one of the pieces she saw a mound of cold gray ashes. At the base of the mound was the charred skull, a hideous misshapen thing with stray patches of hair to show that discomposure was all but completed.

Her leaden feet edged her toward the door. She saw he was no longer interested in her. She opened the door and ran with alarming speed out of the house.

He stood watching the ugly remains of Aunt Sarah. From some distant crevice came the muffled voice of the image.

"The furnace. Back into the furnace to stay!"

He took his eyes from the floor. He remembered Vera had been there. Now she was gone. It was too late to do anything about that now. He rushed to the servants' closet, found the necessary equipment, and came back to the living room to clear away the evidence.

He watched the blazing fire through the open door of the furnace. There would be no evidence now. He was angry for not having completed the cremation the first time. He glanced at his watch. One o'clock.

Exhaustion and furnace heat combined to make him drowsy. His eyes closed. His head drooped to one side lolling grotesquely.

He came awake with a start. His eyes raced to the watch. One-forty. Can't afford to fall asleep like that again, he warned himself. The fire was dying away. The last particle of Aunt Sarah's wretched bones had turned to dust. He couldn't understand what odd desire had ever provoked him to keep her on the mantelpiece. His warped logic convinced him that she had still exerted her influence while she had been in the vase. But now she was gone forever. Now he would be all right. He would never again have anything to fear.

Except Vera!

She knew! And she would tell Ned Anderson.

He would have to stop her. Hurting Vera was the last thing he wanted. But if he did not silence her she would go to Ned. And Ned would believe her. And Ned would think he was insane.

That could never happen because he knew he was *not* insane! Now that Sarah was finally gone he was on the road to recovery. He'd even be able to stop the psychiatric treatments. Of what use would they be to him?

The fire died out. He sat for a while, knowing what he had to do, deciding on the best method of doing it. There wasn't much time. Time, it seemed, had always been his enemy.

He climbed the cellar stairs and entered the kitchen. The wall clock told him it was two-thirty. He could be at Vera's house by two-forty if he hurried. He knew the house well. He could slip in without being heard, silence her, and slip out. All within the space of fifteen minutes.

He passed through the living room, pausing to check once more for any traces of what had happened. The rug was spotless.

The stillness of the room was jarred by the sound of the front door slamming.

Ned Anderson came to a halt in the doorway of the living room. He looked like anything but a doctor with his collar opened and his gray hair windswept and disarrayed. He was fighting to catch his breath.

An icy hardness pervaded his gentle old features. It told Jeffrey everything. Vera had been to see him. Now they both knew. Jeffrey staggered a step backward. For a moment a fuzziness clouded his thoughts. Events were piling up too fast for him to keep up with them.

"I've had a long night, Jeffrey," the old man spoke between short gasps, "a long hard terrible night."

"You look tired, Ned."

"I think you'd better sit down, Jeff," He entered the room as Jeffrey sat on the sofa. "Vera is at her home, suffering from a severe case of shock. She is unable to speak or to comprehend..." He stopped as he noticed Jeffrey was not reacting.

He was accepting the news with stoic calm. His reaction was an inner one. A state of shock! There was still time! Ned did not know yet. But he came here because he suspected. He must be watched.

"I want to know what happened, Jeffrey!"

"I don't know what you mean, Ned."

The doctor moved in front of him. His back was to the mantel. "Vera came home a little over two hours ago. Her neck was covered with blood. Someone had tried to strangle her. I know you saw her here..."

"How do you know that?"

"Her mother told me she came to your house at nine-thirty."

"But Vera didn't tell you, did she? I mean she couldn't have told you if she's in a state of shock."

His reply astonished the old man.

"You're not going to deny seeing her, are you?"

"I haven't seen her for three days."

The doctor looked into his eyes. There was a transparent film over them, a wall that had cut him off from any further rational contact.

"Jeffrey, you realize I'm your friend, don't you?"

"Don't let him tell you that, Jeffrey!"

"Yes, I realize that, Ned."

"And you know I wouldn't try to hurt you?"

"Be careful! He has a plan! He'll put you away!"

"Yes."

"I told you I had a long night. Perhaps I can best explain why I'm here if I tell you how much has happened tonight. So I want you to listen and try...please try, Jeffrey...to understand."

Jeffrey got up from the sofa and walked to the mantelpiece. For a moment the sight of the bloodstains immobilized him. He had forgotten to clean the mantel. He turned to face the doctor, covering the stains with his back.

"Is there any reason why we can't discuss it tomorrow?"

"I must talk now, Jeffrey. I was on my way home at midnight. I bought my morning paper and before I could move away from the newsstand your name hit me smack between the eyes."

He could not conceal the shock. "My name!"

"There was a double murder in a flophouse on Front Street. A man and a young girl. They had both been strangled to death. The papers say it was done by someone of superhuman strength. The girl's neck had been mangled out of shape and punctured in two places."

"I don't understand how my name enters into it."

"The man was carrying your wallet."

The jolt unstabilized him, as if someone had split the room down the middle with a giant hatchet.

"The police proceeded on the stupid theory, presumably for the benefit of headline hungry reporters, that the man was you. That theory won't last very long."

"What do you mean?"

"You'll have to tell them the man was *not* you. If *you* don't tell them somebody else will."

"Will *you* tell them, Ned?"

The doctor hesitated. "How did that man get your wallet?"

"He was a pickpocket."

Ned's expression told him the old man thought he was lying.

"It was one o'clock by the time I reached home. I had no sooner walked in the door when the phone rang. It was Paul Carter, the Stevens family doctor. He urged me to come and see Vera at once. I went as fast as I could. I spent an hour with Vera. As I told you she was unable to say anything. But when I was through examining her it was not necessary for her to say anything. Shall I go on, Jeffrey?"

There was no doubt now that Ned had come with but one intention. He would put him away. Someplace where he would be alone again. Alone forever. There was no use depending upon Ned to help him anymore. But there was someone he could depend upon!

"You'd better continue," he told the doctor.

"Very well. I read the newspaper story again, carefully. I knew you had gone to Front Street yesterday. I had no idea how long you had stayed but I was reasonably sure that, on your first visit, you would have difficulty meeting or talking to anyone. So I knew the murdered man was not you."

Jeffrey turned from him and faced the mirror. The reflection of the old grandfather clock began to ripple gently.

"Judging from the amount of blood on both bodies and the amount found on the window ledge I knew the killer's hands must have been covered with blood when he left the room. The person who tried to strangle Vera had bloodstained hands..." he paused. "Like the stains on your mantel," he concluded.

The mirror was a mass of frenzied vibrations. The room became distorted.

"You're quite a brilliant man, Ned. Let's hear the rest of it."

"Please, Jeffrey. You don't have to hear..."

"I insist, Ned! You say you're my friend, you want to help me?"

The doctor eyed him cautiously. "The window in the room was twenty, feet from the ground. That can be a dangerous jump for a man in a hurry. When you walked to the fireplace just now you were limping."

The room was no longer reflected. There was only the friendly mist. And in the distance, taking shape to come to his aid, was the image.

"Is that all, Ned?"

"Why did you try to kill Vera?"

"I haven't said I did try to kill her. You were trying to trap me, weren't you, Ned?"

"How did she find out about Aunt Sarah?"

"So you know about Aunt Sarah too!"

"I'm afraid I've only suspected," the doctor sighed. "You see, twice a week for six weeks just wasn't enough time to know anything. If I had any idea you were so close to what happened tonight I would have…"

"You would have what, Ned?"

The old man regarded him with sober concern. "I would have seen to it that you had gotten a rest."

"In an institution? No Ned, you couldn't have done that."

The image was at the mirror's edge. Its ghastly face was aflame with hatred. It snarled like a chained animal straining to break loose. It wanted to kill!

"You couldn't have put me in an institution. Do you know why, Ned?"

"Jeffrey, listen to me. You must understand it won't be for always. You're not beyond salvation."

Jeffrey laughed hysterically.

"I'm not even in need of salvation. Look into the mirror, Ned."

"Jeff…"

"Look into the mirror and you'll see why no one can ever harm me again. My salvation is in there."

The doctor walked to the mirror. He looked into it. His expression turned to pity.

"There is nothing in the mirror, Jeffrey."

He jerked his head around in a sudden moment of panic. The image was still there, still awaiting the order that would unleash the stored up fury.

"You're wrong, Ned. Look closely."

"The poker, Jeffrey! By the fireplace! Take the poker and…"

"And you'll see how well protected I am. Go on, Ned. Look!"

"Hold the poker behind your back, Jeffrey! That's right! Now wait! Wait for just another moment..."

"See my slave, Ned? With him I can do anything and nobody will ever suspect!"

"Ready, Jeffrey! Get ready! Lift the poker high in the air..."

"...between us we eliminated Aunt Sarah. We did humanity a favor, did you know that, Ned? Take a good look at him..."

"Now, Jeffrey. Now!"

"...take a good last look at him..."

"Look out, Jeffrey! He has a gun! Bring the poker down! Kill him. Kill him."

The poker swiftly, accurately found its mark on the tender aging scalp. Ned fell to the floor, the grayness of his hair receding under the warm red flow of blood.

"Again Jeffrey. Once more to be sure!"

The room quaked in the aftermath of two rapid gunshots. The poker crashed on the stone hearth before the fireplace. The small automatic slipped out of Ned Anderson's dead fingers.

Jeffrey clutched at the two small holes in his stomach. He gripped the mantelpiece. His hand pressed hard against the wound, trying to hold the blood in.

He shrieked at the image as it began to melt like burning wax before his eyes.

"Come back! Come back! I'm all right! He can't put us away now! What are you, afraid of! Come back here!"

The image did not hear him. Its hot searing features were swallowed up by the fading mist.

He looked at the floor. Ned Anderson was dead. There, was only one voice left to silence. He could do it alone.

He moved toward the door. Pain shot out from every direction and tore into his garbled stomach. His face perspired. He clung dearly to the fragments of life that was left. There was enough, more than enough he told himself to get him to Vera's house.

He opened the front door. The cold clear air gave him invigorating impetus. He passed through the huge iron gate and went into the dark empty street. A ten-minute walk from there. Plenty of time. Put her out of the picture Then safety.

His heart pumped furiously as he realized he was going in the wrong direction. Vera's house was the other way. Turn around! Turn around!

His feet would not obey. They moved faster. Faster in the wrong direction! He ordered them to slow down! He was the master of his own feet! Why did they move in the wrong direction? They took him faster and faster.

Turn around, he urged. Back to Vera's!

They were running now, still in the wrong direction. His heart could not keep up. It pumped at top speed. His feet moved faster. Something snapped. The pumping stopped. His legs crumbled. The ground smashed into his face. His cheek rested against the soft green earth.

The river shimmered gently in the pale moonlight. A giant elm flexed a thousand green muscles in the tolerant wind. And the stars looked down on a corner of creation to find a man at peace.

THE END

COLD GHOST

By CHESTER S. GEIER

All Hager had to do was slow the dogsled to a walk, and his partner died. A perfect crime—no chance to get caught!

In the valley, with the sheltering hills now behind them, the bitterly cold wind drove at the sled with unchecked ferocity. Gusts of snow came with the wind, thick and dry, the separate particles of it stinging on contact.

The dogs made slow progress through the deep drifts. Hager's smoldering irritation blazed into abrupt rage. From his position at the rear of the sled, he lashed out with the driver's whip that he held in one heavily mittened hand, shouting behind the wool scarf covering the lower half of his face. The dogs lunged in their traces, whining. A couple floundered in the powdery footing and were immediately snapped at by their companions behind them.

Interior Illustration by Rod Ruth

Hager huddled before the fire, trembling with cold that filled him with terror.

The snow was falling swiftly and with a sinister steadiness. It seemed to hang like a vast white curtain over the valley, obscuring the hills and the fanged outline of mountains beyond. The wind seized portions of the curtain and twisted it into fantastic shapes—the shapes of demons, Hager thought suddenly. For the scene through which he moved was a kind of hell, a white and frozen hell, with the howl of the wind like the despairing shrieks of tormented souls.

Hager pictured himself as one of them. And Cahill, huddled in furs on the sled, another. He cursed behind the scarf as he thought of Cahill. This was Cahill's fault, their being out here in the storm. If it weren't for Cahill, he would be back at the cabin, snug and warm, logs blazing cheerfully in the fireplace.

It was a rotten time for Cahill to have taken sick, Hager fumed. But it had happened. And it had left him with nothing else to do but pack their catch of furs, harness up the sled, and start out with Cahill for the doctor in Moose Gulch.

He almost regretted having taken the furs. With Cahill an added burden on the sled, it was too large a load for the dogs to pull with the necessary speed and endurance. But he hadn't dared to leave the entire season's catch unguarded at the cabin. If some wanderer appeared in his and Cahill's absence, the furs would be an irresistible temptation.

Fearing, thus, to leave the furs behind, and now endangered by their weight, Hager found the situation maddening. And the storm was making matters worse. It was near the end of winter, but the climate had chosen this moment to be at its most unco-operative.

Hager muttered blackly against the storm, wondering why he had allowed his trapper's dream of wealth to lure him to this far northern corner of Alaska. It was a cold, bleak and hostile country. Tiny settlements, like Moose Gulch were few and far between. Of course, furs were at their best and most plentiful here. He and Cahill had proved that, for their catch was a large one. Hager's thoughts soared briefly above his bitter mood as he thought of the money the furs would bring. And of the things that the money would bring back in civilization.

Added to what he had so far managed to save, his share would make almost enough to start a fox breeding ranch. Or a mink ranch. Almost enough—but not quite. That meant he would have to spend another winter in this location, and Hager flinched at the thought. He hated loneliness and the bitter, subzero cold. Most of all he hated the cold. Only a fur breeding ranch, with large, warm living quarters, would have made it bearable.

Hager didn't know when the idea came to him. It must have been lying dormant for a long time in a far, dark corner of his mind, only now surging to the fore. Subconsciously he must have prepared himself for this moment of inspiration. He wasn't sure. He was aware only of an interval while he plodded behind the sled, drawn by the struggling and panting team, cursing the dogs, cursing Cahill and the fierce cold that mischievously searched out the most tender portions of his face beneath the hood of his parka. There was that moment, and then—

AND then he found himself toying with the thought of murdering Cahill.

With the other out of the way, the entire proceeds from the sale of furs would be his. There would be no necessity to split. He could start the fur ranch at once. He wouldn't have to spend another winter in this vicious cold. He—

A dozen fascinating new possibilities opened up to Hager. It was as though he had been blind and was able to see only now. Breath-taking vistas blossomed before his awakened eyes. There was music in what he visioned, music and the voices of women, bright lights, color, movement, and the warmth of gentler climes.

The brightest part of the picture was that Cahill's death need not be outright murder. The man was sick. His life depended on getting him into the hands of the doctor in Moose Gulch as quickly as possible.

If Hager were simply to delay in reaching the settlement, Cahill would die as surely as though from the thrust of a knife or the impact of a bullet. Exposure to the biting cold would finish him. And nobody would know. Hager could always claim that he had hurried as best he could under the difficult, hampering circumstances of the storm, but that Cahill had died on the way. As easy as that. If Marshal Art Maddox stuck his long nose into the matter, Cahill's unmarked body would be proof that there had been no foul play.

Hager felt satisfied that his scheme was without loopholes. The idea had become a definite plan. And now his square lips hardened with determination behind the scarf. He looked at Cahill, dozing feverishly on the sled, with deep-set gray eyes that were bleak and implacable.

Cahill would never reach Moose Gulch alive.

With his grim purpose giving new drive to his actions, Hager glanced about him. It was difficult to see through the curtain of snow that hung between him and the landscape, but by squinting steadily through momentary rifts made by the frigid, lashing wind, he was able presently to discern that they were near the pass leading out of the valley. Beyond the pass, he knew, was a forest, dipping down to the banks of a frozen stream. The stream ran for several miles until it branched into a river, which in turn led directly into Moose Gulch. With these landmarks to guide him, a traveler through the snow-bound wilderness could reach the settlement easily and quickly. But Hager didn't intend to do that. He now had time to kill. He chuckled darkly over the accuracy of the phrase.

Plodding toward the pass, he deliberately slowed his steps. He no longer used the whip or shouted at the dogs for greater speed. The animals were grateful for the respite. They slackened their pace, tongues lolling and bushy tails waving as they bobbed in their plowed path through the white drifts.

Cahill dozed on. Once or twice he moved restlessly amid the furs piled about him. It was as though some deep, vague instinct warned him that something was wrong.

Hager watched the other sharply for a time, then desisted to give his attention to maneuvering the sled through the pass. The forest appeared, the trees wraith-like under their thick, white mantles of snow. Hager didn't follow the dip in the land that led toward the frozen stream. He guided the dogs in the opposite direction and began watching Cahill again. He hoped that the man would not awake until less familiar territory surrounded them.

Cahill didn't awake. He dozed and tossed, his lips moving occasionally in a soundless mutter. His gaunt, leathery face was pale under its growth of grizzled whiskers.

The snow-covered land rose, became rocky and difficult. The dogs began laboring with increasing weariness in their efforts to keep pulling the heavy sled. Hager realized he couldn't go in this direction much longer. When a ravine suddenly presented itself, relatively free of snow, he decided to call a halt.

UNFASTENING the dogs, he left the ravine and began searching through the snow for brushwood. It took time, but Hager was in no hurry. He gathered an armful and finally returned to the sled.

Cahill was awake. He had propped himself feebly among the furs, his gaunt face blank and drab with sickness. His filmed blue eyes fastened on Hager.

"Water," he whispered. "Water, Matt."

"Coming up," Hager said. "Just you wait a minute, Ben, and you'll get all the water you want."

Cahill fell back among the furs, and Hager leisurely shaved kindling and stacked the wood and then set it ablaze. The ravine was shielded from the wind, and the wood ignited without difficulty. At last Hager went to the sled and removed the small pack he had fortunately thought to bring along. His experience with the wilderness had trained him never to overlook the smallest precautions.

Hager took a handled pan from the pack. He filled it with snow and then held the pan over the flames. When the snow melted, he filled a tin cup with the liquid and went over to Cahill. He had to steady the cup as the other drank.

Finally Cahill nodded. His eyes seemed to clear. He glanced about him, and a dim worry moved in his face.

"Matt, where are we?"

"Somewhere near Boot Valley."

"You...you mean we're lost?"

"I sort of got mixed up in the storm. Nothing to worry about."

Cahill shivered suddenly. "We got to reach town, Matt. Got to see the doctor."

Hager nodded. "How do you feel?"

"It's getting worse. I can feel it getting worse. I'm cold now, Matt. Before...before I was..." Cahill's voice trailed off. He had to make an effort before he was able to speak again. "Got...got to see the doctor, Matt. Can't waste any time."

"I know," Hager said. "But the team needs a little rest. They've had a lot of heavy hauling, and there's still a distance to go."

Cahill nodded miserably, shivering. He burrowed into the furs, still shivering, breathing rapidly through parted lips. Slowly the chill left him. His eyes clouded again. Then his lids fell, and he dozed once more.

Hager brewed tea and drank it slowly, squatting before the fire. Then he packed and lighted his pipe. He stared into the flames with narrowed eyes, seeing his dreams pictured there. They were pleasant dreams.

Hager remained in the ravine until the supply of wood was gone. Then he fastened the dogs back into their traces and resumed his position behind the sled. With shouts and cracks of the whip, he guided the animals out of the ravine, following the downward slope of the land this time.

The snow stopped falling after a while, but the wind and the cold increased. The cold hung on the air like an enormous, transparent weight. Somehow it seemed to give an impossible crystalline purity to the snow blanketing the trees and the land. In doing so, it emphasized and magnified its very presence. It made itself something almost alive and sentient, icily malignant, overbearing, utterly cruel and without mercy.

Hager cursed the cold with redoubled venom. Despite the thickness of his fur parka and the layers of clothing beneath the cold seemed to soak into him like an all-penetrating liquid. He had to wave his arms and stamp his feet to fight back a creeping numbness.

BUT the terrible chill could not subdue the flame of purpose burning in Hager's mind. That part of him remained keenly alert. The sled was moving in the direction of the stream, and he was careful to judge the distance carefully. He didn't want to approach too close. At just the right moment he turned the sled at angle back toward the way from which it had come. It was his plan to keep zigzagging, approaching the stream and then retreating, always at a tangent. A great deal of time would be consumed in this way, with very little actual forward progress toward Moose Gulch.

He repeated this maneuver again and again. Cahill roused a few times to inquire weakly about their progress. Always Hager gave the same answer.

"We're getting there, Ben. It won't be long now. Don't you worry."

After that Cahill was silent. It seemed evident to Hager that the man was sinking rapidly. But not as rapidly as Hager wished. He knew he couldn't bear the paralyzing cold much longer, and his hatred of it grew.

The sled reached a group of slab-like rock outcroppings that offered shelter from the slashing wind. Hager stopped the sled behind their protection for a short rest. The additional delay suited his plans.

While the dogs huddled together in the snow, Hager went around the sled to get the pack. He glanced at Cahill's face—and his muscles became tense. Cahill's eyes were open. Cahill was watching him with a terrible steadiness and a soul-searing clarity. Cahill... *knew*.

Hager realized that Cahill must have been awake for quite some time, watching the actions of the sled. The man had clearly discovered Hager's deception.

Hager felt transfixed by the accusing brightness in the other's eyes. He sensed that his guilt was written vividly and unmistakably in his face. He fumbled for words that would form an excuse, an apology, some sort of plausible lie—anything that would remove the dreadful knowledge in Cahill's eyes. But no words came.

After a strained, bitter moment Cahill spoke. His voice was low, yet somehow curiously distinct. "You're trying to kill me, Matt. I see it now. You aren't going straight toward Moose Gulch. You're tracking back and forth to waste time. You...want me to die!"

"That isn't true," Hager blurted. "I...I got lost. The storm and cold got me mixed up."

Cahill went on as though he hadn't heard. "It's the furs, isn't it, Matt? You want all the money for yourself. With me out of the way, you won't have any trouble."

"I got mixed up, I tell you," Hager insisted.

Cahill said nothing further. With a burst of energy as sudden as it was amazing, he gripped the sides of the sled and began pushing himself erect. His strangely clear eyes were fixed on Hager.

Mastering a brief surge of panic, Hager threw himself forward, forcing Cahill back into the sled. Cahill struggled a moment, but the reserve strength he had managed to summon quickly gave out. He fell back into the sled and lay limp and quiet, his eyes closed, breathing harshly and rapidly.

Hager watched for several minutes, the cold creeping slyly into him with the inactivity. Then, assured that Cahill would make no further trouble, he obtained the pack. He fed the dogs this time, tossing them pieces of dried meat. They would need renewed strength and energy to take him the remaining distance to Moose Gulch. Finally, gathering brushwood, Hager built a small fire and brewed tea. He ate a couple of thick sandwiches as he drank the tea, chewing with methodic slowness and glancing at Cahill.

THE other hadn't stirred since making his accusation. But when Hager finished eating, Cahill's eyes opened once more. He looked at Hager for a long, breathless moment. Only a vestige of the unnatural brightness that had been in his eyes remained now. With what must have required a tremendous effort, he spoke.

"You aren't going to get away with this, Matt. I...I'm going to get you. I'm going to make you pay."

A moment longer Cahill looked at Hager. And then the last remnant of brightness left his eyes. His lids fell slowly. He looked exhausted and seemed to be resting. But several minutes later, acting on a sudden realization, Hager felt for Cahill's pulse and found that the man was dead.

Triumph spread through Hager like a heady warmth. It was over. The money from the furs would be his alone. He would have the fur ranch, now. But there was no hurry about that. He would travel a little first and have some fun.

The best part of it was that he would never have to worry. Cahill's body was completely unmarked. It was very obvious that he had died of illness. There couldn't possibly be any suspicions.

Then Hager recalled the threat Cahill had made before dying. Cahill had promised revenge, but there was nothing he could do now. Hager shrugged the memory away. The dead were dead. They could do no harm.

Hager now lost no time in reaching Moose Gulch. He drove the dogs relentlessly, trotting behind the sled. Elation gave him a strength that took him easily over the miles.

A short time before he entered the settlement it began to snow again. Hager was pleased. The snow would cover up the tracks he had left in the event that Art Maddox did any snooping.

He went directly to the doctor's home, carrying the body of Cahill inside. He cleverly played the part of a man reluctant to believe that his partner had died.

"Isn't there something you can do, Doc?" he asked anxiously. "Maybe it isn't too late."

The other straightened from his examination of Cahill and shook his white thatch. His round, ruddy features were sympathetic. "I'm afraid it's all over. Ben Cahill's as dead as he'll ever be. Most likely he passed away some time before you were able to reach town. Nothing left to do now but turn him over to the undertaker. That's me, in case you don't know. In Moose Gulch it takes two, three jobs to keep a man fairly busy."

Hager sighed and looked properly grief-stricken. "Well, I'll leave you to take care of things, Doc. Do a good job—nothing but the best, you know. Ben was the finest partner a man could ever have."

Hager left and proceeded to visit acquaintances in the settlement, spreading the news of Cahill's death. He was showered with condolences, which he accepted with a suitable air of melancholy. Later, eating supper in the tiny dining room of Moose Gulch's small, frame hotel, he was joined at the table by Art Maddox.

The marshal was a tall, raw-boned man with a long nose and protruding eyes that looked deceptively mild. His presence filled Hager with a vague dread.

"Heard Ben Cahill took sick and died while you were bringing him into town," Maddox began. "Sure is too bad. How did it happen?"

Hager explained, adhering closely to essential facts, though he omitted certain others and stretched a point here and there. He finished, "I tried to get Ben into town as fast as I could, but it was snowing hard and I almost got lost a couple of times. Ben was sick bad, and with the cold and all, he died on the way."

"It kind of looks like you expected that to happen," Maddox said.

Hager grew tense. "What do you mean?"

"The way you took the furs along kind of makes it look like you expected Ben Cahill to die. Besides, you ought to have known that the furs would slow you down on the trip to town."

"I was afraid to leave the furs at the cabin," Hager defended. "Suppose somebody stole them while me and Ben were gone? A whole season's catch. I just couldn't take a chance."

Maddox nodded with evident reluctance. "That's true enough, I guess. I was just sort of wondering about it." He stood up. "Well, sorry to have bothered you."

HAGER made a generous gesture. "No bother at all." He watched as Maddox left the room, grinning inwardly. Maddox apparently suspected something in his snooping, suspicious way, but the only point of attack he'd been able to find was one for which Hager had a satisfactory explanation. Hager felt certain that he wouldn't be questioned again. And with the snow blotting out the erratic trail the sled had left, he was confident that he had nothing to fear from Maddox any longer.

The grin crept out around his square lips. He was safe. He had committed the perfect crime.

Hager checked in at the hotel, and after a pleasant evening spent at one of Moose Gulch's two saloons, he returned and went to bed. He had a restless night. The hotel was warm enough, and the covers on the bed thick, but a strange feeling of cold seemed to envelop him. And though he emptied the bottle of whisky he had brought with him, the cold persisted.

He slept fitfully. Once he dreamed that he was tied, naked, to the sled and being driven by Cahill through a terrific snow storm. The cold was so intense it seared him like fire. He awoke, shivering, a vivid recollection of Cahill's gaunt, accusing features in his mind. Again he seemed to hear Cahill's dying promise.

"You aren't going to get away with this, Matt. I'm going to get you. I'm going to make you pay."

And now, shuddering with that weird cold that seemed to enclose him like a huge, vengeful fist, Hager wondered.

The cold remained with him in the days that followed. It not only remained. It grew more unbearable.

Hager began to have a persecuted feeling. The cold stayed with him wherever he went. Even near hot stoves, or in heated rooms, he felt chilled. No one else seemed to notice it. The cold seemed intended for him alone. More and more, he wondered about Cahill's threat.

He was materialistic. He didn't believe in ghosts. But he knew that he was being haunted by an unnatural cold that nobody else seemed able to feel.

He cast about for a method of escaping the cold. The obvious solution was to leave Moose Gulch, as he had intended all along. In his mind the cold was somehow connected with the settlement, through Cahill, who was buried there. A trip to one of the warm, southern regions in the States, he decided, should bring relief.

He sold the furs and with the money took passage on a plane that operated between the settlement and a large town some distance away. Continuing to travel by plane, he presently arrived in Seattle.

Still the cold remained with him. The miles he had put between Moose Gulch and himself hadn't done any good.

Nothing seemed to help. Heavy clothes, nourishing foods, whisky, vigorous exercise—nothing brought him the warmth he was beginning to crave as an addict craves dope.

Desperately, he resumed his trip, traveling by air and then by train, and finally grasping at any means of transportation that happened to be most convenient. The cold traveled with him. It enveloped him like a shell. It was an invisible prison, shutting him away from the world of warmth.

The climate grew increasingly mild and balmy as he progressed southward. But the chill that always surrounded him grew worse.

More often, now, he thought of Cahill's grim promise. *"I'm going to get you. I'm going to make you pay."* It repeated itself over and over in his mind. It was emphasized by the invisible blanket of cold wrapped inescapably about him.

Once, in a hotel room where he had been drinking steadily, Hager's despair rose in him to the point of madness. He leaped from the bed, hurling an empty whisky bottle against the wall, screaming mingled curses and entreaties.

"Damn you, Cahill, leave me alone! Haven't you had enough? How much longer are you going to keep torturing me? Leave me alone, do you hear? Leave me alone!"

Cahill didn't seem to hear. Or if he did, he paid no attention. The cold stayed.

HAGER began to lose weight. His stocky figure became gaunt, his cheeks sunken. Dark hollows cupped his feverishly bright eyes. His hands trembled. He jerked nervously at sudden noises.

In Los Angeles he yielded to a wild impulse and visited a doctor. He explained his symptoms, omitting their true cause, and pleaded for help.

The doctor gave him a complete physical examination, though it was evident from the man's expression of perplexity that he had learned nothing. "I can't understand it," he told Hager. "There's nothing seriously wrong with you. All you need is plenty of food and rest. You're probably just imagining things."

Hager groaned, paid his bill, and fled.

Several days later found him in Mexico. It was warm—but he didn't feel it. He knew with a terrible certainty that he would never feel warmth again. And he was tired of futilely trying to escape something from which there was no escape. He rented a small house on the outskirts of a town far from the Border and hired an elderly Mexican named Pancho to attend to his needs.

Pancho was a good servant. But he was evidently greatly puzzled by Hager. According to the stories Pancho told his cronies in the town, his *gringo* master insisted that a hot fire be kept going constantly in the fireplace. And in this warm weather, too! As if that alone wasn't enough, the *gringo* also kept himself wrapped thickly in blankets. It was all very strange. The *gringo*, he said, was being tormented by a demon.

The people of the town, a simple folk to whom the supernatural was as real as the sun in the sky, were sympathetic. A priest at the church promptly volunteered his aid. He had, as Pancho subsequently explained to Hager when he appeared with the man, an enviable reputation for his skill in exorcizing devils and evil spirits.

Hager seized at the hope. He clutched at the priest eagerly.

"Try it! Pray for me! Do something—anything!"

The priest nodded gravely and began his task.

It worked.

Hager felt warm again.

A wild delight filled him. For the first time he became aware that the room was stifling, but the mere fact that he was able to feel it seemed the most wonderful thing in the world. He had a sense of freedom as complete as though he had been released into the sunlight after long confinement in a lightless dungeon.

He wrung the priest's hand, forced money on him, and then told Pancho he was throwing a *fiesta* for the entire town that evening. Pancho was to take care of the details immediately. No expense was to be spared.

For the rest of the day, Hager soaked himself in the sunlight, reveling in the delicious warmth. And when evening came he attended the *fiesta* in high spirits. He ate *tortillas*, drank wine, and danced with innumerable dark-eyed *senoritas*.

It was late when he returned to the house with Pancho. He found a robed figure waiting patiently at the door. It was the priest. Something about the man's solemn expression filled Hager with dread.

"What's the matter?" he demanded. "Has something happened?"

In his halting English, Pancho translated the gist of the priest's explanation. "The *padre* say he no can help you, *senor.* He say he have how you call vision. It tell him you must pay."

There was more. But Hager didn't need any more to know that he was being refused further help for the crime he had committed.

A short while after the priest left he felt the cold again.

Pancho built a fire in the fireplace, and Hager crouched before it, huddled in blankets and shivering. He was still there when

Pancho went to bed. And he was still there when Pancho awoke in the morning. But he was no longer shivering. He no longer felt the cold.

He was dead.

It had been a warm night. The fire had been, hot, the blankets numerous and thick. Yet Hager had *frozen* to death.

THE END

Out in the alien desert, down in the caves, the creatures of legend spawned. But evil has many faces, many arms. The most horrible is...

THE ARM OF ENMORD

By JACK SHARKEY

THE colony on Arcturus Beta had been well established for nearly a half-century before anyone paid any real attention to the legend. In any colonization of an alien planet, nervous tension ran high among the pioneers who had come there to live and build and flourish, and each of the Earth Colonies on the planets of Sol and the nearer stars had its complement of tales calculated to scare the pants off newcomers to the group. There were the so-called Fire Ferns of the Martian Desert, which early scouting parties swore they'd seen destroying the listlessly stolid scaly Martian fauna, or the Ocean Things of Venus, which defied all efforts to capture them, due to their uncanny (and fortuitous) power to become one with the water in which they slithered and coiled. Legends were easy to come by, when men's nerves neared the snapping point and alien winds threatened their flickering campfires. They were invented, spread by word-of-mouth communication, and soon became part of the "history" of a newly settled planet. No one really believed them, but no planet was without them, either. Colonists were much like children who fear the bogeyman, yet force themselves to listen to any and all information they can glean about their nebulous nemesis, delighting in their own shiverings. And so legends were born, thrived awhile, then died into a kind of nostalgic notoriety.

Until Arcturus Beta.

The original landing had been made by a party of men mostly Teutonic in origin (Space Psychology insisted that the lesser the differences in a crew's makeup—and that included nationality—the greater the chances for success of an expedition.), and so the "creatures" in their legends were vaguely Viennese.

Had they been American, there would have been Devil Men.

The French would have chosen *Hommes Diaboliques,* or the Spanish decided upon *Los Hombres del Diablo.*

And so it was by merest chance they came to be called the *Teufel Menschen...*

"...and that's why I insist there's more to this thing than mere legend," said Drake Talbot, smacking his fist into his palm.

Stacey laughed and shook her head at him, setting the golden curls flying at the back of her head. "Drake, darling, you're so intense!" she said, taking his hands and attempting to draw him down on the sofa beside her.

Drake pulled his hands away. "Even you think I'm a fool."

Stacey's smile faded. "I'm sorry. I didn't mean it to sound quite like that, Drake. It's just that—well—*everybody* knows about planets, and legends, and how they get started. And yet you're always so insistent about these Teufs!"

Drake's face, its frowning creases sharpened and highlighted by the glow from the fireplace, looked oddly sad and alone. "No one likes to admit there are things man doesn't understand, or cannot control, Stace. A*ll* these legends have some basis in fact."

Stacey sighed, and began to refill their glasses with the red-gold wine that came from the soil of their adopted planet. So well did the vineyards thrive in that soil that someone had even nicknamed the place Arcturus Bacchus. "We've been over that so many times, dearest. The Fire Ferns actually *did* look like they swallowed up those Martian animals, and their orange-and-yellow fronds *did* look like they were on fire—especially when a man had been out in the desert sun for a long time— But..."

"Let's not go over it again, Stace. The animals, it turned out, dug their burrows beneath these plants, and only seemed to be eaten by them when they were actually just wriggling down into the soil. I know all that. And I also know that one-third of all ships that try to cross the Venusian Ocean are never seen again."

"Drake, there are storms, tidal waves, maybe even whale-like creatures who dote on boats, in that ocean," Stacey snapped.

Drake shrugged. "I see there's no point in even discussing it with you." He sat beside her, moodily watched the reflected play of the flames in the depths of his wine, and then began to sip at it, staring into the fireplace.

"But that's my point!" said Stacey. "You *don't* 'discuss' it. You argue, you browbeat, you rant and rave..."

Drake put down his glass. "It's getting late," he said. "I'll walk you home."

"Afraid to let me out alone after dark?" she goaded, reaching for her cloak. "Afraid the Teufs will get me?"

Drake took her by the shoulders and stared into her face, his eyes filled with pain. "If I say 'Yes', you'll only laugh."

Stacey's heart melted when she saw the hurt in his eyes. "No, Drake, I won't laugh. I don't believe it, but—" she kissed him softly on the lips, "—I appreciate it."

He helped her on with her cloak, drew on his own, and they walked to her house in friendly, handholding silence. At her door, she turned to face him once more.

"Thank you," she said, smiling, and kissed him once more.

"Goodnight, Stace." Drake said, softly, and vanished into the cool, green-blue night, his footsteps fading quickly out of earshot.

Stacey closed the door, and turned up the kerosene lamp upon the table. The colony had electricity, but its use was still restricted to the industrial end, of their life on the planet. In time, the village would become a town, then someday a city. Right at the moment, it boasted of barely one hundred men and women, some married, all the rest engaged. In a colony, sent out from Earth to thrive, no bachelors or spinsters were allowed. Stacey felt quite fortunate in her betrothal to Drake. They had had no say in the matter, themselves. All she'd known when she took the flight to Arcturus' second planet was that the man was the correct age, mental level, race, personality and state of health to match her own similar qualifications for an ideal marriage. The whole thing had been done by a mechanical brain back in New Manhattan.

But something a brain could not compute had entered into the picture. Stacey had fallen in love with Drake at first sight.

She wouldn't have minded getting married right then and there. But the brain back on Earth had, wisely enough, decreed a three-month waiting period. It could afford no mismatches when the life of a colony depended upon it. They had to wait and see, and be sure. Had Stacey been even the least bit cool toward the idea, she'd have been flown back to Earth, and another girl sent in her place to be Drake's bride.

The thought of another sharing his love made her tremble. The waiting period still had three weeks to run, and then she'd be his forever. Stacey smiled, and slipped off her cloak, with a delicious shiver of anticipation.

"Hello, Stacey," said a voice.

She spun about, panicky, her heart fluttering wildly, her eyes seeking the source of the sound.

"Tymbel!" she said, suddenly angry.

Tymbel sat up lazily from where he'd been half-lying in her easy chair. "Greetings, dear cousin," he said, smoothly.

"If you don't leave here immediately, I'm going to sound the alarm!" she threatened, reaching for the door handle.

"Easy. Easy does it, Stacey," he cautioned her, grinning toothily. "This loyal citizen role suits you fine, but you're not turning me in, and you know it."

"And why not?" asked Stacey, her nostrils quivering.

"Because you're a woman, and you're dying to know where I've been. That's why."

Stacey drew herself up. "You think mere idle curiosity could make me forget my duty to the colony?"

"The alarm is in the center of the square, right outside your door," said Tymbel, gesturing dramatically. "Go ahead. Start ringing it."

Stacey shuddered with mixed anger and pride, then she sat down. "All right, Tymbel. Where were you? I was worried sick when you weren't here when I arrived."

"That's better. Much better," said Tymbel, leaning back once more in the confines of the chair.

Stacey fidgeted. If anyone should come... She knew the penalty for harboring a fugitive was banishment, and that meant leaving Drake, forever, separated by millions of miles, for the rest of her life. She fought the sickness taking hold of her.

"You have one minute to tell me and then, whether you've finished or not, I m sounding the alarm!" she warned him.

The lazy grin left his face as he realized that she meant it.

"All right then, I'll tell you," he said. "All my life, since I was just a kid, I dreamed of traveling to outer space. It was high adventure to me, then. To be a pioneer on alien soil, to fight off heaven knows what creatures that threatened the Earthmen, you know the story: The Flash Gordon type of existence. And so I signed for the Arcturus Colony, and came up here. And what was it like? The journey through space was boring. The ship flew entirely on instruments, had no portholes. I might as well have been inside a submarine for all the joy I got out of crossing the universe. And when I got here, it was just another job. The thrill of being on another planet wore off in a matter of days, and it was just like Earth all over again. Hard work, low pay, and not even another town to go to, to relieve the monotony. I got tired of it in a big hurry."

"Your letters had that whole story between the lines," said Stacey. "I could tell you hated it, as much as you tried to be cheerful about it."

"And when I knew you were coming..." said Tymbel, "...well that did it. Another member of the family to come and see me here was too much for me to take. By letter, I could at least live a false life of high adventure, and fool the people at home, partly, that I'd realized all my childhood dreams. But not once you came. You'd soon see that I was no one, just as I was back on Earth. Just another day laborer, building houses, factories, barns."

"I'm sorry, Tymbel," said Stacey. "I didn't realize..."

He waved her to silence, and shrugged. "Hell, Stacey, you couldn't know. No one's blaming you. But that did it. The day your name was on the incoming passenger list was the day I left my toolbox behind me and headed for the hills. I understand that Kathy—"

"She's remarried." Stacey nodded. "The village voted you out of your wife, and Henry McCallister's wife had just died, so—"

"Spare me the gruesome details," said Tymbel, lightly, though a note of bitterness crept into his voice. "I hope she's happy with him. I know she wasn't really happy with me. Hell!" he shrugged, trying for nonchalance he didn't feel. "That's all water under the bridge, now, anyhow."

"Tymbel," said Stacey, "what are you going to do?"

"I'm going to let them capture me. There's no chance of survival outside the colony. It's a miracle I lasted these last few months. I had to hover around the rim of this place, stealing fruit and vegetables, now and then a lost lamb. I made out okay. But now I'm ready to go back."

Something in his tone twitched at Stacey's mind. The minute's grace she'd given him had already passed, but she had to know what he was up to. "You've always been a schemer, Tymbel," she said. "So I know you wouldn't give in without a fight. You want to be sent back. Why?"

"Have you read the regulations on deportees?" asked Tymbel, with a slow smile.

"I—I believe so. I couldn't quote them, though."

"The part I like goes: '...shall be sent back to Earth, along with his monies, chattels, and the like...' That's where I make my fortune, Stacey."

"But you have nothing but your tools, and some clothes...?" said Stacey, her interest kindling rapidly.

"Oh?" said Tymbel, raising his eyebrows in mock surprise. *"Is that all I have?* Perhaps not so, cousin."

"Don't play games with me," Stacey said, with sudden irritation. "You've found something. What?"

"I don't suppose you were on this planet two minutes before someone was playing on your hackles with the legend of the Teufs, Stacey. Am I right?"

A cold something clutched at her spine. It seemed odd Drake discussing the legend not so long ago, and now Tymbel. A strange uneasiness began to ooze through her veins. "Yes. I've heard all about it, with all its ramifications. Why?"

"Stacey..." Tymbel leaned forward in the chair till his face was inches from hers his manner intense. "It's *not* a legend."

Her heart seemed to stop, then took up a faster throbbing. Two men, so completely dissimilar, to tell her the same thing on the very same night. It was rather unnerving.

She managed a laugh that rang falsely. "Drake was just telling me the same thing, tonight. I suppose you're going to tell me you've come upon their hideaway, and found your way through the labyrinth, to the treasure?"

"You don't believe the legend, do you!" he said, with a funny grin. "You think it's all a bunch of— Or maybe you don't *want* to believe it."

Stacey stood up. "Your time's up, Tymbel," she said, stiffly. "You'd better run. I'm going to give the alarm."

"Stacey, Stacey," Tymbel shook his head. "Is my 'crime' such a great one? It's not as though I'm a murderer, you know."

"Deserting a colony is one of the worst crimes in interstellar settlement," said Stacey, her voice shaking. "It can mean life or death to the other colonists. Fortunately," she said, with more scorn than she'd intended, "you were easily replaced."

"Then doesn't that," said Tymbel, easily, "somewhat lessen the heinousness of my deed?"

"Well—"

"Besides, I haven't told you why I've come here, tonight."

"Why *did* you?" asked Stacey, her curiosity getting the better of her.

"Because I need your help," Then, as she stiffened, he added hastily, "Oh, come now! Nothing like collusion with a criminal. I know you too well to even attempt that. No, I need your help in getting me my legal rights."

"In what way?" she asked.

"I need a witness that is above reproach, to see me get the treasure. I don't trust this village, and it doesn't trust me. I need someone who'll swear that *I*, and I alone, found the treasure."

"They'd never believe me," said Stacey. "They know you're my cousin. I haven't been here long enough to establish—"

"*You?*" said Tymbel, with genuine surprise. "Who's talking about *you?* I'm referring to that noble creature to whom you've become affianced."

"Drake?" said Stacey. "Why Drake?"

"Because he's on the Council. Because he was born and bred on this planet, and they all love and trust him. Because he's too much of a fool to lie and say that he discovered the treasure, and leave me out in the cold. That's why."

"You expect me to *use* him? For *you?*" The scorn in her voice would have singed a more sensitive man's ears.

"And for him," said Tymbel.

"For him? How so?" Stacey asked, in puzzlement.

"He's forever insisting that the legend is true. Wouldn't he love to have proof of this? Can you think of a lovelier wedding present for the groom?"

Stacey's hand, which had been reaching for the door handle once more, fell to her side. "As usual, Tymbel, you've succeeded," she said, softly. "How do you always manage to get your own way?"

Tymbel's forefinger tapped his temple, lightly. "Because I've got it up here, cousin," he grinned, content with his triumph.

"When?" asked Stacey, resigning herself to his plan.

"Tomorrow soon enough?"

Stacey nodded. "Tomorrow. And just how do I get Drake to go to the treasure? If he once sees you, he'll turn you in."

Tymbel pulled a ragged sheet of paper from within his sweat-soiled shirt. "I have a map that'll take you to the entrance of the labyrinth, cousin. Get him there, then leave the rest to me."

Stacey took the crudely drawn map from him. "And if he asks where I got this map?"

Tymbel eased himself out of the chair and strode toward the door. He opened it, and poised there, silhouetted against the cool green-blue of the night. "You're a woman. You'll think of something. Fibbing comes easy to the weaker sex."

Stacey opened her mouth to reply, but his grin stopped her.

"Goodnight, cousin," said Tymbel. He closed the door and was gone.

The crowd screamed and gabbled in a tongue that Stacey could not fully comprehend. They pushed her and shoved her aside, to get to the man, his eyes rolling in his head, who staggered and stumbled down the cobbled street of the village. He mumbled a tale that was incomprehensible to Stacey's ears, yet his meaning found its way into her mind. His wife and child were taken, gone.

His beautiful wife and baby son had been taken. Over and over in Stacey's mind rang the phrase *"Teufel Menschen"*. And the scouting party had gone out, and had found no trace of any such cave as the man had described, nor had they found his wife. The wife whom he claimed to have last seen being dragged down into the opening in the ground, screaming futilely at the Things that enfolded her with their glistening arm-structures as they hobbled and hopped away into the gloom. The scouting party had found his son, alive and well. But the man would not even look upon his son's face. He only buried his eyes in the crook of one arm, and pointed his other hand at the crib wherein the baby cooed and kicked its tiny pink legs, and sobbed out a single word, over and over: *"Enmord!"* Then Stacey saw the man wither, go into convulsions, and die, with his hair oddly gray for he had been young. And she saw his son growing up, the idol of the village maidens, and saw his son leading a laughing girl by the hand, under the bright light of Arcturus at noon, across the plains toward the nearby hills. And she saw him take the girl unerringly to the mouth of a cave, and heard the laughter die on the girl's lips as the son *changed*... And reached out for her as she fell into a strange swoon. Then the son's eyes looked up greenly from the limp form of the girl he held in his arm-structures, and looked right into Stacey's own eyes.

"Tomorrow soon enough?" asked the Thing, in Tymbel's voice.

Stacey screamed and screamed, and woke up. She lay safe in her own bed, in the village on Arcturus Beta. The sheets were drenched with cold perspiration.

Drake, she thought desperately. I've got to tell Drake! I must go at once.

"I quite agree, darling," said Drake, holding her hand to prevent its trembling again. "It was more than a mere dream."

"I don't know what to think—what to believe anymore," she said in a low, quavering voice. "It was so real. So horribly real."

"I can well imagine," said Drake. "Parts of your dream are historically verified, in the log of the original colony here. That man was Carl Von Huber, and the wife was Machtilde Koner. Their son Franz *did* disappear, later in life, with one of the girls from the village. It was assumed they'd died in the desert beyond the hills."

"It was so real," she reiterated. "What are we to do?"

"*We,* darling, are to do nothing," said Drake, kindly. She clutched at his hand.

"You're not going out there alone!"

"Stacey, darling, you should know better. According to the legend, these things, the Teufs, as we call them nowadays, have no strength over a man. Only over women and children. Carl insisted, before he went mad, that had he not been so far from Machtilde when the Teufs attacked, she'd have been perfectly safe. They could not even have shown themselves had he been by her side. So you needn't worry about me."

"But why must you go?" she begged, suddenly in tears, her eyes pleading.

"It's been my long-felt desire to prove the truth of the Teufs' existence. That's one reason. And the other—"

"Tymbel was right," said Stacey. "You *are* a kind of noble fool. You'd risk your life so he'd come into what was rightfully his by discovery."

"There *is* no risk, I tell you," said Drake, irritably.

"Then if you go, *I* go," she said, her chin jutting stubbornly.

"No. That's out, completely!" said Drake. "I'd never permit you to venture out there."

"But you're a man. I'll stay close to you. Then I'll be safe. You said so, yourself!"

"I won't risk it!" said Drake. "You're staying here."

"Very well, then," said Stacey. "I won't let you have the map, then."

"Stace!" said Drake, exasperated. "That's not fair of you. Don't you know I'm only thinking of your safety?"

"Don't you think I care about yours?" she shouted. "You fool, if anything happened to you out there, I'd—I'd kill myself!"

"Don't say that!" he snapped, taking her by the shoulders and gripping till he hurt her. "You don't know the terrible risk—"

"Please, Drake, please!" she cried.

He released her and turned his back. "If you insist upon this folly, there's only one thing I can do."

"You'll take me?" she asked, hopefully.

His head moved slowly from side to side. "I'll stay here, too. You mean too much to me Stace. I'd rather lose the way to the treasure than lose you."

Stacey looked at his back, the muscles of which had come all limp, in his disappointment. She couldn't bear the hurt she knew he was feeling. Numbly, she took out the map and placed it upon the table. "All right, then, Drake," she said, "I can't rob you of your dream. Take the map and go."

Drake turned, looked at her, then at the map. He took her face between his big strong hands, gently. "I'll come back," he promised.

"Be careful, darling," she said.

Drake kissed her, tenderly, then took the map and left the room. Stacey watched his form, handsome and broad shouldered, as he moved up the cobbled street toward the village limits. She shut the door and then leaned against it, sobbing.

And all at once she had a thought. There was no time to lose. She grabbed up her cloak from the chair where it had been dropped, and hurried out into the street, keeping that distant figure in view...

"Drake. Drake Talbot!" called a voice.

Drake looked about him, squinting in the bright light that cascaded from the greenish skies over the hills. Then he saw the man, waving. "Tymbel?" he called back.

"Over there," Tymbel answered. Then, as Drake's long strides brought him nearer, "I thought you weren't coming, after awhile... Where's Stacey?"

Drake frowned. "I wasn't fool enough to bring her out here. If the legend is true, you know the danger. I could kill you for even thinking of having her come near this place."

Tymbel shrugged. "She'd have us with her. The Teufs can't abide the near presence of a man, or have you forgotten?"

"I think you've forgotten what it is to *be* a man!" Drake spat contemptuously. "To risk her life so that you could get a little richer!"

A grin split Tymbel's face. He remained unsullied by the insult. "Not a *little* richer, Talbot old man. The rumors of the treasure were grossly underestimated. It's a fortune," he said, his eyes lighting up.

"So take it and be damned with it," Drake said.

Tymbel shrugged. "Come along, then. I'll need you as a witness. Or did Stacey explain everything to you?"

"Of course she did. We have no secrets from one another."

"That's what I figured she'd do. She's too simple to lie," said Tymbel, chuckling. "Just as well. I knew you'd come."

"All right, let's get it over with. Where is this cave you mentioned?"

"Follow me, if you will," said Tymbel, turning and striding away across the slope of the hill. They vanished behind a curve of rolling, warm ground.

An instant later, from the opposite direction, Stacey appeared, looking about her in bewilderment. In her hand she clutched a copy of the map, drawn up before her visit to Drake that morning. She hadn't originally intended to use it to follow him. She'd assumed she'd be able to talk him into letting her go along. The copy had been for the sole purpose of leaving behind, in the event that anything should happen to the two of them. Something to let the town know the danger that was actual, not legendary, and exactly where it lay on the planet. But now she'd followed to the end of the map, and there was nothing in sight. No cave, no Drake, no Tymbel.

Stacey, whose movements had been quick until that moment, slowed her pace all at once, and the beginnings of fear started in her mind. This locale, if the map were to be believed, was the territory of the Teufs. It looked very much as she'd seen it in her dream, when young Franz had taken the laughing girl out to her doom. In fact—

Stacey halted her stride with a shudder. She *recognized* the place. That copse of shrubbery over to the right, the tall, tree-like thing that flourished all over Arcturus Beta, very like an elm tree of Earth, but too geometrically symmetrical in its division of shady branches. It was right where it had been in her dream. It was older, by nearly half a century, than as she'd seen it, but there was no mistaking its location. And, if her dream had been accurate in that respect, then the entrance to the labyrinth should lie just beyond the curve of the hill.

Forcing herself to ignore the cold dread in her heart, she trod the same path that the merry maiden of generations past had taken, toward the entrance to what might well spell her own destruction. But Drake was there, somewhere, and she had to go to him.

And as she came over the rim of the hill, she saw him. The recognition was too brief in duration for her to shout. And then he'd vanished, with Tymbel going before him, into a black hole in the earth. "Drake!" she called, finally finding her voice.

But either the hills muffled the noise, or the distance was too great, for he did not reappear. She hesitated for only a moment, then hurried down the hillside toward the mouth of the cave.

It grew in size as she approached it, until she was at the very brink of the entrance, which she was uneasily surprised to find stood twice as tall as herself. Beyond the opening was only blackness and silence.

"Drake?" she called, into the darkness. "Drake, it's Stacey!"

The cave seemed to take the words from the air and bury them in its walls. There was no echo, not even that hollowness of sound that should have overcome her voice on entering the hollow in the earth.

And then she seemed to hear Drake's voice, in the midst of an incalculable distance, calling back, "Stacey, where are you?" But she couldn't be sure. They were the words she *wanted* to hear. And they'd been so very faint that they could very well have been supplied by her own mind. She called out again, but this time there was no trace of a response.

Stacey put one foot over the brink of the cave, and set it down, half-expecting hundreds of green Things to leap from the walls of the tunnel and carry her off. But there was no movement, no sound. She took another step, and was then standing within the cave itself. Nothing happened. She could detect only the sound of her own labored breathing.

It took great courage to take the next step, for still, etched in her mind, for the rest of her life, she saw the face of that terrified girl who had followed Franz to this very spot. But all at once, after that third step, it became easy. She hurried into the darkness, calling Drake's name.

And then she stopped. For, ahead of her, it was dark no longer. The walls of the cave glowed a pallid fluorescent blue, over a suddenly non-rocky floor. The floor of the lighted cave was made of sand, pale white sand, and felt soft and comfortable as she walked into the light.

She was at the start of the labyrinth. She could see the openings at odd intervals along the length of this strange tunnel, each opening onto a tunnel itself. Once she ventured into this place, she'd never find her way out unaided. Even if there were no Teufs to carry her off, she might well starve if she became lost in the maze. No, she'd better go back and wait, and hope, out on the hillside.

Stacey turned around.

Behind her, the blue-lit tunnel continued backward, with no trace of the darkened section through which she'd entered. She looked around her, frantically, left and right and above and below, seeking the entrance. It was not to be found.

"It's *got* to be this way!" she said aloud, running back a few paces toward where it should be. It was not. And when she turned and looked back again, the section of tunnel that she'd just quit didn't look the same, somehow. As though she'd blundered into one of the cross tunnels by mistake.

Her terror returned with full force, gripping her heart in a cold vise. "*Drake!*" she screamed.

There was no answer, no echo.

Stacey stumbled forward, trembling. Her hand fell upon the wall to her right, and she drew it away, with a sense of shock. The walls were warm, and soft, like—like bare flesh.

Stacey's mind flooded with icy panic. Yelling her lover's name, over and over, she began to run…

It seemed hours later that she first saw the golden light. She'd lost her cloak somewhere in the endless twistings behind her, and one of her shoes had fallen, and she'd kicked off the other one. But the change in lighting filled her with new hope.

"It must be the outside!" she muttered, half doubled over, trying to catch her breath. "It has to be the way out!"

She breathed deeply, to restore a little of her failing strength, and hurried toward the light across the sandy floor.

It was not the outside.

And she was no longer alone.

"Tymbel!" she cried, half-delirious with relief at seeing another human being.

He jumped to his feet from where he'd been crouching, a guilty look upon his face. "Stacey, how did you get here?" he asked, nervously.

Then she saw where he'd been crouching, and moved forward into the high-vaulted chamber that glowed with the golden light. The treasure of the Teufs lay before her in all its alien splendor. Her heart seemed to catch in her throat at the beauty of it all. Necklaces, rings, coronets, strange-looking weapons, loose gems, things that seemed to be utensils for eating yet were odd in concept and design, everything glittering and gleaming and glowing in a riotous jumble of haphazard design, precious stones and precious metals piled here and there as though the bearers had just dumped them and let them lie where they fell.

"Then it's true!" she exclaimed. "It's all true!"

Then the thought that should have been foremost in her mind came to her, a little late, "Drake," she said to Tymbel. "Where's Drake?"

Tymbel looked abashed, and his eyes could not meet hers. "I— I don't know where he is," he answered.

"Don't *know?*" she said, moving toward him. "I saw you come into this cave together. He was with you. What's happened to him?"

Tymbel suddenly fell to his knees before her and began to whimper. "Don't. Don't be mad, Stacey. I didn't mean it. It was an accident."

Her voice surprised her, coming out so much steadier than she felt. "You didn't mean what, Tymbel? What have you done?"

Tymbel was sobbing, in misery, the remorse choking him while he spoke. "Stacey, I've always been afraid, always been a coward. You know that. I needed this money, this gold, this treasure. He—he wasn't going to let me take it."

"Wasn't going to? But Drake didn't care about—" The import of his words was sinking into her mind. "What did you do?"

"He heard you," said Tymbel, desperately. "He heard you calling to him. I didn't. I thought he was imagining things, until I saw you here, now. He wanted to go back. He blamed me for your coming here. He said I'd never have the treasure. He'd have me sent back to Earth a pauper. I couldn't stand it, Stacey. I—"

"What did you do?" she asked, with deadly calm.

"I hit him. He turned his back and I hit him. He fell and struck his head against the wall, and didn't move anymore. I got scared, then, and tried to wake him up. He—he didn't wake up."

"He's dead," said Stacey, in an empty voice. "You killed him."

"I didn't mean it. I didn't mean it." Tymbel sobbed, his face bent to the sand. "I'm sorry, Stacey…"

Something stirred in Stacey's blood as she looked upon the craven creature that groveled on the sand before her. A cold, mortal hatred overcame her. Without even being aware of moving, she found her right hand lifting, by its thick handle, one of the alien weapons. It was a short, deadly war club, similar in use to a mace. Jewels glinted on the handle as she raised it.

Tymbel looked up, alerted by a sixth sense, and saw her, and the cold determination of her face, and screamed, "Don't kill me, Stacey. You need me! You can't get out of here without me! They'll get you!"

Stacey hardly heard him. There was a loud roaring in her ears, and a red haze before her eyes, and she felt a quiver go through her upraised arm as it fell. As in a vast distance, she heard a thud, and then another and another.

When the haze cleared, she was standing over what was left of Tymbel. His head was a bloody sponge. The weapon lay on the sand at her feet, dripping redly onto the absorbent white sand.

Then Stacey looked up and saw Enmord.

Either she'd not noticed before, when she entered the chamber, or it had not been there to notice. There was a niche, an alcove, in the far wall. Set into the aperture was a stone slab, a stained stone slab that was a sacrificial altar, and above it squatted the placidly evil stone face of Enmord. His thick, grotesque body was just human enough in shape to make the differences all the more horrible. Of his four arms, three met in front of the bloated torso in a strange sort of clasp of the long fingers. The fourth arm was pivoted, and raised above the center of the altar, a many-bladed dagger in its rocky grasp.

And then she saw the Things, sitting on their haunches, their eyes sparking greenly in their greenish faces. There were many of them, and they all squatted and looked at her, hungrily. Then one of them hopped in her direction, like a misshapen frog.

Stacey backed away, unable even to cry out, so great was her terror. Another hopped, and then another. One of them opened its mouth, and emitted a sound like a gurgling yawn.

Immediately, they all bounded toward her, leaping and plopping across the soft white sand. Stacey's mind sent out an alarm through her nervous system, and she turned about and fled, with the Things hopping resolutely after her.

There was nowhere to flee to, but she had to run away. They had only to wait until she dropped from exhaustion and then take her, without a struggle. Stacey pushed the thought from her mind, and ran, wildly, down the tunnel. Abruptly, ahead of her, she saw more of the hopping green Things come into the tunnel. She gave a weak cry, and veered into the tunnel on her right, hurling herself beyond her own endurance away from her hideous pursuers. And yet again they were before her, and not behind.

And the realization came to her. When she'd come into the labyrinth, and had turned about, the tunnel was before her, always. Might the way out not lie forward, but backward?

Gripping herself with the force of her will, she closed her eyes and made herself take a backward step. Then another.

And then she backed into something that gave, and took hold of her. Stacey screamed and spun about, her fists up-raised to beat at her assailant. And then she saw that she was once more outside the mouth of the cave, and that the person who had taken her into his arms was none other than Drake.

"Darling!" she cried out, piteously, and sagged into his embrace. "I found the way out. And you're alive! You're all right!"

The mouth of the tunnel was suddenly crammed with the green Things, staring at her, but not moving beyond the brim of the blackness. She shuddered and clung to Drake, even more tightly.

"The Teufs!" she said. "It's all true. The Teufs, the treasure, and Enmord, the name from my dream. I saw him, Drake, the altar...and his arm!"

And still Drake had not spoken a word to her.

And then she realized that Drake didn't *feel* right...

She turned back her head and looked into his eyes, and saw the green glow therein.

"Darling," said Drake, "*I* am the Arm of Enmord."

THE END

FOUR MEN AND A SUITCASE

By RALPH ROBIN

*Which would you think is more important: nuclear fission or the price of a
fifth of whisky? Well, as the man said when he met his 450-pound cousin for
the first time: all of that is relative! Take Frank, for example. He lived—if
lived is the right word—on Skid Row. To Frank, the shape of Heaven
resembled something turned out by Libby-Owens, provided it was filled with the
right stuff. Yet he traded an entire quart bottle of the best in spirits for an egg-
shaped whatsis that drank sour milk and formed pictures of squares and
circles. Most of his friends thought Frank was off his rocker for wasting good
liquor—and eventually he proved they were right!*

BILL was standing on River Street wishing he had twenty-five
cents for a drink. He had seventeen cents. It would have been
easy enough to bum ten cents if he could have got up the nerve to
stop someone, but without a drink first he never had the nerve.

Three other men who looked alike and looked like Bill—as four
Orientals might look alike to a tourist—were in a huddle a few
yards away.

One of them turned from the others and walked over to Bill.

"Listen. We're going to split a pint. Want in? How much you
got?"

"Twelve cents," Bill said.

The man shook his head and started to walk away.

"Wait. I've got seventeen cents. It's all I got. Let me in for
that much."

"I'll ask them."

Trembling, Bill watched the men: he could not hear them.
There was a nodding of heads, and they waved him over.

"This is Frank. That's Smitty. I'm Lester."

"My name's Bill."

"We're going to drink it in Frank's room," said Lester, the man
who had approached Bill. "He has a room."

"Yes, sir, I have a room," Frank said.

Illustration by Robert Kay

Lester counted the quarters, dimes, nickels, and pennies. He held the money in his cupped hands and they marched him to the nearest liquor store, where he bought a pint of blend.

The four men went to Frank's room, which was big enough for them to sit on the edge of the bed if they didn't stretch their legs. There was nothing to be seen in the room except the bed, a broken rocking chair, and a half-filled bottle of milk on the windowsill. The milk looked soured.

Lester opened the whiskey. He measured with his fingers; placed his thumb firmly near the neck of the bottle.

"That about right for Bill? Might as well let him have his first, then share and share alike."

"Let's see," said the host, squinting. Not much light came through the dirty window. "That's about right. Mind you don't go below it, Bill."

"Check," said Smitty.

Bill put his thumb beside Lester's and they raised the bottle to Bill's mouth. He drank and let go the bottle, and it snapped back. Lester drank and handed it to Frank.

Bill felt a little more like a man. He stretched his arms in the air; he kicked forward and backward.

His heel rapped something hard. "Watch it," Frank said.

"Watch what?"

"Just watch what you're kicking."

"All right. I didn't mean any harm."

"Frank's pretty careful with that suitcase," Lester said.

"He don't want nothing to happen to that suitcase," Smitty said.

"That's enough about that suitcase," Frank said.

Bill's eyes followed the bottle as it went around. He wished he had another seventeen cents.

"It's a mighty important suitcase," Frank said.

"Frank's going to make a lot of money out of that suitcase some day. Soon's he figures out how to handle the deal."

"Shut up, Smitty. You fellows promised to keep your mouths shut. After all we don't know this guy from a hole in the ground."

"Who's doing all the talking?" Lester said.

"I won't bother your suitcase," Bill said. "I won't bother you fellows at all. I've had the drink I paid for and I'll beat it." His feelings were hurt, and anyway he wanted to get out on the sidewalk and start mooching before the drink wore off.

"Aw, don't be like that," the host said. "Here, have another pull—I'll pay for it, fellows."

But he didn't bring out any money, and Lester and Smitty looked unhappy while Bill took a timid swallow from the bottle.

"I think Bill's okay," Frank said. "Maybe he'll have some ideas how to handle the deal. You promise to keep your mouth shut, Bill, and I'll show you what I got in that suitcase."

Bill wasn't interested, but he was hoping the bottle would come back to him once more before it was empty. "I'll keep my mouth shut," he said.

"Make him swear," Lester said importantly.

"Swear you won't tell anybody," Frank said.

Bill held up his right hand. "I swear I won't tell anybody. So help me God."

Frank nodded. "You'll have to get off the bed," he said.

The three guests crowded at the door, while Frank dragged out the suitcase. It was made of fiber and was very large. It was almost a small trunk.

Frank pulled up the frayed top, lifted something carefully in his arms, and put it on the bed. Smitty shoved the suitcase back under the bed.

At least four feet long, the object on the old army blanket seemed a giant egg. It was shaped like an egg and in the dim light it looked the color of a brown hen's egg. But it didn't have the rigid shell. It lay quivering where Frank had placed it—quivering softly, like an egg hard-boiled and peeled.

"What is it, Frank?" Bill asked. Not that he cared.

"Damned if I know, but wait till you see what it does. It's going to be worth a lot of money to me, when I figure out how to handle the deal."

"Frank gave a fellow a whole unopened quart for it," Smitty said.

"It was worth it," Frank said seriously.

"What's it do?" Bill asked. He casually held out his hand and Frank passed the bottle to him. He drank, never taking attentive eyes from Frank's face. He quickly handed the bottle to Smitty.

"Yell at it," Frank said.

"Boo."

"Naw. Yell at it good like you were going to hurt it. And get close up."

"Hey, this isn't a trick, is it? It won't do something to me?"

All his life people had played tricks on Bill.

Lester snickered.

"What've you got in your blood?" Frank demanded. "You always been that yellow?"

Shamed, Bill bent his head over the bed and yelled, as he would have liked to yell at Frank: "I'll tear you apart with my bare hands."

But he couldn't help jerking his head back.

Light traced a circle in the center of the egg-like thing; the circle filled with light, was a glowing disk. Black dots and lines shot across the disk.

"Is it some kind of television set?"

"That's what I thought," Smitty said.

Indeed, something like a television image was forming.

The image sharpened. It was at first a square, as if neatly drawn, cut cater-corner by a straight line into two triangles. One triangle abruptly vanished. The remaining triangle drifted to the center of the disk. A square appeared on each side of the triangle, so that each side was one side of a square. New lines crisscrossed each square in to little squares.

On two sides of the triangle the little squares drifted away, mixed together, and formed a large square. It was the same size as the other large square.

"That reminds me of something in school...a long time ago," Bill said. He remembered but did not speak of a tall Miss Bruce in a yellow dress proving on the blackboard that the square of the hypotenuse is equal to the sum of the squares of the other sides.

"It likes that one," Lester said. "It often starts with that one."

"You talk like it's alive."

Lester and Smitty looked at Frank.

"It is alive," Frank said. "I'll show you something."

He picked up the bottle of milk from the windowsill. A sour smell filled the room as he pulled the cap out.

"He gets it from the chefs in restaurants," Smitty explained. "Spoiled milk. He tells them he drinks it hisself."

Frank swirled the milk, loosening the chunks of curd. He bent over the bed.

He squeezed the narrower end of the egg. A slit opened in the soft, tan surface. Frank poured in some sour milk and let the slit close. Bill could barely see the place, even knowing where it was.

"It eats!"

"When I feed it," Frank said.

Bill looked at the lighted circle. "The picture's fading."

"It always does when you treat it nice."

"Yell at it, Frank," Smitty said.

"You damn rotten egg. I'm going to kick the living hell out of you," Frank shouted.

Now there was a new picture. It was a cross, formed of two straight lines that cut the bright disk like a pie into quarters. And there was a different figure in each quarter. A short straight line. A circle. A thing like a letter O. A figure like the nose of a bullet. Bill did not remember and the others had never seen Cartesian curves.

"That won't do you any good," Smitty screamed. "He's going to kick the living hell out of you."

The picture faded. The bright area dimmed; diffused into the mottled tan skin.

"It's something, all right," Bill said. "You ought to get a lot of money for something like that." *I wish they didn't have to treat it that way, he thought. I don't like hearing them yell at it. I wish I hadn't yelled at it.*

"I am going to get a lot of money for it. Soon as I figure out how to handle the deal. Got any ideas, Bill?"

Frank had the whiskey bottle again, and it was almost empty. Bill looked at it sort of absentmindedly." Here...finish it," Frank said grandly.

Bill took the bottle quickly, afraid the others would object. He gulped what was left in the bottle, wiped his mouth, and looked thoughtful. "A circus might give a lot of money for it."

"There won't be no circus here for three months," Smitty said.

"Those circus guys aren't honest," Lester said. "I worked for a circus one time and I know. They'd gyp you, Frank."

"Circus is one thing I'm considering," Frank said. "Got any other ideas, Bill?"

"How about some rich man? Some big banker might find a thing like that mighty handy for tickling his friends at his big parties."

"He'll tickle his friends hisself," Smitty said.

Lester roared.

"This is serious," Frank said. "That's a good suggestion, Bill. Have another drink."

"The bottle's empty," Lester said. "Mr. Seventeen Cents polished it off."

"I vote we get another pint and figure out how to handle this deal. I won't forget you fellows, you help me."

"You've been singing that song for a long time, Frankie," Lester said. "I don't think you're ever going to figure out how to handle the deal. I got a proposition. I know where I can lay my hands on some capital. Why don't you sell it to me? I'll give you two full Quarts—" Smitty's eyes were wide"— and that'll make you one hundred per cent profit on your investment and no more worries about how to handle the deal."

"It's not for sale. I've told you that before, goddamn it."

"Okay, okay. No harm in asking."

"How about that pint?" Smitty said.

"Are we all in?" Lester jerked his head toward Bill.

"I guess I'll blow," Bill said. "I don't have any more money."

"No, stick around, Bill," said the host. "You've got some pretty good ideas. Course we can't stake you any more. Say! Those shoes look almost new. Where'd you get them?"

"Fellow left them in an open car." Bill looked around nervously.

"We know a guy loan you fifty cents on shoes like that," Frank said.

"But I need them—"

"What've you got in your blood?"

Frank and Smitty pulled out the coins they had been saving for a meal. Lester was sent with the money and the shoes, for they had drunk enough to trust him. And he was back before anybody got anxious, with another pint.

The bottle went around.

For once the drinks didn't make Bill feel happier. He leaned against the dirty wall and wiggled his toes in and out of his torn socks. He wished he had his strong shoes back. He wished he had a pint all his own. He wished he was by himself.

He looked at the egg-shaped freak shivering gently on the army blanket. *Poor old egg,* he thought. *Poor old egg.* He didn't know whether he meant himself or the freak on the bed. Sadness was prickling in his eyes and nose. He did not want to burst into tears.

"How about it, Bill? How about it, Bill, boy? Any more ideas how to handle the deal?"

"Sell it—sell it—to the people who make movies in Hollywood—the big directors," Bill stammered. Then he blurted:" But you oughtn't to treat it the way you do. You oughtn't to yell at it and hurt its feelings. If that's what you've got to do to make it do things, you ought to just give it to somebody who will give it a good home. Somebody kind."

"Tie that. He's sorry for it," Lester said.

"He thinks we're brutes," Smitty said in falsetto.

Frank said, "It's all business with me. Just a matter of figuring out how to handle the deal. But if I have to kick the living hell out of it to make me some money, don't think you or anyone else is going to stop me."

"I didn't—"

"We thought you were a good guy and here you are drinking our whiskey—"

"You took my shoes."

"— and telling me how to treat my own property. This is a free country and a land of opportunity and you're not going to tell me what to do."

"That's giving it to him," Smitty said. "That's laying it on the line."

"I'll show him what I can do with my property." Frank put his mouth close to his property and screamed, "I'll cut you in pieces, goddamn you, and flush you down the can."

Its middle glowed again; then darkened; then began to glimmer with stars. Then the moons appeared. There were four moons in different phases, from a thin crescent to a full face.

"It's beautiful," Bill murmured, "but you shouldn't make it do it that way. I think it's something from—far away. I think it's trying to tell us. You should treat it right. And you should take it to—" He searched his mind for someone in authority. "You should take it to the President."

They laughed; they hooted; they thumped each other. They jumped up and down. They slapped Bill's shoulders in mock admiration.

"The President. Take it to the President. Yes, sir, Napoleon, your majesty, we'll hop the next freight going straight to Washington."

They dug their hands in their clothes, imitating Napoleon.

"Or the cops," Bill said tensely. "They'd know where to take it."

There was silence.

"The cops," Smitty said. He spat on the floor.

"Copper-hearted," Frank said. "A cop-crier."

He bent over the bed. "Show us something different," he screamed. He pulled back his hand and slapped the soft form. The marks of his fingers were dark on its side.

Lester looked worried. "Be careful, Frank. You'll ruin it."

"You keep out of this too!"

The stars and the moons vanished. A single gray figure took their place as the background brightened.

"That stinks," Frank said.

"It looks like a toadstool," Smitty said.

Bill said slowly, "I've seen a picture like that."

"That makes it stink worse." Frank slapped his property again, on the other side. "Show us something better."

"Why—" Bill started. It was the last word he said.

The city crumpled, and the screaming began.

THE END

A BIT OF THE DARK WORLD

By FRITZ LEIBER

"I'm betting it will give the readers a spine-tingling scare," Fritz Leiber said to us when he delivered this eerie story of a cosmic horror. "I set myself a challenge," he said. "Is it still possible today to write convincingly the tale of a terror with which science cannot cope?" The decision is yours.

"There was a crack in his head and a little bit of the Dark World came through, and pressed him to death,"

—*Rudyard Kipling in "The Phantom Rickshaw"*

THE antique-seeming dip-nosed black Volks touring car with its driver and two other passengers besides myself was buzzing up a saddle ridge of the Santa Monica Mountains, swinging close past the squat brush-choked peaks with their strange up-jutting worn rocky pinnacles that looked like primeval monoliths or robed and hooded stone monsters.

We were moving with top down and slowly enough to glimpse sharply the occasional little pale lizard skitter or grasshopper whirl up out of our way over the gray crushed stone.

It was a brilliantly clear day with compact clouds that emphasized the dizzying inverted depth of the blue sky. Between clouds, the sun was dazzlingly bright. More than once, as we headed straight toward the low-trending distant incandescent orb along a switchback stretch, I was stung by its beams and suffered the penalty of black patches swimming in my vision for a minute.

We had met only two cars and glimpsed only half a dozen houses and cabins since leaving the Pacific Coast Highway—a remarkable loneliness considering that Los Angeles was a scant hour's drive behind us. It was a loneliness that had drawn Viki and myself apart with its silent intimations of mysteries and revelations, but not yet driven us together again (though there was a hint that it would) by reason of its menace.

Illustration by Dan Adkins

Franz Kinzman, sitting in front to the left, and his neighbor who had volunteered to do this stretch of the driving (a Mr. Morton or Morgan or Mortenson, I wasn't sure) seemed less affected by the landscape, as one would expect seeing they were both rather more familiar with it than Viki or I. Though it was hard to gauge reactions merely from the attitude of the back of Franz's close-cropped gray head or Mr. M.'s faded brown duck hat pulled low to shade his eyes.

We had just passed that point of the Little Sycamore Canyon road where all the Santa Barbara Islands are visible like an argosy of blue-gray faintly granular clouds floating on the surface of the pale blue Pacific, when I suddenly remarked, for no profound major reason that I was aware of at the time, "I don't suppose it's any longer possible today to write a truly gripping story of supernatural horror—or for that matter to undergo a deeply disturbing experience of supernatural terror."

OH, there were enough minor reasons for the topic of my remark. Viki and I had worked in a couple of cheap monster movies. Franz Kinzman was a distinguished science-fantasy writer as well as a research psychologist, and the three of us had often gabbed about the weird in life and art. Also, there had been the faintest hint of mystery in Franz's invitation to Viki and myself to spend with him the weekend of his return to Rim House after a month in LA. Finally, the abrupt transition from a teeming city to a forbidding expanse of nature always has an eerie sting—as Franz immediately brought up without turning his head.

"I'll tell you the first condition for such an experience or artistic inspiration," he said as the Volks entered a cool band of shadow. "You've got to get away from the Hive."

"The Hive?" Viki questioned, understanding very well what he meant, I was sure, but wanting to hear him talk and have him turn his head.

Franz obliged. He has a singularly handsome, thoughtful, noble face, hardly of our times, though looking all of his fifty years and with eyes dark-circled ever since the death of his wife and two sons in a jet crash a year ago.

"I mean the City," he said as we buzzed into the sun again. "The human stamping ground, where we've policemen to guard us and psychiatrists to monitor our minds and neighbors to jabber at us and where our ears are so full of the clack of the mass media that it's practically impossible to think or sense or feel deeply anything that's beyond humanity. Today the City, in its figurative sense, covers the whole world and the seas and the airways too and by anticipation the spaceways. I think what you mean, Glenn, is that it's hard to get out of the City even in the wilderness."

Mr. M honked twice at a blind hairpin turn and put in the next remark. "I don't know about that," he said, hunching determinedly over the wheel, "but I should think you could find all the horror and terror you wanted, Mr. Seabury, without going away from home, though it'd make pretty grim films. I mean the Nazi death camps, brainwashing, sex murders, race riots, stuff like that, not to mention the atom bomb."

"Right," I countered, "but I'm talking about supernatural horror, which is almost the antithesis of even the worst human violence and cruelty. Hauntings, the suspension of scientific law, the intrusion of the un utterly alien, the sense of something listening at the rim of the cosmos or scratching faintly at the other side of the sky."

As I said that, Franz looked around at me sharply with what seemed an expression of sudden excitement and apprehension, but at that moment the sun blinded me again and Viki said, "Doesn't science fiction give you that, Glenn? I mean horrors from other planets, the extraterrestrial monster?"

"No," I told her, blinking at a fuzzy black globe that crawled across the mountains, "because the monster from Mars or wherever has (at least as visualized by the author) so many extra feet, so many tentacles, so many purple eyes—as real as the cop on the beat. Or if he's a gas, he's a describable gas. The exact sort of goon men will be meeting when the spaceships start traveling the starways. I'm thinking of something…well ghostly, utterly weird."

"And it's that thing, Glenn, that ghostly, utterly weird thing— that you believe can't be written about effectively any more, or experienced?" Franz asked me with an odd note of suppressed eagerness, eyeing me keenly although the Volks was traveling a jouncy section. "Why?"

YOU started to sketch the reasons yourself a moment ago," I said. My newest black globe was slipping sideways now, pulsing, starting to fade. "We've become too smart and shrewd and sophisticated to be scared by fantasies. Most especially we've got an army of experts to explain away the supernatural sort of thing the instant it starts to happen. The physicist boys have put matter and energy through the finest sieves—there's no room left in it for mysterious rays and influences, except for the ones they've described and catalogued. The astronomers are keeping tabs on the rim of the cosmos with their giant telescopes. The Earth's been pretty thoroughly explored, enough to show there aren't any lost worlds in darkest Africa or Mountains of Madness near the South Pole."

"What about religion?" Viki suggested.

"Most religions," I replied, "steer away from the supernatural today—at least the religions that would attract an intellectual person. They concentrate on brotherhood, social service, moral leadership—or dictatorship—and fine-drawn reconciliations of theology to the facts of science. They're not really interested in miracles or devils."

"Well, the occult then," Viki persisted. "Psionics."

"Nothing much there either," I asserted. "If you *do* decide to go in for telepathy, ESP hauntings—the supernormal sort of thing—you find that territory has all been staked out by Doctor Rhine, riffling his eternal Zener cards, and a bunch of other parapsychologists who tell you they've got the whole benign spirit world firmly in hand and who are as busy classifying and file-carding as the physicists.

"But worst of all," I went on as Mr. M. slowed the Volks for a potholed uphill stretch, "we've got seventy-seven breeds of certified psychiatrists and psychologists (excuse me, Franz!) all set to explain the least eerie feeling or sense of wonder we get in terms of the workings of our unconscious minds, our everyday human relationships, and our past emotional experiences."

Vicki chuckled throatily and put in, "Supernatural dread almost always turns out to be nothing but childhood misconceptions and fears about sex. Mom's the witch with her breasts of mystery and her underground baby-factory, while the dark hot bristly demon dissolves to Dear Old Dad." At that moment the Volks, avoiding another dark spill of gravel, again aimed straight at the sun. I dodged it in part but Viki got it full in the eyes, as I could tell from the odd way she was blinking sideways at the turreted hills a moment later.

"EXACTLY," I told her. "The point is, Franz, that these experts are experts, all joking aside, · and they've divvied up the outer and inner world between them, and if we just start to notice something strange we turn to them at once (either actually or in our imaginations) and they have rational down-to-earth explanations all ready. And because each of the experts knows a lot more about his special field than we do, we have to accept their explanations—or else go off our own merry way, knowing in our heart of hearts that we're behaving like stubborn romantic adolescents or out-and-out crackpots."

"The result is," I finished, as the Volks got past the potholes, "that there's no room left in the world for the weird—though plenty for crude, contemptuous. Wisecracking, fun-poking imitations of it, as shown by the floods of corny monster films and the stacks of monster and madness magazines with their frac-tionally-educated hip cackling and beatnik jeers."

"Laughing in the dark," Franz said lightly, looking past us back the road, where the thin dust the Volks raised was falling over the cliff toward the thorny dark ravines far below.

"Meaning?" Viki asked. "People still are afraid," he stated simply, "and of the same things. They've just got more defenses against their fears. They've learned to talk louder and faster and smarter and funnier—and with more parroted expert-given authority—to shut them out. Why, I could tell you—" He checked himself. He really did seem intensely excited beneath the calm philosopher's mask. "I can make it clear," he said, "by an analogy."

"Do," Viki urged.

Half turned in his seat, Franz looked straight back at the two of us. A quarter of a mile ahead or so the road, climbing a little again, plunged into a stretch of heavy cloud-shadow. I noted this fact with relief—as I now had no less than three dark fuzzy globes crawling along the horizon and I yearned to be out of the sun. From the way Viki was squinting I could tell she was in the same fix. Mr. M, with his pulled-down hat and Franz, faced around, seemed less affected.

Franz said, "Imagine that mankind is just one man—and his family—living in a house in a clearing in the midst of a dark dangerous forest, largely unknown, largely unexplored. While he works and while he rests, while he makes love to his wife or plays with his children, he's always keeping an eye on that forest.

"After a while he becomes prosperous enough to hire guards to watch the forest for him, men trained in scouting and woodcraft— your experts, Glenn. The man comes to depend on them for his safety, he defers to their judgment; he is perfectly willing to admit that each of them knows a little more about one small nearby sector of the forest than he does.

"But what if those guards should all come to him one day and say, 'Look, Master, there really is no forest out there at all, only some farmlands we're cultivating that stretch to the ends of the universe. In fact, there never was a forest out there at all, Master— you imagined all those black trees and choked aisles because you were scared of the witch doctor!'

"Would the man believe them? Would he have the faintest justification for believing them? Or would he simply decide that his hired guards, vain of their little skills and scoutings, had developed delusions of omniscience?"

THE cloud-shadow was very close now, just at the top of the slight climb we'd almost finished. Franz Kinzman leaned closer to us against the back of the front seat and there was a hush in his voice as he said, "The dark dangerous forest is still there, my friends. Beyond the space of the astronauts and the astronomers, beyond the dark tangled regions of Freudian and Jungian psychiatry, beyond the dubious psi-realms of Dr. Rhine, beyond the areas policed by the commissars and priests and motivations-research man, far, far beyond the mad beat half-hysterical laughter…the utterly unknown still is and the eerie and ghostly lurk, as much wrapped in mystery as ever."

With an exhilarating chilling and glooming, the Volks rolled into the sharply edged cloud shadow. Switching around in his seat Franz began eagerly, intently, rapidly to search the landscape ahead, which seemed suddenly to expand, gain depth, and spring into sharper existence with the screening off of the blinding sun.

Almost at once his gaze fixed on a smoothly ridged gray stone pinnacle that had just come into view on the opposite rim of the canyon valley beside us. He slapped Mr. M. on the shoulder and pointed with his other hand at a small parking area, surfaced like the road, on the hillside bulge we were crossing.

Then, as Mr. M, swung the car to a grating stop in the indicated area just on the brink of the drop, Franz rose in his seat and, looking over the windshield, pointed commandingly at the gray pinnacle while lifting his other hand a little, fingers tautly spread, in a gesture enjoining silence.

I looked at the pinnacle. At first I saw nothing but the half dozen rounded merging turrets of gray rock springing out of the brush-covered hilltop. Then it seemed to me that the last of my annoying after-images of the sun—dark, pulsing, fringe-edged, had found lodgment there.

I blinked and swung my eyes a little to make it go away or at least move off—for after all it was nothing but a fading disturbance in my retinas that, purely by chance, momentarily coincided with the pinnacle.

It would not move away. It clung to the pinnacle, a dark translucent pulsing shape, as if held there by some incredible magnetic attraction.

I shivered. I felt all my muscles faintly chill and tighten at this unnatural linkage between the space inside my head and the space outside it, at this weird tie between the sort of figures that one sees in the real world and the kind that swim before the eyes when one closes them in the dark.

I blinked my eyes harder, swung my head from side to side.

It was no use. The shaggy dark shape with the strange lines going out from it clung, to the pinnacle like some giant clawed and crouching beast.

AND instead of fading it now began to darken further, even to blacken, the faint lines got a black glitter, the whole thing began horridly to take on a definite appearance and expression, much as the figures we see swimming in the dark become faces or masks or muzzles or forms in response to our veering imagination—though now I felt no ability whatever to change the trend of the shaping of the thing on the pinnacle.

Viki's fingers dug into my arm with painful force. Without re-alizing it, we'd both stood up in the back of the car and were leaning forward, close to Franz. My own hands gripped the back of the front seat. Only Mr. M hadn't risen up, though he was staring at the pinnacle too.

Viki began, in a slow rasping strained voice, "Why, it looks like—"

With a sharp jerk of his spread-fingered hand Franz com-manded her to be silent. Then without taking his eyes away from the crag he dipped in the side pocket of his coat and was next reaching some things back toward us.

I saw, without looking at them directly, that they were blank white cards and stub pencils. Viki and I took them—so did Mr. M.

Franz whispered hoarsely, "Don't say what you see. Write it down. Just your impressions. Now. Quickly. The thing won't last long—I think."

For the next few seconds the four of us looked and scribbled and shivered—at least I know I was shuddering at one point, though not for an instant taking my eyes away.

Then, for me, the pinnacle was suddenly bare. I knew that it must have become so for the others too at almost the same instant, from the way their shoulders slumped and the strained sigh Viki gave.

We didn't say a word, just breathed hard for a moment or so, then passed the cards around and read them. Most of the writing or printing had the big sloppiness of something scribbled without looking at the paper, but beyond that there was a visible tremor or shakiness, especially in Viki's notes and my own.

Viki Quinn's:

> Black tiger, burning bright.
> Blinding fur—or vines.
> Stickiness.

Franz Kinzman's:

> Black Empress.
> Glittering cloak of threads.
> Visual glue.

Mine (Glenn Seabury's):

> Giant Spider.
> Black lighthouse.
> The web.
> The pull on the eyes.

Mr. M, whose writing was firmest:

> I don't see anything. Except three people looking at a big bare gray rock as if it was the door to Hell.

And it was Mr. M, who first looked up. We met his gaze. His lips sketched a tentative grin that seemed both sour and uneasy.

HE said after a bit, "Well, you certainly had your young friends pretty well hypnotized, Mr. Kinzman."

Franz asked calmly, "Is that your explanation, Ed—hypnotic suggestion—for what happened, for what we thought happened?"

The other shrugged. "What else?" he asked more cheerfully. "Do you have another explanation, Franz?—something that would account for it not working on me?"

Franz hesitated. I hung on his answer, wild to know if he'd known it was coming, as he'd seemed to, and how he'd known, and whether he'd had any comparable previous experiences. The hypnotism notion, though clever, was pure nonsense.

Finally Franz shook his head and said firmly, "No."

Mr. M. shrugged and started the Volks.

None of us wanted to talk. The experience was still with us, pinning us down inside, and then the testimony of the cards was so complete in its way, the parallelisms so exact, the conviction of a shared experience so sure, that there was no great immediate urge to compare notes.

Viki did say to me, in the offhand way of a person checking a point of which he's almost certain, " 'Black Lighthouse'—that means the light was black? Rays of darkness?"

"Of course," I told her and then asked in the same way, "Your 'vines,' Viki, your 'threads,' Franz—did they suggest those fine wire figures of curved planes and space you see in mathematical museums? Something linking a center to infinity?"

They both nodded. I said, "Like my web," and that was all the talk for a bit.

I took out a cigarette, remembered, and shoved it back in my top pocket.

Viki said, "Our descriptions...vaguely like descriptions of tarot cards...none of the actual tarots, though..." Her remarks trailed off unanswered.

MR. M, stopped at the top of a narrow drive that led down sharply to a house of which the only visible part was the flat roof, topped with pale jagged gravel. He jumped out.

"Thanks for the lift, Franz," he said. "Remember to call on me—the phone's working again—if you people should need a lift...or anything." He looked quickly toward the two of us in the back seat and grinned nervously. "Goodbye, Miss Quinn, Mr. Seabury. Don't—" he broke off, said simply, "So long," and walked rapidly down the drive.

Of course we guessed he'd been going to say, "Don't see any more black tigers with eight legs and lady's faces," or something like that.

Franz slid across into the driver's seat. As soon as the Volks got moving I knew one reason the steady competent Mr. M. might have wanted to drive the mountainous stretch, Franz didn't exactly try to make the old Volks behave like a sports car, but his handling of it was in that direction—skittish, a bit dashing.

He mused loudly, "One thing keeps nagging me: why didn't Ed Mortenson see it?—if 'see' is the right word."

So at last I was sure of Mr. M.'s name, Mortenson. It seemed a triumph.

Viki said, "I can think of one possible reason, Mr. Kinzman. He isn't going where we're going."

"Imagine one of the awful bird-catching spiders of South America translated into human form, and endowed with intelligence just less than human, and you will have some faint conception of the terror inspired by this appalling effigy."

—M. R. James in *"Canon Alberic's Scrapbook"*

RIM House was about two miles beyond Mr. Mortenson's place and likewise on the downhill (down-cliff, rather!) side of the road. It was reached by a decidedly one-lane drive. On the outside of the drive, edged by white-painted stones, was a near-vertical drop of over one hundred feet. On the inside was a forty-five degree brush-dotted rocky slope between the drive and the road, which was climbing sharply along this stretch.

After about one hundred yards the drive widened to become the short, narrow, jutting plateau or terrace on which stood Rim House, occupying about half of the available space. Franz, who had taken the first part of the drive with confident briskness, slowed the Volks to a crawl as soon as the house came in view so we could scan the outside layout while still somewhat above it.

The house was built to the very edge of the drop, which here plunged down further and even more sharply than it had along the drive. On the uphill side of the house, coming down to within two feet of it, was a dizzily expansive slope of raw earth with hardly a thing growing in it, smoothly geometrical as a, little section of the side of a vast brown cone. Along the very top of it a row of short white posts, so distant I couldn't see the cable joining them, marked the road we had left. The slope looked forty-five degrees to me—these things always look impossibly steep—but Franz said it was only thirty—a completely stabilized landslide. It had been burned over a year ago in a brush fire that had almost got the house and still more recently there had been some minor slides started by repairs to the road above, accounting for the slope's unvegetated appearance.

The house was long, one-storey, its walls finished in gray asbestos shingles. The nearly flat roof, also finished in gray asbestos, sloped gently from the cliff side in. Midway the length of the house was a bend, allowing the house to conform to the curving top of the cliff and dividing it into two equal sections or angles, to call them that. An unroofed porch, lightly railed (Franz called it "the deck") ran along the nearer angle of the house fronting north and thrusting several feet out over the drop, which as ·this point was three hundred feet.

On the side of the house toward the drive was a flagstone yard big enough to turn a car in and with a lightly roofed carport up against the house on the side away from the drop. As we drove down onto the yard there was a slight clank as we crossed a heavy metal plate bridging a small neat ditch that ran along the foot of the raw earth slope, carrying off the water that would come down it— and also the water that would drain from the roof—during Southern California's infrequent but sometimes severe winter rains.

FRANZ backed the car around before we got out. It required four movements-swing to the corner of the house where the deck started, back with a sharp turn until the rear wheels were almost in the ditch, forward with a reverse turn until the front wheels were at the cliff edge by the metal bridgelet, then back into the carport until the rear of the car was almost up against a door that Franz told us led to the kitchen.

The three of us got out and Franz led us to the center of the flagged yard for another look around before we went inside. I noticed that some of the gray flags were actually solid rock showing through the light soil cover, indicating that the plateau was not an earth terrace cut by men but a rocky flat-surfaced knob thrusting out of the hillside. It gave me a feeling of security which I especially welcomed because there were other impressions— sensations, rather that were distinctly disturbing to me.

They were minor sensations, all of them, barely on the threshold of awareness. Ordinarily I don't think I'd have noticed them—I don't consider myself a sensitive person—but undoubtedly the strange experience of the thing on the pinnacle had keyed me up. To begin with there was the hint of the nasty smell of burnt linen and with it an odd bitter brassy taste; I don't think I imagined these things, because I noticed Franz wrinkling his nostrils and working his tongue against his teeth. Then there was the feeling of being faintly brushed by threads, cobwebs, or the finest vines, although we were right out in the open and the nearest thing overhead was a cloud a half mile up. And just as I felt that— the faintest feeling, mind you—I noticed Viki lightly and questingly run her hand across the top of her hair and down the back of her neck in the common gesture of "feeling for a spider."

All this time we were talking off and on—for one thing Franz was telling us about buying Rim House on quite inexpensive terms five years back from the heir of a wealthy surfing and sports-car enthusiast who had run himself off a turn in Decker Canyon.

Finally there were the sounds that were, I thought, breathing on the verge of audibility in the remarkably complete silence that flowed around us when the Volks' motor was cut off. I know that everyone who goes from the city to the country is troubled by sounds, but these were on the unusual side. There was an occasional whistling too high-pitched for the ear's normal range and a soft rumbling too low for it. But along with these perhaps fancied vibrations, I three times thought I heard the hissing rattle of fine gravel spilling down. Each time I looked quickly toward the slope, but never could catch the faintest sign of earth on the move, although there was admittedly a lot of slope to be scanned.

THE third time I looked up the slope, some clouds had moved aside enough so that the upper rim of the sun peered back down at me. "Like a golden rifleman drawing a bead" was the grotesque figure of speech that sprang to my mind. I looked hurriedly away. I wanted no more black spots before my eyes for the present. Just then Franz led us up on the deck and into Rim House by the front door.

I was afraid that all the unpleasant sensations would intensify as we got inside—especially somehow the burnt-linen smell and the invisible cobwebs—so I was greatly cheered when instead they all vanished instantly, as though faced-down by the strong sense of Franz's genial, sympathetic, wide-ranging, highly civilized personality that the living room exuded.

It was a long room, narrow at first where it had to give space to the kitchen and utility room and a small bathroom at this end of the house, then broadening out to the full width of the building. There was no empty wall space, it was completely lined with shelves—half of books, half of statuary, archeological oddments, scientific instruments, tape recorder, high-fi set and the like. Near the inner wall, beyond the narrow section, were a big desk, some filing cabinets, and a stand with the phone.

There were no windows looking out on the deck. But just beyond the deck, where the bend in the house came, was a big view window looking out across the canyon at the craggy hills that completely cut off any sight of the Pacific. Facing the view window and close to it was a long couch backed by a long table.

At the end of the living room a narrow hall led down the middle of the second angle of the house to a door that in turn let out into a most private grassy space that could be used for sunbathing and was just big enough for a badminton court—if anyone felt nervy enough to leap about swatting at the bird on the edge of that great drop.

ON the side of the hall toward the slope was a big bedroom—Franz's—and a large bathroom opening into the hall at the end of the house. On the other side were two only slightly smaller bedrooms, each with a view window that could be completely masked by heavy dark drapes. These rooms had been his boys', he remarked casually, but I noted with relief that there were no mementoes or signs whatever left of youthful occupancy; my closet, in fact, had some women's clothes hanging in the back of it. These two bedrooms, which he assigned to Viki and myself, had a connecting door which could be bolted from both sides, but now stood unbolted but shut—a typical indication, albeit a minor one, of Franz's civilized tactfulness: he did not know, or at least did not presume to guess, the exact relationship between Viki and myself, and SQ left us to make our own arrangements as we saw fit—without any spoken suggestion that we should do so, of course.

Also, each door to the hall had a serviceable bolt—Franz clearly believed in privacy for guests—and in each room was a little bowl of silver coins, no collector's items, just current American coinage.

Viki asked about that and Franz explained deprecatingly, smiling at his own romanticism, that he'd copied the old Spanish California custom of the host providing guests with convenience money in that fashion.

Having been introduced to the house, we unloaded the Volks of our trifling luggage and the provisions Franz had picked up in LA. He sighed faintly at the light film of dust that had accumulated everywhere during his month's absence and Viki insisted that we pitch in with him and do a bit of house cleaning. Franz agreed without too much demurring. I think all of us were eager to work off the edge of this afternoon's experience and get feeling back in the real world again before we talked about it—I know I was.

Franz proved an easy man to help houseclean—thoughtful for his home but not at all fussy or finicky about it. And while wielding broom or mop Viki looked good in her sweater, toreador pants, and highbound sandals, she wears the modern young-female's uniform with style rather than the customary effect of dreary intellectuality mated to a solemnly biologic femaleness.

When we'd done, we sat down in the kitchen with mugs of black coffee—somehow none of us wanted a drink—and listened to Franz's stew simmer.

"You'll want to know," he said without preface, "if I've had any previous eerie experiences up here, if I knew something was apt to happen when I invited you up for the weekend, whether the phenomena-pretentious term, isn't it?—seem to be connected with anything in the past of the region or the house or my own past—or with current activities here, including the scientific-military installations of the missile people—and finally whether I have any overall theory to account for them—such as Ed's suggestion about hypnotism."

Viki nodded. He'd adequately, stated what was in our minds.

"About that last, Franz," I said abruptly. "When Mr. Mortenson first made that suggestion, I thought it was completely impossible, but now I'm not quite so sure. I don't mean you'd deliberately hypnotize us, but aren't there kinds of self-hypnosis that can be communicated to others? At any rate, the conditions were favorable for suggestion operating—we'd just been talking about the supernatural, there was the sun and its afterimages acting as an attention-capturer, then the sudden transition to shadow, and finally you pointing decisively at that pinnacle as if we all had to see something there."

"I don't believe that for one minute, Glenn," Viki said with conviction.

"Neither do I, really," I told her. "After all, the cards indicate we had remarkably similar visions—our descriptions were just different enough to make them fearfully convincing—and I don't see where that material could have been suggested to us during the trip out or at any earlier time when we were together. Still, the idea of some obscure sort of suggestion has crossed my mind. A blend of highway hypnosis and sun-hypnosis, maybe? Franz, what were your earlier experiences? I take it there were some."

HE nodded but then looked at us both thoughtfully and said, "I don't think I should tell you about them in any detail, though. Not because I'm afraid of you being skeptical or anything like that, but simply because if I do, and then similar things happen to you, you'll be more likely to feel—and rightly—that the power of suggestion may have been at work.

"Still, I ought to answer your questions," he continued. "So here goes, briefly and in a general way. Yes, I had experiences while I was up here alone month before last—some of them like this afternoon's, some of them quite different. They didn't seem to link up with any particular folklore or occult theory or anything else, yet they frightened me so that I went down to LA and had my eyes checked by a very good oculist and had a psychiatrist and a couple of psychologists I trust give me a thorough check-up. They pronounced me fit and unwarped—likewise my eyes. After a month I had myself convinced that everything I'd seen or sensed had been hallucinatory, that I'd simply had a case of nerves, a fit of the horrors, from too much loneliness. I invited you two along partly to avoid restarting the cycle."

"You couldn't have been completely convinced, though," Viki pointed out. "You had those cards and pencils all ready in your pocket."

Franz grinned at the neatly scored point. "Right," he said. "I was still keeping in mind the off-trail chance and preparing for it.

And then when I got in the hills the set of my ideas changed. What had seemed completely inconceivable, in LA became once more a borderline possibility. Queer. Come on, let's take a turn on the deck—it'll be cool by now."

We took our mugs along. It was moderately cool, all right, most of the canyon-valley had been in the shadow for at least two hours and a faint breeze flowed upward around our ankles. Once I'd got used to being on the edge of the terrific drop, I found it exhilarating. Viki must have too, for she leaned over with deliberately showy daring to peer.

THE floor of the canyon was choked with dark trees and un-undergrowth. This thinned out going up the opposite face until just across from us there was a magnificent upthrusted and folded stratum of pale tan rock that the canyon wall cut in cross-section and showed us like a geology book. Above this fold was more undergrowth, then a series of tan and gray rocks with dark gullies and caves between them, leading by steps to a high gray summit-crag.

The slope behind the house completely cut off the sun from us, of course, but its yellow rays were still striking the tops of the wall across from us, traveling up them as the sun sank. The clouds had all blown away east, where a couple were still visible, and none had replaced them.

In spite of being in a much cheerier "normal" mood, I'd braced myself just a bit for the eerie little sensations as we'd come out onto the deck, but they weren't there. Which somehow wasn't quite as reassuring as it ought to have been. I made myself study and admire the variegated rocky wall opposite.

"God, what a view to wake up to every morning!" Viki said enthusiastically. "You can feel the shape of the air and the height of the sky."

"Yes, it's quite a prospect," Franz agreed.

THEN they came, the little ones, faint-footed as before, feather-treading the sensory thresholds—the burnt-linen odor, the bitter brassy tang, the brushing of skyey cobwebs, the vibrations not quite sound, the hissing rattling spill of ghost gravel…the minor sensations, as I'd named them to myself…

I knew Viki and Franz were getting them too, simply because they said no more and I could sense them both holding very still.

…and then one of the last rays of the sun must have struck a mirror-surface in the summit crag, perhaps an outcropping of quartz, for it struck back at me like a golden rapier, making me blink, and then for an instant the beam was glitteringly black and I thought I saw (though nothing as clearly as I'd seen the black all-knowing spider-centipede on the pinnacle) a black shape—black with the queer churning blackness you see only at night with your eyes closed. The shape coiled rapidly down the crag, into the cavern gullies and around the rocks and finally and utterly into the undergrowth above the fold and disappeared.

Along the way Viki had grabbed my arm at the elbow and Franz had whipped round to look at us and then looked back.

It was strange. I felt frightened and at the same time eager, on the edge of marvels and mysteries about to be laid bare. And there had been something quite controlled about the behavior of all of us through it. One fantastically trivial, point—none of us had spilled any coffee.

We studied the canyon wall above the fold for about two minutes.

Then Franz said, almost gaily, "Time for dinner. Talk afterwards."

I felt deeply grateful for the instant steadying, shielding, anti-hysterical and, yes, comforting effect of the house as we went back in. I knew it was an ally.

"When the hard-boiled rationalist came to consult me for the first time, he was in such a state of panic that not only he himself but I also felt the wind coming over from the side of the lunatic asylum!"

—*Carl Gustav Jung in "Psyche and Symbol."*

WE accompanied Franz's stew with chunks of dark pumpernickel and pale brick cheese and followed it with fruit and coffee, then took more coffee to the long couch facing the big view window in the living room. There was a spectral yellow glow in the sky but it faded while we were settling ourselves. Soon the first star to the north glittered faintly—Dubhe perhaps.

"Why is black a frightening color?" Viki put before us.

"Night," Franz said. "Though you'll get an argument as to whether it's a color or absence of color or simply basic sensory field. But is it intrinsically frightening?"

Viki nodded with pursed lips.

I said, "Somehow the phrase 'the black spaces between the stars' has always been an ultimate to me in terror. I can look at the stars without thinking of it, but the phrase gets me."

Viki said, "My ultimate horror is the idea of inky black cracks appearing in things, first in the sidewalk and the sides of houses, then in the furniture and floors and cars and things, finally in the pages of books and people's faces and the blue sky. The cracks are inky black—nothing ever shows."

"As if the universe were a gigantic jigsaw puzzle," I suggested.

"A little like that. Or a Byzantine mosaic. Glittering gold and glittering black."

Franz said, "Your picture, Viki, suggests that sense of breaking-up we feel in the modern world. Families, nations, classes, other loyalty groups falling apart. Things changing before you get to know them. Death on the installment plan—or decay by jumps. Instantaneous birth. Something out of nothing. Reality replacing science fiction so fast that you can't tell which is which. Constant sense of déjà-vu—I was here before—but when, how?' Even the possibility that there's no real continuity between events, just—inexplicable gaps. And of course every gap—every crack—means a new perching place for horror."

"It also suggests the fragmentation of knowledge, as somebody called it," I said. "A world too big and complex to grasp in more than patches. Too much for one man. Takes teams of experts—and teams of teams. Each expert has his field, his patch, his piece of the jigsaw puzzle, but between any two pieces is a no man's land."

"Right, Glenn," Franz said sharply, "and today I think the three of us have plunged into one of the biggest of those no man's lands." He hesitated then and said with an odd diffidence, almost embarrassment, "You know, we're going to have to start talking sometime about what we saw—we can't let ourselves be gagged by this fear that anything we say will alter the picture of what the others saw and warp their testimony. Well, about the blackness of this thing or figure or manifestation I saw (I called it 'Black Empress,' but Sphinx might have been a better word—there was the suggestion of along tigerish or serpentine body in the midst of the black fringy sunburst)—but about its blackness, now, that blackness was more than anything else like the glimmering dark the eyes see in the absence of light."

"Right," I said.

"Oh yes," Viki chimed.

THERE was a sense," Franz went on, "that the thing was in my eyes, in my head, but also out there on the horizon, on the pinnacle I mean. That it was somehow both subjective—in my consciousness—and objective—in the material world—or..." (He hesitated and lowered his voice) "...or existing in some sort of space more fundamental, more primal, and less organized than either of those.

"Why shouldn't there be other kinds of space than those we know?" he went on a shade defensively. "Other chambers in the great universal cave? Men have tried to imagine four, five and more spatial dimensions. What's the space inside the atom or the nucleus feel like, or the space between the galaxies or beyond any galaxy? Oh, I know the questions I'm asking would be nonsense to most scientists—they're questions that don't make sense operationally or referentially, they'd say—but those same men Can't give us the ghost of an answer to even the question of where and how the space of consciousness exists, how a jelly of nerve cells can support the huge flaming worlds of inner reality—they fob it off with the excuse (legitimate in its way) that science is about things that can be measured and pointed at, and who can measure or point at his thoughts? But consciousness is—it's the basis we all exist in and start from, it's the basis science starts from, whether or not science can get at it—so it's allowable for me to wonder whether there may not be a primal space that's a bridge between consciousness and matter...and whether the thing we saw may not exist in such a space."

"Maybe there are experts for this sort of thing and we're missing them," Viki said seriously. "Not scientists, but mystics and occultists, some of them at any rate—the genuine few among the crowd of fakers. You've got some of their books in your library. I recognized the titles."

Franz shrugged. "I've never found anything in occult literature that seemed to have a bearing. You know, the occult—very much like stories of supernatural horror—is a sort of game. Most religion too. Believe in the game and accept its rules—or the premises of the story—and you can have the thrills or whatever it is you're after. Accept the spirit world and you can see ghosts and talk to the dear departed. Accept Heaven and you can have the hope of eternal life and the reassurance of an all-powerful god working on your side. Accept Hell and you can have devils and demons, if that's what you want. Accept—if only for story purposes—witchcraft, druidism, shamanism, magic or some modern variant and you can have werewolves, vampires, elementals. Or believe in the influence and power of a grave, an ancient house or monument, a dead religion, an old stone with an inscription on it—and you can have things of the same general sort. But I'm thinking of the kind of horror—and wonder too, perhaps—that lies beyond any game, that's bigger than any game, that's fettered by no rules, conforms to no manmade theology, bows to no charms or protective rituals, that strides the world unseen and strikes without warning where it will, much the same as (though it's of a different order of existence than all of these) lightning or the plague or the enemy atom bomb. The sort of horror that the whole fabric of civilization was designed to protect us from and make us forget. The horror about which all, man's learning tells us nothing."

I STOOD up and moved close to the window. There seemed to be quite a few stars now. I tried to make out the big fold of rock in the hillside opposite, but the reflections on the glass got in the way.

"Maybe so," Viki said, "but there are a couple of those books I'd like to look at again. I think they're back of your desk."

"What titles?" Franz asked. "I'll help you find them."

"Meanwhile I'll take a turn on the deck," I said as casually as I could, moving toward the other end of the room. They didn't call after me, but I had the feeling they watched me the whole way.

As soon as I'd pushed through the door—which took a definite effort of will—and shoved it to without quite shutting it behind me—which took another—I became aware of two things: that it was much darker than I'd anticipated—the big view window angled away from the deck and there was no other obvious light source except the stars—two, that I found the darkness reassuring.

The reason for the latter seemed clear enough: the horror I'd glimpsed was associated with the sun, with blinding sunlight. Now I was safe from that—though if someone unseen should have struck a match in front of my face just then, the effect on me would have been extreme.

I moved forward by short steps, feeling in front of me with my hands at the level of the rail.

I knew why I'd come out here I thought. I wanted to test my courage against the thing, whatever it was, illusory or real or something else, inside or outside our minds, or somehow as Franz had suggested, able to move in both regions. But beyond that, I realized now, there was the beginning of a fascination.

My hands touched the rail. I studied the black wall opposite, deliberately looking a little away and then back, as one does to make a faint star or a dim object come clear in the dark. After a bit I could make out the big pale fold and some of the rocks above it, but a couple of minutes' watching convinced me that it was possible endlessly to see dark shapes crossing it.

I looked up at the heavens. There was no Milky Way yet, but', there would be soon, the stars were flashing on so brightly and thickly at this smog-free distance from LA. I saw the Pole Star straight above the dark star-silhouetted summit-crag of the hillside across from me, and the Great Bear and Cassiopeia swinging from it. I felt the bigness of the atmosphere. I got a hint of the stupendous distance between me and the stars, and then—as if my vision could go out in all directions at will, piercing solidity as readily as the dark—I got a lasting, growing, wholly absorbing sense of the universe around me.

LYING behind me, a gently swelling, perfectly rounded section of the earth about a hundred miles high masked off the sun. Africa lay under my right foot through the earth's core. India under my left, and it was strange to think of the compressed incandescent stuff that lay between us under earth's cool mantle—blindingly glowing plastic metal or ore in a space where there were no eyes to see and no millionth of a free inch in which all that dazzling locked-up light could travel. I sensed the tortured ice of the frigid poles, the squeezed water in the deep seas, the fingers of mounting lava, the raw earth crawling and quivering with an infinitude of questing rootlets and burrowing worms.

Then for moments I felt I looked out glimmeringly through two billion pairs of human eyes, my consciousness running like fuse-fire from mind to mind. For moments more I dimly shared the feelings, the blind pressures and pulls, of a billion trillion motes of microscopic life in the air, in the earth, in the bloodstream of man.

Then my consciousness seemed to move swiftly outward from earth in all directions, like an expanding globe of sentient gas. I passed the dusty dry mote that was Mars. I glimpsed milkily-banded Saturn with its great thin wheels of jumbled jagged rock. I passed frigid Pluto with its bitter nitrogen snows. I thought of how people are like planets—lonely little forts of mind with immense black distances barring them off from each other.

Then the speed of expansion of my consciousness became infinite and my mind was spread thin in the stars of the Milky Way and in the other gauzy star islands beyond it—above, below, to all sides, among the nadir stars as well as those of the zenith—and on the trillion-trillion planets of those stars I sensed the infinite variety of self-conscious life—naked, clothed, furred, armor-shelled, and with cells floating free-clawed, handed, tentacled, pinchered, ciliated, fingered by winds or magnetism—loving, hating, striving, despairing, imagining.

For a while it seemed to me that all these beings were joined in a dance that was fiercely joyous, poignantly sensuous, tenderly responsive.

Then the mood darkened and the beings fell apart into a trillion-trillion-trillion lonely motes locked off forever from each other, sensing only bleak meaninglessness in the cosmos around them, their eyes fixed forward only on universal death.

Simultaneously each dimensionless star seemed to become for me the vast sun it was, beating incandescently on the platform where my body stood and on the house behind it and the beings in it and on my body too, aging them with the glare of a billion desert noons, crumbling them all to dust in one coruscatingly blinding instant.

HANDS gently grasped my shoulders and at the same time Franz's voice said, "Steady, Glenn," I held still, though for a moment every nerve cell in me seemed on the verge of triggering, then I let out an uneven breath edged with laughter and turned and said in a voice that sounded to me quite dull, almost drugged, "I got lost in my imagination. For a minute there I seemed to be seeing everything. Where's Viki?"

"Inside leafing through *The Symbolism of the Tarot* and a couple of other books on the arcana of the fortune-telling cards, and grumbling that they don't have indexes. But what's this 'seeing everything,' Glenn?"

Haltingly I tried to tell him about my "vision," not conveying a hundredth of it, I felt. By the time I finished I could see the blur of his face against the black wall of the house barely well enough to tell that he nodded.

"The universe fondling and devouring her children," his brooding comment came out of the dark. "I imagine you've run across in your reading, Glenn, the superficially sterile theory that the whole universe is in some sense alive or at least aware. There are a lot of terms for it in the jargon of metaphysics: cosmotheism, theopantism, panpsychism, panpneumatism—but simply pantheism is the commonest. The idea that the universe is God, though for me God isn't the right term; it's been used to mean too many things. If you insist on a religious approach, perhaps what comes closest is the Greek idea of the Great God Pan, the mysterious nature deity, half-animal, that frightened man and woman to panic in lonely places. Incidentally, panpneumatism is the most interesting to me of the obscurer concepts: old Karl von Hartmann's notion that unconscious mind is the basic reality—it comes close to what we were saying inside about the possibility of a more fundamental space, linking the inner and outer world and perhaps providing a bridge from anywhere to anywhere."

As he paused I heard a faint spill of gravel, then a second, though I got none of the other minor sensations.

"But whatever we call it," Franz went on, "there's something there. I feel—something less than God but more than the collective mind of man—a force, a power, an influence, a mood of things, a something more than subatomic particles, that is aware and that has grown with the universe and that helps to shape it." He had moved forward now so that I saw his head silhouetted against the thick stars and for a moment there was the grotesque illusion that it was the stars rather than his mouth that was speaking. "I think there are such influences, Glenn. Atomic particles alone can't sustain the flaming inner worlds of consciousness, there must be a pull from the future as well as a push from the past to keep us moving through time, there must be a ceiling of mind over life as well as a floor of matter beneath it."

AGAIN, as his voice faded out, I heard the feathery hisses of gravel running—two close together, then two more. I thought uneasily of the slope behind the house.

"And if there are those influences," Franz continued, "I believe that man has grown enough in awareness today to be able to contact them without ritual or formula of belief, if they should chance to move or look this way. I think of them as sleepy tigers, Glenn, that mostly purr and dream and look at us through slitted eyes, but occasionally—perhaps when a man gets a hint of them—open their eyes to the full and stalk in his direction. When a man becomes ripe for them, when he's pondered the possibility of them, and then when he's closed his ears to the protective, mechanically-augmented chatter of humanity, they make themselves known to him."

The spills of gravel, still faint, as illusions, were coming now in a rapid rhythm like—it occurred to me at that instant—padding footsteps, each footstep dislodging a little earth. I sensed a faint brief glow overhead.

"For they're the same thing. Glenn, as the horror and wonder I talked about inside, the horror and wonder that lies beyond any game, that strides the world unseen and strikes without warning where it will."

At that instant the silence was ripped by a shrill scream of terror from the flagged yard between the house and the drive. For an instant my muscles were chilled and constricted and there was a gagging pressure in my chest. Then I lunged toward that end of the deck.

Franz darted into the house.

I PLUNGED off the end of the deck, almost fell, twisted to my feet—and stopped, suddenly at a loss for my next move.

Here I couldn't see a thing in the blackness. In stumbling I'd lost my sense of direction—for the moment I didn't know which ways were the slope, the house, and the cliff edge.

I heard Viki—I thought it had to be Viki—gasping and sobbing strainingly, but the direction of that wouldn't come clear, except it seemed more ahead of me than behind me.

Then I saw, stretching up before me, a half dozen or so thin close-placed stalks of what I can only describe as a more gleaming blackness—it differed from the background as dead black velvet does from dead black felt. They were barely distinguishable yet very real. I followed them up with my eyes as they mounted against the starfields, almost invisible, like black wires, to where they ended—high up—in a bulb of darkness, defined only by the patch of stars it obscured, as tiny as the moon.

The black bulb swayed and there was a corresponding rapid jogging in the crowded black stalks—though if they were free to move at the base I ought to call them legs.

A door opened twenty feet from me and a beam of white light struck across the yard, showing a streak of flagstones and the beginning of the drive.

Franz had come out the kitchen door with a powerful flashlight. My surroundings jumped sideways into place.

The beam swept back along the slope, showing nothing, then forward toward the cliff edge. When it got to the spot where I'd seen the ribbony black legs, it stopped.

There were no stalks, legs or bands of any sort to be seen, but Viki was swaying and struggling there, her dark hair streaming across her face and half obscuring her agonized expression, her elbows tight to her sides, her hands near her shoulders and clawed outward—exactly as though she were gripping and struggling against the vertical bars of a tight cage.

The next instant the tension went out of her, as though whatever she'd been struggling against had vanished. She swayed and began to move in blind tottering steps toward the cliff edge.

That snapped my freeze and I ran toward her, grabbed her wrist as she stepped on the verge, and half-dragged, half-whirled her away from it. She didn't resist. Her movement toward the cliff had been accidental, not suicidal. Franz kept the flashlight on us.

She looked at me, one side of her blanched face twitching, and said, "Glenn."

Franz yelled at us from the kitchen door, "Come on in!"

"But the third Sister, who is also the youngest—! Hush! Whisper whilst we talk of her! Her kingdom is not large, or else no flesh should live; but within that kingdom all power is hers. Her head, turreted like that of Cybele, rises almost beyond the reach of Sight. She droops not; and her eyes, rising so high, might be hidden by distance, but being what they are, they cannot be hidden... This youngest sister moves with incalculable motions, bounding with tiger's leaps. She carries no key; for, though coming rarely amongst men, she storms all doors at which she is permitted to enter at all. And her name is Mater Tenebrarum, Our Lady of Darkness.

—Thomas de Quincy in "Suspira de Profundis"

As soon as we got Viki inside she recovered very rapidly from her shock and at once insisted on telling us her story. Her manner was startlingly assured, interested, almost gay, as if some protective door in her mind were already closed against the absolute reality of what had happened.

At one point she even said, "It all still could have been a series of chance little sounds and sights, you know, combined with suggestion working powerfully—like the night I saw a burglar standing against the wall beyond the foot of my bed, saw him so clearly in the dark that I could have described him down to the cut of his mustache and the droop of his left eyelid...until the dawn coming on turned him into my roommate's black overcoat with a tan scarf thrown around the hanger and hook."

While she'd been reading, she said, she'd become aware of the ghost-spills of gravel, some of them seeming to rattle faintly against the back wall of the house, and she'd gone out at once through the kitchen to investigate.

Groping her way, moving a few steps beyond the Volks toward the center of the yard, she had looked toward the slope and at once seen moving across it an incredibly tall wispy shape that she described as "a giant harvestman, tall as ten trees. You 'know harvestmen, some people call them daddy longlegs, those utterly harmless pitifully fragile spiders that are nothing but a tiny brown inanimate-looking ball with eight bendy legs that are like lengths of half-stiffened brown thread."

She'd seen it quite clearly in spite of the darkness, because it was "black with a black shimmer." Once it had vanished completely when a car had turned the bend in the road above and its headlights had feebly swept the air high above the slope (that would have been the faint brief overhead glow I'd sensed)—but when the headlights swung away the giant black glimmering harvestmen had come back at once.

She hadn't been frightened (wonderstruck and terribly curious, rather) until the thing had come treading rapidly toward her, its shimmering black legs drawing closer and closer together until before she realized it they were a tight cage around her.

Then, as she discovered they weren't quite as thin and insubstantial as she'd imagined, and as she felt their feathery, almost bristly touch against her back and face and sides, she'd suddenly snapped and given that one terrific scream and started to struggle hysterically. "Spiders drive me wild," she finished lightly, "and then there was the feeling I'd be sucked up the cage to the black brain in the stars—I thought of it as a black brain then, no reason why,"

FRANZ didn't say anything for a bit. Then he began, in a rather heavy, halting way. "You know, I don't think I showed much foresight or consideration when I invited you two up here. Quite the opposite, in fact, even if I didn't then believe that. Anyway, I don't feel right about it. Look here, you could take the Volks right now...or I could drive...and—"

"I think I know what you're getting at, Mr. Kinzman, and why," Viki said with a little laugh, standing up, "but I for one have had quite enough excitement for one night. I have no desire to top it off with watching for ghosts in the headlights for the next two hours." She yawned. "I want to hit that luxurious hay you've provided for me, right this minute. Night—night, Franz, Glenn." With no more word she walked down the hall and went in her bedroom, the far one, and closed the door.

Franz said, in a low voice, "I think you know I meant that very seriously, Glenn. It still might be the best thing."

I said, "Viki's got some kind of inner protection built up now. To get her to leave Rim House, we'd have to break it down. That would be rough."

Franz said, "Better rough, maybe, than what else might happen here tonight."

I said, "So far Rim House has been a protection for us. It's shut things out."

He said, "It didn't shut out the footsteps Viki heard."

I said, remembering my vision of the cosmos, "But Franz, if we're up against the sort of influence we think we are, then it seems to me pretty ridiculous to imagine a few miles of distance or a few bright lights making any more difference to its power than the walls of a house."

He shrugged. "We don't know," he said. "Did you see it, Glenn? Holding the light I didn't see anything."

"Just like Viki described it," I assured him and went on to tell my own little tale. "If that was all suggestion," I said, "it was a pretty fancy variety," I squeezed my eyes and yawned; I was suddenly feeling very dull reaction, I suppose. I finished with,

"While it was happening, and later while we were listening to Viki, there certainly were times when all I wanted was to be back in the old familiar world with the old familiar hydrogen bomb hanging over my head and all the rest of that stuff."

A Bit of the Dark World

Illustration by
Dan Adkins

"But at the same time weren't you fascinated!" Franz demanded." Didn't it make you crazy to know more!—the thought that you were seeing something utterly strange and that here was a chance really to understand the universe—at least to meet its unknown lords!"

"I don't know," I told him wearily. "I suppose so, in a way."

WHAT did the thing really seem like, Glenn?" Franz asked. "What kind of being? If that's the right word."

"I'm not sure it is," I said, found it difficult to summon the energy to answer his questions "Not an animal. Not even an intelligence as we understand it more like the things we saw on the pinnacle and the crag." I tried to marshal my fatigue-drugged thoughts. "Halfway between reality and a symbol," I said. "If that means anything."

"But weren't you fascinated?" Franz repeated.

"I don't know," I said, pushing to my feet with an effort. "Look, Franz, I'm too beat to be able t do any more thinking now. It's just too hard to talk about these things. G'night."

"Goodnight, Glenn," he said as I walked to my bedroom. Nothing more.

Midway getting undressed, it occurred to me that my dazed sleepiness might be my mind's defense against having to cope with the unknown, but even that thought wasn't enough to rouse me.

I pulled on my pajamas and put out the light. Just then the door to Viki's bedroom opened and she stood there, wearing a light robe.

I had thought of looking in on her, but had decided that if she were sleeping it was the best thing for her and any attempt to check on her might break her inner protection.

But now I could tell from her expression, by the bit of light from her room, that they were shattered.

At the same moment my own inner protection—the false sleepiness—was gone.

Viki closed the door behind her and we moved together and put our arms around each other and stood there. After a while we lay down side by side on the bed under the view window that showed the stars.

Viki and I are lovers, but there wasn't an atom of passion in our embraces now. We were simply two, not so much frightened as completely overawed people, seeking comfort and reassurance in each other's presence.

Not that we could hope to get any security, any protection, from each other—the thing looming above us was too powerful for that—but only a sense of not being alone, of sharing whatever might happen.

THERE wasn't the faintest impulse to seek temporary escape in lovemaking, as we might have done to shut out a more physical threat; the thing was too weird for that. For once Viki's body was beautiful to me in a completely cold abstract way that had no more to do with desire than the colors in an insect's wing-case or the curve of a tree or the glitter of a snowfield. Yet within this strange form, I knew, was a friend.

We didn't speak a word to each other. There were no easy words for most of our thoughts, sometimes no words at all. Besides, we shrank from making the slightest sound, as two mice would while a cat sniffs past the clump of grass in which they are hiding.

For the sense of a presence looming around and over Rim House was overpoweringly strong. Dipping into Rim House now too, for all the minor sensations came drifting down on us like near-impalpable black snowflakes—the dark burnt taste and smell, the fluttering cobwebs, the bat-sounds and the wave-sounds and once again the feathery spills of gravel.

And above and behind them the sense of a black uprearing presence linked to the whole cosmos by the finest black filaments that in no way impeded it...

I didn't think of Franz. I hardly thought of the things that had happened today, though now and then I would worry at the edge of a memory...

We simply lay there and held still and looked at the stars. Minute after minute. Hour after hour.

At times we must have slept. I know I did, though blacked-out would be a better expression for it, for there was no rest and waking was a nightmarish business of slowly becoming aware and dark aches and chills.

After a long while I noticed that I could see the clock in the far corner of the room—because its dial was luminescent, I thought. The hands pointed to three o'clock. I gently turned Viki's face toward it and she nodded that she could see it too.

The stars were what was keeping us sane, I told myself, in a world that might dissolve to dust at the faintest breath from the nearer presence.

It was just after I noticed the clock that the stars began to change color, all of them. First they had a violet tinge, which shifted to blue, then green.

In an unimportant corner of my mind I wondered what fine mist or dust drifting through the air could work that change.

The stars turned to dim yellow, to orange, to dark furnace-red, and then—like the last sparks crawling on a sooty chimney wall above a dead fire—winked out.

I thought crazily of the stars all springing away from earth, moving with such impossible swiftness that their light had shifted beneath the red into invisible ranges.

WE should have been in utter darkness then, but instead we began to see each other and the things around us outlined by the faintest white glimmer. I thought it was the first hint of morning and I suppose Viki did too. We looked together at the clock. It was barely four-thirty. We watched the minute hand edge. Then we looked back at the window. It wasn't ghostly pale, as it would have been with dawn, but—and I could tell that Viki saw this too by the way she gripped my hand—it was a pitch black square, framed by the white glimmer.

I could think of no natural explanation for the glimmer. It was a little like a whiter paler version of the luminescence of the clock dial. But even more it was like the pictures one imagines in one's eyes in absolute darkness, when one wills the churning white sparks of the retinal field to coalesce into recognizable ghostly forms—it was as if that retinal dark had spilled out of our eyes into the room around us and we were seeing each other and our surroundings not by light but by the power of imagination—which each second increased the sense of miracle that the shimmering scene did not dissolve to churning chaos.

We watched the hand of the clock edge toward five. The thought that it must be getting light outside and that something barred us from seeing that light, finally stirred me to move and speak, though the sense of an inhuman inanimate presence was as strong as ever.

"We've got to try and get out of here," I whispered.

Moving across the bedroom like a shimmering ghost, Viki opened the connecting door. The light had been on in her room, I remembered.

There wasn't the faintest glimmer visible through the door. Her bedroom was dead black.

I'd fix that, I thought. I switched on the lamp by the bed.

My room became solid black. I couldn't see even the face of the clock. *Light is darkness now,* I thought. *White is black.*

I switched off the light and the glimmer came back. I went to Viki where she was standing by the door and whispered to her to switch off the light in her room. Then I got dressed, mostly feeling around for my clothes, not trusting the ghostly light that was so much like a scene inside my head trembling on the verge of dissolution.

Viki came back. She was even carrying her little overnight bag. I inwardly approved the poise that action indicated, but I made no effort to take any of my own things. "My room was very cold," Viki said.

We stepped into the hall. I heard a familiar sound: the whir of a telephone dial. I saw a tall Silver figure standing in the living room. It was a moment before I realized it was Franz, seen by the glimmer. I heard him say, "Hello, operator, Operator!" We walked to him.

HE looked at us, holding the receiver to his ear. Then he put it down again and said, "Glenn. Viki. I've been trying to phone Ed Mortenson, see if the stars changed there, or anything else. But it doesn't work for me. You try your luck at getting the operator, Glenn."

He dialed once, then handed me the receiver. I heard no ringing, no buzz, but a sound like wind wailing softly. "Hello, operator," I said. There was no response or change, just that wind sound. "Wait," Franz said softly.

It must have been at least five seconds when my own voice came back to me out of the phone, very faintly, half drowned in the lonely wind, like an echo from the end of the universe. "Hello, operator."

My hand shook as I put down the phone. "The radio?" I asked.

"The wind sound," he told me, "all over the dial."

"Just the same we've got to try to get out," I said.

"I suppose we should," he said with a faint ambiguous sigh. "I'm ready. Come on."

As I stepped onto the deck after Franz and Viki, I felt the intensified sense of a presence. The minor sensations were with us again, but far stronger now: the burnt taste made me gag almost. I wanted to claw at the cobwebs, the impalpable wind moaned and whistled loudly, the ghost-gravel hissed and splashed like the rapids of a river. All in near absolute darkness.

I wanted to run but Franz stepped forward to the barely glimmering rail. I held on to myself.

The faintest glimmer showed a few lines of the rock wall opposite. But from the sky above it was beating a dead inkier blackness—blacker than black, I thought—that was eating up the glimmer everywhere, dimming it moment by moment. And with the inkier blackness came a chill that struck into me like ice needles.

LOOK," Franz said. "It's the sunrise."

"Franz, we've got to get moving," I said.

"In a moment," he answered softly, reaching back his hand. "You go ahead. Start the car. Pull out to the center of the yard. I'll join you there."

Viki took the keys from him. She's driven a Volks. There was still enough glimmer to see by, though I trusted it less than ever. Viki started the car, then forgot and switched on the headlights. They obscured yard and drive with a fan of blackness! She switched them off and pulled to the center of the yard.

I looked back. Although the air was black with the icy sun light I could still see Franz clearly by the ghost light. He was standing where we'd left him; only leaning forward now, as though eagerly peering.

"Franz!" I called loudly against the weirdly wailing wind and the mounting gravel-roar. "Franz!"

There reared out of the canyon, facing Franz, towering above him, bending toward him a little, a filament-trailing form of shimmering velvet black—not the ghost light, but shimmering darkness itself—that looked like a gigantic hooded cobra, or a hooded Madonna, or a vast centipede, or a giant cloaked figure of the cat-headed goddess Bast, or all or none of these.

I saw the silver of Franz's body begin to crumble and churn. In the same moment the dark form dipped down and enfolded him like the silk-gloved fingers of a colossal black hand or the petals of a vast black flower closing.

Feeling like someone who throws the first shovel of earth on coffin of a friend, I croaked to Viki to get going.

There was hardly any glimmer left—not enough to see the drive, I thought, as the Volks started up it.

Viki drove fast.

THE sound of the spilling gravel grew louder and louder, drowning out the intangible wind, drowning out our motor. It rose to a thunder. Under the moving wheels, transmitting up through them, I could feel the solid earth shaking.

A bright pit opened ahead of us on the canyon side. For a moment it was as If we were driving through veils of thick smoke, then suddenly Viki was braking, we were turning into the road, and early daylight was almost blinding us.

But Viki didn't stop. We headed up the Little Sycamore Canyon road.

Around us were the turreted hills. The sun hadn't yet climbed above them but the sky was bright.

We looked down the road. No dust clouds obscured it any-where, though there was dust rising now from the bottom of the canyon-valley.

The slope swept down straight from us to the cliff edge, without a break, without a hummock, without one object thrusting up through. *Everything* had been carried away by the slide.

That was the end of Rim House and Franz Kinsman.

THE END

DEATH SEEMS SO FINAL

By RICHARD S. SHAVER

The only final step in life is death. But what seems to be the end may be only the beginning...

ALL you know, is that you were in the rear seat of the black Buick sedan. Your wife was sitting there, holding your hand and talking about the dance, and how she had more fun than she had had for ten years. Bill and Mary were in the front seat, and Bill was falling in love, with his wife all over again. All of you were just a little drunk, maybe. Not very. Just a few beers.

You are going down the street east of the American Legion Building, and the Buick skids just a little on the ice.

Mary cries, "Bill! Stop! There's a train coming."

You don't even catch the full meaning of her voice, because your brain is a little numb.

You see the blinker light winking at you like a blood-shot eye, and the huge searchlight of the locomotive bearing down upon you. Your wife's fingers cut into your arm and it hurts. Then the car is spinning.

Then a lot of things happen all at once. The grinding, crushing blow of steel against steel. A cloud of hissing steam released in your face. The huge eye of light that blinds you as you hold on to your wife and she screams.

The eye keeps right on coming at you and you can't escape it. The car seems to topple end over end with you inside it. You can't find your wife now. Something has torn you away from her. There is still the grinding of steel, and then—silence.

Everything is very quiet. You try to move and you can't move. You are motionless, and there is no feeling in your body. There is feeling and yet, no feeling. It's like the surgeon's knife, cutting through frozen flesh. *Your flesh.* It's like feeling the knife as it cuts, and yet feeling no pain. You lie there, wondering about the others. At first it doesn't matter much.

FACES gather around you. You stare up at them, every thought moving around in your mind like crystal clear waves. You see your wife. Her face tells you that she is unhurt. Then you know that she is shocked. Her eyes become distended with horror. There is a face with a trainman's cap above it. There is a face with a policeman's cap, and badge. You would like to tell them that everything is all right. That you aren't hurt. You hear their voices.

"Reed? Reed, why did it have to happen?"

It's your wife, and she's sobbing and then screaming. You try to smile and say:

"Don't worry, Hon. I'm okay. Honest I am."

But they're dragging her away. *They're dragging her away from you.* The voices are loud, then soft. There are many, and then but a few. There is a voice that comes more clearly than the others. It's Doc. Webber. He acts as though something awful has happened. You want to speak to him. Maybe you *do* speak, but your facial muscles are frozen. You can't move your lips, or force a sound out.

"I'm paralyzed," you tell yourself. "I'm okay, only I'm paralyzed. Webber will understand."

"Better call the coroner," Webber says.

Call the coroner?

What in the devil is he talking about?

Me, *I'm* not dead. *I* don't want the coroner. Webber rolls up his stethoscope and pushes it into his pocket. You see him standing there, looking down at you. Where does he get that stuff? He's nuts. *You're not dead.*

You know that no one is talking now. All of a sudden they stop. The black monster on the track is puffing and steaming. You hear it. You can't turn your head or roll your eyes to look. There is a little circle of faces staring down at you. You can't feel. Not *really* feel. Just that dull, painless feeling that comes from being frozen stiff all over.

Some of the faces are crying. Some of them are regarding you with dull, curious eyes. Eyes that have never seen anything like you. Eyes that are enjoying what they see, in a drunken, animal way.

"Damn you," you scream inside. "Damn you ghouls. Go away. Get out of here. I'm not dead. *I'm not dead.*"

Inside you're sobbing and screaming and swearing. All that pent up emotion is trying to escape, and can't. Your thoughts tumble over and over each other. Bewildered, frightening thoughts.

Then there is another face. It is Ben Parish, the coroner. *Now*, you think. Now they'll leave me alone. They won't think I'm dead. Ben will tell them I'm okay. That Doc Webber is crazy.

You played poker with Ben Parish last Saturday night. You asked him how many corpses he had to pronounce dead, before he

Illustration by William A. Gray

7

earned enough dough to get into that poker game. He didn't laugh. He didn't think it was funny.

Now he isn't laughing. He's looking down at you, his hands thrust deep into his coat pockets.

He shrugs and says:

"There couldn't be any doubt, could there? Not with him in that condition?"

He turns away.

In *what* condition? Is he nuts? Is he trying to say that you're *dead*?

Suddenly the panic is worse. It's so bad that it chokes you. It engulfs you in a fear that is worse than anything else in the world.

Something black drifts up over your face. It falls over your eyes hiding everything from sight. You do not feel it. You recognize it, because you remember. You remember seeing the dead covered with black.

They are taking you away.

They are taking you where they take the dead. They don't understand. They can't. You need a nurse. A pretty nurse in a stiff, white uniform. You need a doctor and a hospital. You need an operation. Yes, by God, you need an operation. This is insane. It's—it's—

But you can't move and you can't speak. You suffer pain, but it isn't physical. It's mental.

They are taking you away, and you can't reason with them.

You lie there in the black sea of a lost world. You hear sounds. The sound of men talking in low voices. The sound of wood against wood. Metal scraping metal. Then you are alone. Completely alone.

THE siren starts gibbering in a low moan. They are driving slowly. They are showing respect for their dead. People—your friends, are lining the sidewalk. People you danced with and drank beer with, staring through the big windows of the ambulance, looking at the black, man-shape inside.

Suddenly you're all burned up inside. You're angry at them all. They are fools. Unreasoning fools. They are incapable of understanding even simple things. They should know that you're alive.

And Doc Webber's voice is whispering softly:

"Better call the coroner."

*   *   *

You know where you are now. There is only one place for them to take you. You don't feel with your body. You feel with that vibrant, suffering mind. You know that the ambulance is turning and bumping over a rutted driveway. You know, because you have memories. You hear. Oh, yes, you hear clearly. The voices are here again. They aren't hushed now. They are loud and clear. They are the voices that come when dead men stop being souls and become bits of business.

"Too bad it had to be him. Always liked him."

You're being moved. No sensation of moving. Just sounds that piece themselves into an explanation of what is happening. Sounds that bring back memories.

"All of them were drunk. Funny, though, him the only one hurt. Tough on his wife."

"Damn you, Jim Dunn," your mind screams. "Any time you bury me, you'll hear about it. Let me go. Tell my wife I'm all right."

It doesn't come out. The words don't come from your lips. You know Jim Dunn's smooth, puffed face. You talked to him tonight, at the dance. Now he's taking you to *his* place, Dunn's Funeral Parlor. You've been there before, with him. You've been living two blocks from it for fifteen years. You'd made lousy jokes about his business.

"Stiff competition, huh, Jim?"

The joke always fell flat with Jim.

He didn't like to be kidded, not about his business. But, he wasn't going to bury *you*. No one was.

Or was he? You can't speak. You can't move. You can only think—and hear. There aren't any voices now. The black stuff still covers your eyes. You are in a room, and you know all about that room. You're on top of a long table. You've seen the table before.

You remember the afternoon Dunn had you visit the Funeral Parlor. He had a body there, working on it. It wasn't allowed, that visit, but no one checked up on you and it didn't do any harm.

"We have to get the family's permission before we embalm them," Dunn said. "We let them lay overnight sometimes."

Your mind is suddenly like a cornered rat. It is baffled. It's a wild thing, clawing uselessly at the heavy bars of a cage. You can't break those bars. Inside you, you're sweating and swearing and praying, all at once. You're the human animal—cornered.

They can't. They can't, you tell yourself time after time. If you could only call your wife? If she would come? It's no use. Rest.

Rest and save it. Save the fight that's left inside you. You're alone now and you're beginning to understand that by *their* standards, you maybe *are* dead. Maybe. They all think you are. Webber said so. Ben Parish said so.

"There couldn't be any doubt could there...in that condition?"

In what condition?

You lay quietly because you *can't* move, not even your eyelids. You keep on thinking, though. You think of everything. Any way out? No, there is no way out. No way.

THERE is a light. It is harsh and bright, but it does not hurt your eyes. Instead, it shocks your mind back into renewed thought. The black cloth drifts away. You remember all the things that happened when you stood in this room watching Dunn working. No pain. No feeling. Just voices.

"His wife called last night. She's taking it pretty well. Now, if this bothers you, get out of the room. I wouldn't have let you in here if you had known him personally. Sometimes I let friends in. Not often."

You think, sure, you let them in. *I've* been here. I was here, once, and I wish I had never come. I wouldn't have known about this. That would have been better.

A quavery, uncertain voice.

"I'm not accustomed to this sort of thing. Maybe I can't take it. Don't like the sight of blood very much."

Your mind starts to scream and scream.

"Get him out of here," you shout.

216

"He isn't going to watch. I don't want anyone to watch. I don't want..."
They didn't know. You couldn't tell them.

"Don't like the sight of blood very much."

Far away, an electric motor was humming. Just a small electric motor.

"Badly cut up," Dunn's voice said.

"Have to use facial restoration. Won't have to touch the legs or hips."

"Won't have to touch..."

"You don't have to touch me at all. I'm alive. I'm all right. Leave me alone."

You are writhing in mental pain. You are fighting—against everyone. Against the world. You're sweating and sobbing inside, *all inside.*

The motor goes on humming. Then you're glad because Dunn's fingers drift over your eyes and close them. You're glad because you don't have to look. That makes it easier, because you know you couldn't stand to see it—not even a little bit.

"I'm getting out of here," a frightened voice says, and chokes. The door slams. Jim Dunn chuckles. It's just a tiny sound. A joke he put over on humanity. He is humming. His voice doesn't have any more tone to it than that cursed motor.

Humming—singing—and you dead.

No, not *really* dead.

SO MANY voices. You know where you are now. You know because there are so many voices, and all the little sounds are familiar to you. The sound of a squeaky door—a water tap being turned off—the creaking of a certain step. These are sounds that you lived with for years and years.

The voices come to you and drift away again, quickly.

"Your husband is at rest. Take it bravely. He didn't suffer. We have that to be thankful for."

Why, you ask? You want to open your eyes and reach for your wife's hand. You know that she is there. You hear the muffled, sobbing sounds. Then even those are gone.

He didn't suffer.

What did she think was happening now? What did this woman's voice think was happening inside you?

"Suffer little children to…"

Only two words from your wife's lips. Two stunned words.

"Oh! God?"

Two words. That was all.

Then lots of words, all washed into one sea and drowning there. Words forgotten before they were spoken. You remember a man's voice. A neighbor's voice. All you remember about him? Once he borrowed a shovel and didn't bring it back. You never liked him after that.

"He was drunk. They all were drunk. Tough, but he had it coming to him."

Then music. Terrible, wheezing organ music. Words moved around in your mind like lazy, poisonous snakes, spitting their venom into you. A gentle, old lady's voice, secretly tense with excitement.

"I always said, death is *so* final."

Is it? You should know. You have all the answers. You should be able to sit up and tell that old voice that she's off her trolley. She's batty. She's got a lot to learn.

Something goes "plop."

It's the soft gentle plop of a door closing when there is air pressure in the room.

The sound of a coffin closing and the air fighting back with little sucking, futile sounds of pressure against softly padded silk.

Maybe you *will* die now. Maybe you will die because there is no more air.

You know that isn't it. You aren't breathing. You haven't been breathing for a long time. Your mind just keeps on functioning clearly. It moves like a well-plotted graph. Up and down. Hatred and love. Hope and despair. Up and down. Your thoughts—plotted on a graph.

Thinking—thinking…

ONLY sounds now but no voices.

Creaking casters—engines roaring to life—bumping sounds against the walls of your prison.

It's hard to concentrate on individual thoughts. You know only the white-hot terror inside you. You know that you left a woman behind—crying.

"Guess he had it coming."

My God, they don't know the half of it.

The slow, lazy creak of metal against metal. Wood against metal:

"There could be no doubt...in that condition."

Sound. Maybe a voice, far away. No words. A droning voice. Then, like heavy voltage shooting into you. No pain. No *physical* pain. Just the pain of fear...

"Plop—plop—plop."

Then faster and faster.

"Plopplopplop."

An avalanche of sound. Heavy, crushing sound, echoing around you. Then, silence. Dead silence. Your mind didn't mean to create that pun.

Memory. Memory so sharp that it slices at your thoughts like a razor.

Formaldehyde turns the flesh to a resinous substance. It preserves perfectly. Sometimes as long as five hundred years.

"Very interesting, Undertaker Dunn, dealer in defunct bodies. Very fascinating. *But how long after that does the mind continue to function?"*

You wonder.

"Death seems so final."

No more voices. No more sound. All of it gone. You laugh weirdly inside yourself. Hysterical laughter that has no outlet.

Dead silence. I'll say it's dead silence. How long is five hundred years? How long is time? How can the mind remain active and be tortured within you? What trick has death played on *you?* Will the mind go on thinking, even with the body gone?

No answer. No answer within that pain warped mind. You'll have plenty of time to answer those questions. Plenty of time. Your bed is made. It's your deathbed. Lie in it.

"I always said, death is *so* final."

THE END

If you've enjoyed this book, you will not want to miss these terrific titles...

ARMCHAIR SCI-FI & HORROR DOUBLE NOVELS, $12.95 each

D-121   **THE GENIUS BEASTS** by Frederik Pohl
           THIS WORLD IS TABOO by Murray Leinster

D-122   **THE COSMIC LOOTERS** by Edmond Hamilton
           WANDL THE INVADER by Ray Cummings

D-123   **ROBOT MEN OF BUBBLE CITY** by Rog Phillips
           DRAGON ARMY by William Morrison

D-124   **LAND BEYOND THE LENS** by S. J. Byrne
           DIPLOMAT-AT-ARMS by Keith Laumer

D-125   **VOYAGE OF THE ASTEROID, THE** by Laurence Manning
           REVOLT OF THE OUTWORLDS by Milton Lesser

D-126   **OUTLAW IN THE SKY** by Chester S. Geier
           LEGACY FROM MARS by Raymond Z. Gallun

D-127   **THE GREAT FLYING SAUCER INVASION** by Geoff St. Reynard
           THE BIG TIME by Fritz Leiber

D-128   **MIRAGE FOR PLANET X** by Stanley Mullen
           POLICE YOUR PLANET by Lester del Rey

D-129   **THE BRAIN SINNER** by Alan E. Nourse
           DEATH FROM THE SKIES by A. Hyatt Verrill

D-130   **CRY CHAOS** by Dwight V. Swain
           THE DOOR THROUGH SPACE By Marion Zimmer Bradley

ARMCHAIR SCIENCE FICTION CLASSICS, $12.95 each

C-55   **UNDER THE TRIPLE SUNS**
         by Stanton A. Coblentz

C-56   **STONE FROM THE GREEN STAR**
         by Jack Williamson,

C-57   **ALIEN MINDS**
         by E. Everett Evans

ARMCHAIR SCI-FI & HORROR GEMS SERIES, $12.95 each

G-13   **SCIENCE FICTION GEMS, Vol. Seven**
         Jack Vance and others

G-14   **HORROR GEMS, Vol. Seven**
         Robert Bloch and others

If you've enjoyed this book, you will not want to miss these terrific titles...

ARMCHAIR SCI-FI & HORROR DOUBLE NOVELS, $12.95 each

ARMCHAIR SCIENCE FICTION CLASSICS, $12.95 each

ARMCHAIR SCI-FI & HORROR GEMS SERIES, $12.95 each

If you've enjoyed this book, you will not want to miss these terrific titles…

ARMCHAIR SCI-FI & HORROR DOUBLE NOVELS, $12.95 each

D-141 **ALL HEROES ARE HATED** by Milton Lesser
AND THE STARS REMAIN by Bryan Berry

D-142 **LAST CALL FOR DOOMSDAY** by Edmond Hamilton
HUNTRESS OF AKKAN by Robert Moore Williams

D-143 **THE MOON PIRATES** by Neil R. Jones
CALLISTO AT WAR by Harl Vincent

D-144 **THUNDER IN THE DAWN** by Henry Kuttner
THE UNCANNY EXPERIMENTS OF DR. VARSAG by David V. Reed

D-145 **A PATTERN FOR MONSTERS** by Randall Garrett
STAR SURGEON by Alan E Nourse

D-146 **THE ATOM CURTAIN** by Nick Boddie Williams
WARLOCK OF SHARRADOR by Gardner F. Fox

D-148 **SECRET OF THE LOST PLANET** by David Wright O'Brien
TELEVISION HILL by George McLociard

D-147 **INTO THE GREEN PRISM** by A Hyatt Verrill
WANDERERS OF THE WOLF-MOON by Nelson S. Bond

D-149 **MINIONS OF THE TIGER** by Chester S. Geier
FOUNDING FATHER by J. F. Bone

D-150 **THE INVISIBLE MAN** by H. G. Wells
THE ISLAND OF DR. MOREAU by H. G. Wells

ARMCHAIR SCIENCE FICTION CLASSICS, $12.95 each

C-61 **THE SHAVER MYSTERY, Book Six**
by Richard S. Shaver

C-62 **CADUCEUS WILD**
by Ward Moore & Robert Bradford

B-5 **ATLANTIDA** (Lost World-Lost Race Classics #1)
by Pierre Benoit

ARMCHAIR MYSTERY-CRIME DOUBLE NOVELS, $12.95 each

B-1 **THE DEADLY PICK-UP** by Milton Ozaki
KILLER TAKE ALL by James O. Causey

B-2 **THE VIOLENT ONES** by E. Howard Hunt
HIGH HEEL HOMICIDE by Frederick C. Davis

B-3 **FURY ON SUNDAY** by Richard Matheson
THE AGONY COLUMN by Earl Derr Biggers

If you've enjoyed this book, you will not want to miss these terrific titles…

ARMCHAIR SCI-FI & HORROR DOUBLE NOVELS, $12.95 each

D-151 **MAGNANTHROPUS** by Manly Banister
BEYOND THE FEARFUL FOREST by Geoff St. Reynard

D-152 **IN CAVERNS BELOW** by Stanton A. Coblentz
DYNASTY OF THE LOST by George O. Smith

D-153 **NO MORE STARS** by Lester del Rey & Frederik Pohl
THE MAN WHO LIVED FOREVER R. De Witt Miller & Anna Hunger

D-154 **THE CORIANIS DISASTER** by Murray Leinster
DEATHWORLD by Harry Harrison

D-155 **HE FELL AMONG THIEVES** by Milton Lesser
PRINCESS OF ARELLI, THE by Aladra Septama

D-156 **THE SECRET KINGDOM** by Otis Adelbert Kline & Allen S. Kline
SCRATCH ONE ASTEROID by Willard Hawkins

D-157 **ENSLAVED BRAINS** by Eando Binder
CONCEPTION: ZERO by E. K. Jarvis

D-158 **VICTIMS OF THE VORTEX** by Rog Phillips
THE COSMIC COMPUTER by H. Beam Piper

D-159 **THE GOLDEN GODS** by S. J. Byrne
RETURN OF MICHAEL FLANIGAN by S. J. Byrne

D-160 **BATTLE OUT OF TIME** by Dwight V. Swain
THE PEOPLE THAT TIME FORGOT by Edgar Rice Burroughs

ARMCHAIR SCIENCE FICTION CLASSICS, $12.95 each

C-63 **THE OMEGA POINT TRILOGY**
by George Zebrowski

C-64 **THE UNIVERSE WRECKERS**
by Edmond Hamilton

C-65 **KING OF THE DINOSAURS**
by Raymond A. Palmer

ARMCHAIR SCI-FI & HORROR GEMS SERIES, $12.95 each

G-17 **SCIENCE FICTION GEMS, Vol. Nine**
Ben Bova and others

G-18 **HORROR GEMS, Vol. Nine**
Emil Petaja and others

If you've enjoyed this book, you will not want to miss these terrific titles…

ARMCHAIR SCI-FI & HORROR DOUBLE NOVELS, $12.95 each